WILL WILDER

THE RELIC OF PERILOUS FALLS

RAYMOND ARROYO

CROWN BOOKS
FOR YOUNG READERS

NEW YORK

Text copyright © 2016 by Raymond Arroyo
Jacket art copyright © 2016 by Jeff Nentrup
Illustrations copyright © 2016 by Antonio Javier Caparo

All rights reserved. Published in the United States by Crown Books for
Young Readers, an imprint of Random House Children's Books, a division of
Penguin Random House LLC, New York.

Crown and the colophon are registered trademarks of Penguin Random House LLC.

Visit us on the Web! randomhousekids.com

Educators and librarians, for a variety of teaching tools, visit us at RHTeachersLibrarians.com

Library of Congress Cataloging-in-Publication Data
Arroyo, Raymond.
The relic of Perilous Falls / Raymond Arroyo. — First edition.
pages cm. — (Will Wilder ; [1])
Summary: "A thrill-seeking twelve-year-old boy with a mysterious family heritage who
discovers ancient objects of rare power—and must protect them from the terrifying demons
who will do anything to possess them" —Provided by publisher.
ISBN 978-0-553-53959-2 (trade) — ISBN 978-0-553-53960-8 (lib. bdg.) —
ISBN 978-0-553-53961-5 (ebook)
[1. Adventure and adventurers—Fiction. 2. Relics—Fiction. 3. Supernatural—Fiction.
4. Families—Fiction. 5. Prophecies—Fiction.] I. Title.
PZ7.A74352Re 2016 [Fic]—dc23 2015006124

Printed in the United States of America
10 9 8 7 6 5 4 3 2 1
First Edition

To the Arroyo children:
Alexander, Lorenzo, and Mariella, who first heard the tale

CONTENTS

If that the heavens do not their visible spirits
Send quickly down to tame these vile offences,
It will come,
Humanity must perforce prey on itself,
Like monsters of the deep.

—William Shakespeare, *King Lear*

WILL WILDER
THE RELIC OF PERILOUS FALLS

THE COURTYARD OF HELL

Ortona, Italy
December 20, 1943

Nazi bombs hurled half the dome of the Basilica di San Tommaso Apostolo to its marbled floor, exposing a smoke-filled night sky. Even the stars failed to pierce the darkness hanging over the church. Shattered marble and brick, busted statues, and splintered chairs rose on all sides like ugly snowdrifts. A biting cold filled the dilapidated church. Aside from the dust, the only thing moving among the rubble was a darting figure.

A young man, trailed by shadows, scaled a ruined wall that had once served as the cathedral's entrance. He moved with speed and precision. He wore the green uniform of an American soldier and a round brimmed helmet on his head. Reaching the top of the debris, he lay flat, studying the chalky pit before him.

For the last three hours he had fought through the narrow streets of Ortona, desperate to reach the bombed-out church. An elite team of German paratroopers—"The Green Devils"—had taken control of the town days earlier. Crawling on his belly for much of the journey, the soldier painstakingly advanced block by terrible block, alone. Each time he dashed into the open, Nazi snipers fired from multiple positions. He was quick, but there were few places to hide.

Crumbled buildings blocked alleys, and clouds of debris made a clear view of the church all but impossible. Lifeless bodies filled the cobblestone streets. The soldier pressed a sleeve to his nose throughout the journey to block out the unbearable stench. The closer he got to the church, the worse the smell. At least it was a familiar scent. Like rotting fish, it had always been the first sign for him—the sign of what was to come.

The American soldier had reached the town with the First Canadian Infantry Division after being separated from his platoon in Sicily a week earlier. But his Canadian allies knew nothing of his personal mission: to get inside the Basilica of St. Thomas the Apostle in Ortona before it was too late. Now he finally rested on its ruins.

From the canvas satchel on his back he drew a flashlight, aiming its beam at the wrecked high altar below. Chunks of the ceiling had smashed the main altar in two, so the top stone now formed a dilapidated V. He jerked a handkerchief from his pocket and covered his nose. The stink was intensifying. With his free hand he pulled a pair of gloves and a velvet pouch from the satchel. Then he made his move.

Silently, the soldier leapt down the hill of debris and turned sharply to the left, crouching between a huge piece of the roof and the altar. With the flashlight he studied the damaged marble.

The front of the altar had shattered, exposing a shiny gold casket. The soldier carefully freed the bent chest from the broken stone. On the lid was a delicate painting of St. Thomas the Apostle, his hand raised in a blessing. The soldier removed his scuffed pith helmet, ran a hand through his thick black hair, and pressed his ear to the top of the chest. He balanced the flashlight on the edge of the container, the light catching his sharp cheekbones and wild green eyes. Slipping a knife blade into the keyhole on the front of the box, he waited to hear a familiar click. After a few attempts the lock gave way and he pried open the centuries-old, warped golden lid.

"AH-CHOO!" The soldier's sneeze echoed through the church. Outside, cannon fire and gunfire lit up the night sky in bursts. He dimmed the flashlight and spun his head around. Peering into the darkness, he searched for the thing he could feel approaching. But he saw nothing. Remaining stone still, he desperately tried to hold back another sneeze.

"AH-CHOO!"

He had to be quick. One of them, maybe more, was near. Opening the golden casket, the soldier, wearing cotton gloves, lifted out the bones of the Apostle Thomas. First the skull, then the ribs, arm bones, pieces of the legs, and finally the remains of the hands—one of which had touched the side of Jesus. He placed each relic in the velvet sack, then bundled the sacred load into his satchel.

"Herr Jacob Wilder," a gravelly, pinched voice called out from above.

Startled, the soldier tilted his flashlight upward. Blocking a statue of Jesus, a six-foot-tall Nazi officer in a long black leather coat straddled the broken altar stone. His skin had a yellowish tint. A trail of dried blood started at a wound on the left side of his face and ran down into a burgundy-stained collar. Dust covered his head and clothing.

The stench nauseated Jacob Wilder.

"I will not hurt you, Jacob. The Brethren told me I would find you here," the Nazi wheezed in accented English. "Have you got them all?"

Jacob Wilder secured his satchel and yanked the gloves from his hands, saying nothing. He palmed the pith helmet, placing it on his head as he stood.

"I am here to assist," the Nazi hissed, jumping down from the altar. "The Brethren asked me to ensure your safe passage out of the city. Do you have the bones?"

"Your name?" Wilder demanded in a low, firm voice, pulling the brim of his helmet low. He backed up a few feet, as if preparing for a fight. "What is your name?"

The Nazi clacked his tongue as if chastising the American for lacking manners. "Captain Gerhold Metzger of the

SS," he said stiffly. "I am a collaborator with the brothers at Montecassino," he whispered. The officer smiled, but it never reached his eyes.

Wilder pinched the bridge of his nose, stifling a sneeze. "Your *name*, beast?"

"I told you: Metzger," the Nazi gasped, stumbling toward the young soldier. "It is imperative that we see the bones." His eyes darted from side to side. "The skeleton in your bag could be the bones of a pious monk or some beggar with no family. How do you *know* they belong to the apostle? Let us have a look for confirmation's sake."

"Quiet!" Wilder said evenly. "Give me your name—now."

"It is hard to know what is true. If you believe those to be the actual bones of Thomas the Apostle, let us see them," the Nazi pressed, choking on every word. "A bright young man like you already knows the truth. Would a saint allow this to happen to his shrine?" The Nazi released a guttural laugh, his arms jerkily indicating the wreckage surrounding them.

As if wielding a weapon, Jacob Wilder raised a small vial filled with clear liquid and splashed it across the front of the Nazi. "Reveal your name, serpent! Come out of him!"

The officer quaked and grimaced, madly attempting to scrub away the fluid streaking down his face and uniform. His whole body trembled. Then, as if he were a balloon suddenly drained of air, the Nazi crumpled to the ground. In his place stood a pale young man with long, gleaming white hair, a suit nearly as white as his skin, and yellowed eyes.

His elongated, bloodless fingers were adorned with dia-monds, emeralds, sapphires, and rubies.

"Your name?" Jacob Wilder said forcefully.

"Must we?" the silky voice, neither male nor female, responded. "The name will do you no good." Then his ex-pression changed to shock. "You can see me?" the creature muttered with some worry. He waved a jeweled hand in the air and began to squeal, "You *see* me!"

"The black aura around your disguise gave you away. Hu-mans don't have those. You're a liar and the father of lies."

The demon smirked and casually looked down on the deflated Nazi officer. "Is there nowhere for us to rest our weary head? Poor fellow died three days ago. It seemed the ideal time to raise him again. Well, you work with what you have." He glanced up at Jacob and hovered in his direction. "Young Wilder, you have strengths and gifts. A *Seer*, are we? How nice."

Wilder said nothing. He looked down at the demon's startlingly white suit, seemingly lit from within. The color was consistent except for the lower part of the pants, which were streaked with dirt and blood. Sharp animal hooves peeked from beneath the cuffs, where feet should have been.

"Your gifts are extraordinary—and look how the Breth-ren use you. They've made you a common thief, sent to loot the spoils of others!" the demon jeered. He shook a lengthy finger in Jacob's face. "Stealing is still a sin, you know."

The soldier remained silent.

"Why so quiet, Wilder? Your dear brothers lack *our* special gifts. They see nothing. Oh, they play at their rituals, but we have powers they'll never understand. Why are you not the leader of the Brethren? I could help you become leader. They would all follow you instead of that bearded fool. . . ." The demon's yellow eyes flashed. "You question Abbot Anthony the Wise, don't you?"

Jacob's face flushed. "That is what you say." He looked straight ahead, not at the demon.

"Of course you question Anthony. . . . Look where his leadership has gotten you. The world your Brethren created lies in ashes. Their prophecy has failed. The *Sinestri* have risen, and we are conquering the world. *Sieg Heil!* Jacob, we are here for you now. Let us see the trinkets in your bag."

Jacob Wilder extended his flat hands in front of him, touching his thumbs and index fingers together in the form of a triangle. He inhaled deeply.

"Your fortress in America burns, even at this moment," the demon whispered soothingly. "There is nothing to return home to, Wilder. Gathering the bones of the dead won't help you now. But as leader you could rebuild something new—"

A red flash lit up the remaining walls of the Basilica of St. Thomas the Apostle for several seconds. Two Nazi artillerymen noticed the strange light from their second-story window a block away from the church.

"Is that a flare?" a short soldier holding his rifle out the window asked his superior.

Lifting a pair of binoculars to his eyes, a young bony officer scanned the edges of the church. He struggled to see by the flashing cannon fire. "There is a man running on that wall. Shoot!" the officer screamed.

Looking through the scope of his weapon, the sharpshooter saw nothing. Each time an explosion lit up the scene, there was only debris.

"Sir, if someone was there, he is gone," the short soldier said, lowering his rifle. "Or maybe it was only a shadow."

"It was a man, I tell you," the officer said, falling into a nearby chair and rubbing his eyes. "He had a light-colored helmet—not like the Canadians. I saw him!"

"Could have been a statue in the church," the sharpshooter replied, unconcerned.

"No. This was no statue."

"On late watches, sir, the eyes can play tricks on us."

"His hands were glowing," the officer sputtered like a scared child. "The man's hands were red—and they were glowing!"

CHAPTER 1

A RIDE IN THE YARD

All Will Wilder meant to do was ride the donkey at his eight-year-old brother's backyard birthday party. He didn't mean to hurt anyone, he didn't mean to unlock his destiny, and he certainly didn't mean to see the *shadows*. But that is exactly what happened. Life often came at Will while he was focused on something else.

Since Will was twelve and nearly five feet tall, his parents thought he had outgrown riding the donkey they had rented for his brother Leo's birthday.

"Aren't you a little old for a donkey ride, Will? It's for the kids. C'mon," Deborah Wilder said, playfully mussing his spiky black hair in their sweltering backyard. She had a thin face like Will's, full lips, and blue-purple eyes that even the hardest of hearts could not resist for long. It was no wonder her TV show, *Supernatural Secrets*, had so many fans. "You're getting so big, the donkey could ride *you*! Why don't you and your friends go finish that catapult thing you've been working on?" She gave him a quick one-armed hug and made her way back toward the party guests.

"Mom, please, just one time around the yard—or maybe down the block," Will begged.

"No, you'll kill it, you big ox!" she said over her shoulder with a smirk. Deborah swept back her straight brown hair and bent down to fix Will's six-year-old sister Marin's pink dress.

"So now donkey rides have age restrictions?" Will yelled after her. "I didn't know that, Mom! Is there a height limit too?" But Deborah Wilder paid him no attention. She had already mingled back into the crush of family, children, and neighbors in the fun part of the yard.

Marin stuck her tiny pink tongue out at Will, both hands on her hips. "Follow the rules, mithter. Follow the rules," she scolded with a lisp before cartwheeling away.

Sulking in defeat, Will shuffled back toward his three friends, two boys and a girl, who were watching closely from the fence at the rear of the yard. *Since when am I too big?* Will believed he had at least another year, maybe two, before he would officially outgrow amusements like donkey rides. He knew he had to let them go eventually. But not now—especially when money and prestige were on the line.

"Strike one, Will-man," Andrew Stout, a massive kid with blazing red hair, and one of Will's closest friends, bellowed. "Where's my five dollars?"

"I'm not finished yet," Will said.

"Oh, no. You're finished. I said you couldn't get on the donkey, and you ain't on the donkey. So pay up. If you want to try again, it'll be double or nothing."

"Can we check the law on this?" interrupted a rail-thin boy with eyes that looked like black BBs behind his rectangular glasses. Simon Blabbingdale lightly poked Andrew's side with one of the thick paperbacks he always seemed to be carrying. "Is it legal for Sheriff Stout's adolescent son to bet on ponies at a birthday party?" Simon unleashed a series of high-pitched snorts, which he considered laughter. Nobody joined him. Simon and Will had been friends since the first grade. When no one in the cafeteria would sit next to the scrawny, curly-haired kid with glasses, Will did.

"Can it, Simon." Andrew flicked the paperback from his ribs and focused on Will. "We made a deal, Will-man, so pay up. I need the money for our trip." The big kid extended his open palm.

The Wilders had invited Andrew and Simon to join them in Florida at the National Pee-Wee Karate Championships. Leo, an accomplished brown belt, was to compete at the tournament in two weeks' time. Will and his friends would tag along for moral support and hit a few amusement parks between matches.

"What if I told you that I just came up with a new way to get on the donkey?" Will mysteriously threw out, his hands clasped behind his back.

"Let's see it. Double or nothing," Andrew said.

Camilla Meriwether, a girl with wide green eyes, a long

chestnut-colored ponytail, and braces, rapped her knuckles on the fence behind her. "Guys. Can we *please* try to act a little more mature? I mean, it's embarrassing. If Will's parents don't want him riding the donkey, why can't we just have some cake and enjoy the party?"

Andrew and Will eyeballed each other, then in unison turned to Cami. "Uh, no."

Cami was the only girl Will spoke to in his entire class. She was kind, sort of cute, and always spoke her mind—even if he rarely listened to her. "Okay, well, while you little guys play your cowboy games, I'm going to get some punch." She marched over to one of the refreshment tables.

When Cami was out of earshot, Andrew spoke up. "All right, get onto the donkey's back, I'll give you ten bucks. If you don't, you have to pay up. Deal?"

Will furrowed his brow and got in Andrew's face. "Deal." They shook on it and Will started to leave, but a swift tap on the arm from Simon stopped him.

"I was thinking, as long as everybody's making wagers," Simon said, looking over the top of his glasses, "I'll buy you the first souvenir of our trip—no more than five dollars—if you race the donkey around the yard. You can't just ride it. I'm talking a full gallop. If there's no gallop, you pick up the souvenir."

Will considered the offer for barely a second. "I'm going to be ten dollars richer and score a free souvenir. You're on too." He shot the boys a crooked smile, then ran off to appeal the donkey ban to the authority of last resort.

Dan Wilder, Will's father, with his tortoiseshell glasses and blue apron, stood at the barbecue pit on the deck methodically tending his perfectly spaced burgers. He laid them out like houses on a map at one of his city planning meetings. Dan Wilder was an architect, a city councilman, and a planner for the town of Perilous Falls. He had a refined sense of order even when it came to grilling—patties were restricted to the lower grill, veggies on the top.

As dads went, Dan was a handsome one. He had a strong, square jaw, and aside from three slight scars on the left side of his face, Dan could have been on the cover of any grocery checkout aisle magazine. A dad of few words, he usually kept to himself, attentively watching while others chattered on. Indeed, he had overheard Will's donkey pleas all day by the time the boy made his approach.

"Dad, I was wondering . . ."

Without looking up from the smoldering patty at the end of his spatula, Mr. Wilder announced, "The answer . . . son . . . is no." Then, brightening, he added, "Do you want a burger?"

"Unless it can ride me around the yard, no thanks." Will stalked away in a huff to plot his next move.

He climbed onto a picnic table close to his house and studied the landscape like a general planning an invasion. *How to get on that donkey?*

On the opposite side of his yard stood the squinty-eyed, mustached Heinrich Crinshaw. The Wilders' bow-tied next-door neighbor was chairman of the Perilous Falls City

Council and a constant if disagreeable presence at family events. On the surface Mr. Crinshaw seemed a refined gentleman, even warm.

Until he opened his mouth.

In a flat drone, he advised the neighborhood kids to stay on the Wilders' side of the fence, worried that they might leap into his garden and ruin the rare flowers and herbs he spent thousands of dollars maintaining.

"There's nothing over there for you," he croaked to the kids when their parents were out of earshot. Then, bending down to their level, with a smile he added, "Though my dog, Suzy, might like to see you all. She so enjoys children. She ate two last year—bones and all."

Mr. Crinshaw turned away as a couple of the little girls immediately burst into tears.

Will spied Aunt Freda, Deborah Wilder's blond relative, who had made herself snack guardian. Looking like an albino elephant caught in a kelly-green bedsheet, Freda jealously protected the table from approaching guests, gobbling cheese squares and chips as she made her way toward the cake at the other end of the table.

Across from Aunt Freda, near the drink station, Mayor Ava Lynch held a circle of parents spellbound. Her red suit and helmet of hard black hair seemed out of place at a backyard summer party. With the help of some sort of greasy youth cream, her skeletal face was quite animated that day. "No, no . . . this city has got to move beyond the shackles of its history or we will never grow," she brayed, as if giving a campaign speech. At nearly seventy years old, the mayor's booming voice could still fill a yard, even reaching Will. "That's why I decided to cancel this year's Jacob Wilder Day celebrations. The world is changing, and it is high time Perilous Falls evolves with it. We can't pretend we're in the era of Jacob Wilder anymore," she said, chuckling.

Will saw his great-aunt Lucille Wilder's face flush with color at the mention of Jacob Wilder. Fireworks were coming. The compact woman with strawberry-blond hair spun on her heels to face the mayor.

"Who are you to cancel a forty-five-year tradition?" Aunt Lucille asked in a sharp voice, her curls trembling as if to emphasize the point. "My father gave his life for this town, and I'll be stewed if you are going to stamp out his memory. Find another punching bag for your campaign, Ava— preferably someone living. You should all remember, there would be no Perilous Falls were it not for my father, Jacob Wilder." Those watching the little woman with fire in her arresting blue eyes fell silent.

"Oh, Lucille. You have to admit that your father's superstitious tales were wearing thin even when we were children. All that devil stuff . . ." Mayor Lynch laughed, trying to win over the crowd. "I know that your father founded the town—and it is wonderful that you run his little museum, bless your heart—but those antique trinkets and all your daddy's stories won't make a safe and prosperous future for Perilous Falls. We're in the twenty-first century now, honey. People no longer believe the things our parents did.

And we just don't have the resources to celebrate old fables, or even the one who created them."

The red hue of Aunt Lucille's face clashed with the powder-blue silk pantsuit she wore. Like loose pajamas, the material swallowed up Lucille's trim frame—but not her hands, which had balled into fists.

"Your eyes see nothing, Ava, *dear*. They never did. My father was a visionary who had courage and virtues you've never possessed. If you don't agree with his beliefs, or his warnings, say so. But don't disparage a man you never knew. Without my family, you might still be seating customers at Belle's Lounge." Lucille stared holes into the mayor. "My grandfather Abe opened his first iron ore mine here when it was nothing but wilderness. My father tamed that wilderness with a purpose. He established schools and churches, and the city hall that you profane. He always said Perilous Falls was to be the last stronghold against the dark madness of the world. Our faith and our traditions are what sustain this town, *Ms. Mayor*. It is who we are. It is who we will always be. That is the legacy of Jacob Wilder, and I will celebrate him with or without mayoral approval. Now, if you'll excuse me." Aunt Lucille turned a withering glance on the mayor and bolted toward the house.

"Poor woman's lost her mind," Mayor Lynch whispered to those nearest her.

Though in her sixty-sixth year, Aunt Lucille looked far younger as she strode across the yard with the ease and grace of a powerful dancer. She stopped next to Will's mom, throwing an arm dramatically on her shoulder.

"Deb, dear, I totally forgot that I have a physical therapy session today," Aunt Lucille said. "I left my gift for Leo on the kitchen table. Tell him I want to see his new karate moves and take him out on the boat one day this week, just him and me."

"Did Ava say something?" Deborah asked, suddenly serious. "Don't leave. Why don't you two try to settle your differences?"

"Deceit and lies are differences to be avoided, not settled. Ava Lynch's lies have done enough damage to this family . . . ," Aunt Lucille said darkly, shoving both hands into her brocaded silken pockets. Then, smiling, she added, "I would love to stay for the rest of the party, but my physical therapy is so important these days. Let's talk later, dear."

Catching sight of Will on the picnic table as she reached the kitchen door, she threw him an exaggerated kiss and, her finger bouncing as if striking a note on an invisible piano, silently mouthed, "You—be—good." With a wave, she was gone in a flash of blue silk.

Deborah followed Aunt Lucille to the center of the yard and announced, "There's only one more donkey ride to go before we eat. It's the birthday boy's turn!" She motioned for her younger son to come forward.

"Mom, I don't need a commercial." The eight-year-old with the pouty lips and glasses rolled his eyes. Leo reluctantly edged past his friends toward a jumpy donkey leashed to an old bearded fellow.

"You ride as long as you want," Mrs. Wilder cooed to the red-faced Leo. "It's your day. You're the boss." She returned to filling cups with punch and ordered Mr. Wilder to start doling out his precious hamburgers.

From the fence Andrew snapped a ten-dollar bill over his head, nodding knowingly at Will. Simon rotated his hands in a circular motion to spur Will to action.

Feeling the pressure, Will glared at Leo riding the donkey in lazy rings. He struggled to devise some way onto the animal's back.

Just then, something out of the corner of Will's eye drew his attention. A hunched black form crept into the very edge of his vision, sending a chill through his body. The air suddenly reeked, and his nose tingled. Will was afraid to look directly at the form, but he could feel its menace. Given its size, it could have been a crouching bear or even an ogre from one of his kiddie books. But when he mustered the courage to turn his head to face it, he saw nothing.

Shadows and "fuzzy things" appearing in his peripheral vision had been an ongoing problem for Will since he was at least four years old. He had seen them at school, down near the Perilous River, even at friends' houses. His mother had repeatedly taken him to the eye doctor to diagnose the problem. But each time, Dr. Schwartz reported that there was nothing wrong with Will's vision and that the shadows were likely the result of too little sleep. Dr. Schwartz suggested that they "continue to monitor the situation" and that Will get some extra rest.

This shadow is different, Will thought with a shiver. It had density and more shape than the others. It seemed alive. Will might have dwelled on the shadow all afternoon had an idea not flashed into his mind, pushing those thoughts aside. *The catapult.* That's how he would win the bet and get the donkey ride. He'd take his mother's advice after all.

Will had been working on the contraption for three weeks, since the start of summer break. Rather than walking around the block to school, which was right next to his house, Will thought it might be fun to simply fling himself over the fence and into the schoolyard. Once classes resumed in the fall, he reasoned, the catapult could cut his daily travel time in half and allow him to sleep at least an extra five minutes a day.

He had constructed the machine out of an old infant car seat from the family garage, as well as springs and levers rescued from the Hinnom Valley Dump. Aside from launching Marin's stuffed animals and a few books over the fence, the catapult had yet to move anything substantial. Leo regularly begged Will to let him be the first "human trial." Each time, Will would gravely shake his head and deny his younger brother's request.

"It's not ready yet. It's not safe," he'd say seriously. "Soon, Leo, *very* soon."

Will leapt off the picnic table, grabbed his pith helmet from the deck, and ran across the lawn. "Where are you going with that thing?" Dan Wilder yelled from his burger station. "Will?"

A gift from his aunt Lucille, the war-ravaged helmet had once belonged to Will's great-grandfather, Jacob Wilder. At the center of the hat was an impressive brass medallion with an angry pelican, wings spread, feeding its young. The splendor of the helmet ended there. The canvas on the front of the hat had been badly marred by six crisscrossed slashes. A powerful pair of jaws had chomped into the right side of the brim, leaving a healthy bite mark behind. Still, the hat gave Will confidence. It had become part of his standard attire, much like his red sneakers and white socks. And though he sometimes carried it in his backpack, if an adventure was afoot, the helmet was on Will's head—a sure sign of trouble to his parents.

At the makeshift corral at the other end of the yard, Leo told the stooped old man holding the donkey's reins, "I think I'm ready to get off."

"Have it your way," the old gent said, shuffling forward to help the boy down.

"Not so fast, Leo. It's your birthday lap." Will sandwiched himself between the old man and his brother. "It's a special moment."

"I'm getting sleepy going round and round."

Will looked over his shoulder to make sure his mother was occupied with the kids and that his dad was still passing out burgers at the grill.

"I have a surprise for your birthday." Will pushed Leo back onto the donkey. "What have you been wanting to do for weeks?"

Leo's eyes grew huge. "Test the catapult!"

"Everything's set. I've adjusted the weight and added some springs. I think it just might work this time. You could even make it over the fence. But . . ."

"But what? It's my birthday!" Leo drew his eyebrows together and shoved his lower lip out in an exaggerated pout. "Can I use the catapult or not?"

The old man holding on to the donkey was tired of listening. "If it's all the same to you boys, I'm going to get a taste of cake. Then Johnny and I are headin' back to the farm." He tied the animal to the fence post with Leo still aboard and tottered away.

Will had that familiar wild glint in his hazel eyes. "If you agree to let me ride the rest of your birthday lap on the donkey, you can test the catapult."

"Should we ask Mom?" Leo wondered.

"She said you were 'the boss.' I heard her. The choice is yours."

Leo brightened and leapt off the donkey. Within seconds Will had untied the reins from the post and mounted the animal.

"Go get in the catapult, Leo. I'll come by and launch you in a minute," Will instructed his brother. Leo bounded like a small bear across the lawn, adjusting his glasses as he dodged party guests.

"I think you just lost ten bucks, moron," Simon told Andrew as they leaned against the fence. "Now let's see how fast he can move on that thing."

The donkey's owner spotted Will on the animal's back. "Hey, son, you're too big to ride Johnny!" he yelled.

Before the old fellow could form another word, Will had jammed his heels into the animal's backside, determined to win the bet with Simon. The donkey began to buck wildly, lifting its hind legs and kicking at the air. Will tried to get the animal to gallop, but it had other ideas. Round and round it spun, trying to remove the boy from its back.

Parents pulled their children close to shield them from the donkey's killer hooves. A disgusted Mayor Lynch hastily excused herself and headed out the yard's side gate, Heinrich Crinshaw following close behind.

On the deck, Dan Wilder dropped his tongs into the barbecue pit. Terror covered his face. "Not the donkey," he said almost to himself. "Will! Will! Off the donkey!"

The braying animal leapt atop the snack table, sending potato chips and cookies flying in all directions. Ignoring Will's frantic tug on the reins, the donkey started jumping up and down. At the other end of the table, Aunt Freda focused on the trembling birthday cake before her.

"Deborah!" she yelped to her niece. "Should I take the cake to a safer spot or just leave it?" But before Mrs. Wilder could respond, the bouncing donkey sent the table's edge and the cake flying into Aunt Freda's jaw. She tumbled backward, her face covered in frosting.

The donkey's hooves skidded off the table's surface, Will still holding on.

"William David Wilder! Get down!" Deborah Wilder screeched through gritted teeth as she attempted to revive her unconscious aunt.

"That could be kind of difficult right now," Will said, one arm around the donkey, the other holding his pith helmet in place. "Heeee-yaaaa," he boomed, grinding his heels into the sides of the donkey. The animal reared up and began to run toward the tree at the far end of the yard, not far from where Leo impatiently squirmed in the catapult.

"Hurry up and launch me," Leo demanded, holding the sides of the old car seat. "I have a birthday party to get back to." Leo had tied pillows to the front and back of his body to buffer his landing.

Will galloped onward. The lever for the catapult, a slightly warped Louisville Slugger bat, was just eight feet away. Will reached his hand out, ready to throw the switch.

"Almost there," Will grunted. Suddenly the donkey slid to a complete stop, tearing up the grass with its hooves and tossing Will headlong toward the catapult.

"Aaah!" Will screamed as he flew into the lever, cracking the bat. Splinters of wood pierced his skin, slicing his hand and wrist.

PLUUUUNG. Will looked up from his throbbing wrist to see Leo sailing into the upper branches of the tree. His catapult really worked!

Leo flew much higher than Will thought possible, but his brother's body wasn't arcing wide enough, and he was dangerously approaching the top of the fence.

"Mom! DAAAAAAD!" Leo screamed on his descent.

Will realized with a pang of guilt that he should have tightened the tension on the springs. But before he could calculate how much added force would be necessary, Leo smashed shoulder-first into a wooden slat, breaking the top off and flipping into the schoolyard.

"Leo!" Dan Wilder yelled, running toward the edge of his property and his whimpering son. "You're punished, Will," he fumed as he began to scale the fence, still in his blue apron. "I mean—all summer!"

The whole yard fell quiet as everyone listened to the scene on the other side of the sun-bleached wooden slats.

"Are you all right? Can you stand up?" Dan asked Leo.

"My arm hit the board. I can't move it," Leo whined.

"His arm may be broken. He's bleeding, Deb," Dan shouted over the fence. "We're going to have to take him to the hospital."

Will felt a stabbing sensation in his heart. He didn't care about his hand. He had hurt his brother, ruined the party, and possibly spoiled the trip to Florida. All at once, something else arrested his attention.

In his peripheral vision, Will saw a dark form rise on his left.

There is nothing there. I'm just stressed and tired, he told himself. Refusing to look to the side, Will squeezed his eyes shut, hoping the shadow would disappear. With a deep breath, he opened just one eye and turned to the left. There stood a hulking black form—a thing at once fearsome and old. It took the shape of an enormous man and was darker than anything he had ever seen before. A chill ran through Will's body. He stumbled backward against the tree. Then the form melted into a deep black shadow stretching the length of the yard. It covered every inch of ground, even though the sun shone above.

"Will!" Deborah Wilder ran toward her son. "What's wrong?"

"It's so dark—so dark!" Will repeated, his eyes fixed on the pitch-black lawn before him.

"What's so dark?" Cami asked, racing to his side.

Confused partygoers and Will's friends stared at the frightened boy.

The old man struggled to pull the crazed donkey away from Will. But the beast bared its teeth in a perverse smile inches from Will's face—all the while emitting high-pitched squeals that could have passed for cruel laughter.

CHAPTER 2

PUNISHMENT

Aunt Lucille held two long knives in the air, her eyes squinting in concentration. With one swift motion she hurled the blades at a moss-draped oak tree behind her home. The two knives landed in the dead center of a tarnished brass octagon mounted on the tree's trunk.

Then, with the bounce of a teenager, she somersaulted toward the tree—a blur of flipping silk and strawberry-blond hair. She landed on both feet, inches from the tree, the knives still trembling in the bark. Instantly, her hands produced two vials from her belt. She popped them open and sprayed clear liquid all over the brass octagon.

Falling suddenly to her knees, she snatched a crossbow from the ground, leaned all the way back, and fired an arrow toward a tree behind her. The arrow sailed across the clearing and pierced the wood, just inside the brass octagon hanging from the other massive trunk.

Aunt Lucille rolled to her side, grabbing a pair of short spears as she tumbled. Springing up like a kangaroo on a trampoline, she ran into the middle of the clearing, came to an abrupt stop, leapt high into the air with crossed arms, and hurled the spears in opposite directions. Their points impaled the trees to her right and left, sticking firmly inside their respective brass octagons. When she returned to the ground, Aunt Lucille inhaled deeply and extended both arms in front of her, forming a triangle with her thumbs and index fingers.

The electronic chirp of a cell phone startled her. Annoyed, she dropped her arms and sprinted to the edge of the clearing where her cell phone and a towel were arranged atop a charred tree stump.

"Yes?" Aunt Lucille said into the phone, only slightly winded.

"Lucille, oh, I'm glad you're there," Deborah Wilder cried through the receiver. "I thought you'd still be at your physical therapy session."

"Just finished, dear," she said, mopping her brow with a towel.

"We're here at Chorazin General. There was an accident. Leo was hurt."

"They have a terrible emergency unit—why would you go to Chorazin?"

"Because it was closest," Deborah said, an edge in her voice.

"You should have gone to St. Joseph's. How bad is Leo?"

"His arm is broken and his shoulder is dislocated. I could kill his brother!"

"Why?"

"His father and I told Will not to ride that donkey. So what do you think he did? Conned his brother into letting him ride the donkey! Right after you left, he tore through the yard and—"

Aunt Lucille cut her off. "Donkey? Wh-what happened?"

"Complete mayhem. He injured Leo, knocked my aunt Freda out—her false teeth are still somewhere in the yard. Then Will hurt his hand. . . ."

"Was there blood? I mean, is he injured?" Lucille asked, her stomach tightening.

"He cut his hand. There was a little blood. He'll be fine. . . ."

Lucille suddenly felt the heat drain from her face. She lowered herself onto the tree stump to catch her breath. Deborah continued on about the accident, but Lucille could only focus on the words "donkey" and "blood."

"Lucille? Lucille?" Deborah asked after a few moments of silence. "Are you still there?"

"Of course, dear," Lucille said, snapping back to attention.

"Good. Could you do me a favor? Would you mind coming

down here and watching Marin and Will for us—just until the doctors are finished putting the cast on Leo?"

"Happy to help. I'll be right there, dear."

Aunt Lucille put the cell phone aside and placed one hand across her stomach; the other she brought to her face. With her knuckles she gently stroked her chin. It was a pose she often assumed when lost in thought. On this day, the gold ring on her finger, the one her father once wore, touched the soft skin beneath her jawbone. Lucille smiled at the memory of running up to him as a little girl in that very clearing. He would always greet her by brushing the back of his fingers along her chin, his chunky ring lightly grazing her. She could feel his presence—especially now.

Frozen in place, Lucille stared past the baby-blue wood siding of her grand home, a finely built wedding cake of wood and plaster, down the rocky slope that led to the Perilous River. The current had grown violent that day, and the water appeared darker than usual to her.

"The time is near," Lucille whispered to herself. "The time is very near."

Then, like a starter pistol had fired in her head, she took off, swiftly yanking the spears and knives from the trees. She raced up the winding path to Peniel, the museum she had directed for more than forty years.

Hanging off the edge of a soaring cliff behind Aunt Lucille's home, Peniel was the high point of Perilous Falls. The gray-and-white stone structure looked like a medieval fortress. In fact, it had been constructed from bits of monastery and cathedral ruins Jacob Wilder had collected during his many travels. A domed roof, clusters of spired cathedral-like buildings, and a rectangular bell tower rose high above the wall that completely encircled the museum.

It was officially called Peniel: The Jacob Wilder Reliquarium and Antiquities Collection, but the locals simply called it "the museum" since it was the only one in all of Perilous Falls.

Aunt Lucille emerged from the steep, tree-covered path in minutes. She rounded Peniel's forbidding outer wall and entered the complex through the centuries-old black wrought-iron gate. Lifelike gargoyles with hideous faces stared down at her from the roofline of the main building. High above the Gothic main entrance, at the center, perched a statue of a regal young man seated on a throne. He wore a crown atop his head and extended a sharp golden sickle, like a scepter, over the edge of the roof.

Aunt Lucille climbed the central stairs, hiding her weapons behind one of the fat planters outside. She then pushed open the heavy oak doors bearing an image of St. George lancing a fearsome dragon. Lucille had seen the carving so often, she gave it no attention. She determinedly walked past a handful of visitors inspecting the outer library and passed into Bethel Hall.

The light from the stained-glass windows and the amber radiance from the seven gold candelabras spaced throughout the room cast an otherworldly glow from the high Gothic ceilings down to the red jasper and marble floor.

Lucille dodged the exhibit cases populating the room. She pulled an antique key from her pocket and shoved it into the lock of a small door marked "Private" at the rear of the main hall.

"Loo-ceele? Is that you, Lucille?" a voice boomed from a corner of the great room.

"Yes, Bart, it's me. I have to run upstairs to check on something," she said without stopping.

"If you're clickety-clackin' that fast, it must be a *big* sumpthin'," the low voice in a shadowed corner of the hall rumbled.

Lucille pounded up a tight spiral staircase that wound in circles for several floors. At the top of the stairs stood a mahogany door, weathered by age and held together by thick bands of black metal that ran across its front.

At the center of the door was a sculpture of a muscular angel pouring water from a chalice into a black pit. Surrounding the pit were claws and tails and people in anguish. The pit was indicated by a dark hole in the middle of the door—a door that had no knob or ring of any kind.

Aunt Lucille drew a chain from around her neck. A five-inch gold cross with jagged teeth near the bottom hung from the chain. She inserted the cross and both her hands into the dark hole at the center of the door. She expertly turned the cross to the right, then to the left, pushed, then waited. Two pieces of metal with half-circle cutouts slid in from either side of the hole. The metal panels held her wrists firmly in place. Suddenly the sound of aged gears spinning filled the corridor.

CLUNK, CLUNK, CLUNK, CLUNK, CLUNK, CLUNK, CLUNK.

The locks yielded. The metal panels of the "pit" coasted back into place, and the door swung open on its own.

Beyond a small entry hall, past a half-drawn curtain embroidered with winged animals, a spacious stone room was filled with curiosities. Fading purple sunlight bled through the Gothic arched windows. The plum-colored light touched a fractured skull on one bookshelf, a twisted wooden staff on another. Cracked leather-bound books were stacked everywhere. On the right was a narrow black metal door embedded like a safe into the stone wall. Aunt Lucille purposefully walked past it, stepping behind a mahogany desk emblazoned with an oversized *W*. She turned to the imposing fireplace on the rear wall.

Placing her hands on the chiseled angel heads on either side of the fireplace, she spun their chins toward each other. A stone panel just above the mantel snapped back. Out popped an olive-colored book with seven ancient locks along its edge. The molded locks, each in the shape of a distinctive claw, held the covers together.

Lucille reverently laid the volume on the mahogany desk. She brushed the dust off the copper curlicues adorning the outer edges of the cover. Then, pressing her trembling hands to the desktop, she read the gold calligraphy inscribed on a leather panel on the book's cover:

The Prophecy of Abbot Anthony the Wise

The Lord came to me upon the waters and said:
Take thee a great book and write upon it as I instruct thee.
My spirit trembled, for the visions He placed in my head
    frightened me.
Still, I write in obedience:
In those days, when the people have grown hard of heart
and belief has dwindled;
when wickedness has become commonplace; and the Brethren
    have broken their unity;
then shall I raise up a young one to lead them.
He shall be the firstborn of the root of Wilder.
He shall have the sight of the angels
and perceive darkness from light.
Behold, when his time is ripe, he shall come riding on a colt,
    the foal of a donkey, and his blood shall spill.
This shall be the sign that the battle is near
and all must prepare.
For in those days the beasts shall rise from the pit
to test my people. . . .

Lucille stopped reading. Her eyes ran back over the inscription, seeking the words she had come to confirm.

. . . he shall come riding on a colt, the foal of a donkey, and his blood shall spill. This shall be the sign that the battle is near and all must prepare.

She inhaled slowly, trying to steady herself—caught between tears and laughter, panic and elation. Her hopes had been dashed so many times before—for so many decades. Had the time of the prophecy's fulfillment finally come? Lucille scooped up the heavy olive volume, returned it to its hiding place, and twisted the angel heads into alignment with their stone wings. Once the panel had closed, she fled the office.

In the waiting room of Chorazin General Hospital, Wilder voices were raised.

"I agree that he needs to be punished, but not for the entire summer," Deborah pleaded with her husband.

"If we don't show him that we mean business, this will continue, Deb. He needs to be punished—for weeks," Dan said in his steeliest tone. "He can't do whatever he wants."

Will sat in a row of chairs behind his parents, allowing him to hear everything they were saying. Marin entertained herself doing cartwheels on the industrial carpet while Will, his pith helmet on his lap, pretended to watch the TV hanging in the corner of the room.

"I guess we could ask your aunt Lucille if Will could help her at the museum," Deb suggested.

"No. Not the museum—how many times have I said I don't want him there?"

"Oh, for Pete's sake! C'mon, Dan. It's a part of your family history."

"No."

"It's a fascinating place for a child. If you're going to punish him for weeks, he may as well learn something."

Dan Wilder's right eye started to twitch. "Not at Peniel. No. He can't go there."

"Well, then *you* come up with a place for him to spend weeks and weeks. What do you suggest, a junior chain gang?" Deborah's voice was growing more piercing by the moment. "You spent your entire childhood at that museum. Your aunt Lucille raised you, and I don't understand why your son . . ."

Deborah continued, but Will was no longer listening. He was distracted by pictures on the television of terrified people being dragged from an overturned boat. Will walked over to the mounted TV and turned up the volume.

"Earlier today, thirty-six passengers boarded this Modo riverboat for a sightseeing cruise along the Perilous River," the young reporter wearing a baseball cap said, standing at the water's edge. "Within hours the boat struck an unidentified object and capsized, taking on water. Authorities tell us that nearly all the passengers have been accounted for, and there are no known fatalities. Area hospitals are treating the injured. The boat's crewman spoke to us exclusively only moments after emergency workers pulled him from the river. Here is his eyewitness account. . . ."

Two officers held a burly, water-soaked man of about thirty by the arms. He was loud, spoke rapidly, and seemed to be on the verge of tears.

"I can't say for sure what happened. I done this job for ten years and I never seen this kind of thing. We was going along fine, just like always, and I feel this bump, like somethin' big hit the boat. Don't know what the heck it was. Felt like a whale or somethin'. Whole thing started leanin', and I knew we was going over. People were fallin' off the decks. I grabbed hold of one lady and dragged her to shore. She was breathin' and all, but couldn't talk or even close her eyes. She was frozen. Couple others like that too."

The station cut back to the reporter who was once again standing on the bank of the Perilous River before the capsized boat. "As you can see behind me, there is a huge dent in the hull," the reporter said, pointing. "What caused this accident or just how many of the thirty-six passengers were affected is still unclear. In a possibly related story, a fifty-six-year-old fisherman, Billy Reynard, went out on the river early this morning. His family discovered his boat late this afternoon, but no sign of Billy. If you have any information, please contact the authorities. Police are investigating, and they remain on the scene here at the Perilous River. We will update you as we know more. Back to you, Natalie."

Will wanted to tell his mom and dad about the report, but they were still deep in their own conversation.

"It's a bad idea, Deb. She'll fill his head with her crazy notions," Dan argued, holding his head in his hands.

"Then take him down to city hall with you. Maybe he can be a gofer or answer your phones," Deborah offered.

"Can I say something here?" Will asked, turning in his chair.

"Briefly," his father replied, looking at him over the top of his glasses.

"I'm sorry about what happened," Will said, summoning his most angelic tone. "And I know you both think I should be punished. But it was an *accident*. If I had known that the donkey was going to go nuts, I would have just done the circle routine with him."

Deborah Wilder was on her feet, pacing. "You're missing the point, Will. Your little brother's arm is broken in two places, and he dislocated a shoulder. He can't compete in the karate championships, and now our trip is canceled. Aunt Freda is staying here overnight because her blood pressure is spiking, and she has a fractured jaw. So don't for a moment think, young man, that you are going to sweet-talk your way out of a punishment." Her long brown bangs were now angrily bouncing in front of her face. "There will be a punishment. You *will* be punished!"

"It was an accident, Mom," Will begged. "I was supposed to go bike riding with Simon, Cami, and Andrew this week. They're all counting on me."

"You should have thought about that before you jumped on the donkey. Your family is in the hospital because of your choices, son. Your friends are suffering because of you," Deborah scolded.

Will opened his mouth to respond.

"Mr. and Mrs. Wilder?" a nurse called out as she entered

through the double glass doors. "The doctor is ready to see you now."

Deborah was suddenly sunshine again. "Great. Sure. Yes, we're coming," she said as if the cameras were about to roll at the start of her weekly show.

Aunt Lucille suddenly appeared behind the nurse. "I'm sorry I'm late. Dan and Deb, you two go look after Leo. I'll watch the kids in here."

Once Dan and Deborah exited the waiting room, Aunt Lucille set Marin up with a coloring book and called Will over to the vinyl couch near the TV.

"Let me see your hand," Aunt Lucille said urgently. Will extended his bandaged paw. She peeled back the tape and unfolded the gauze. "It's not too bad now, though that's a nasty gash."

"It bled a lot, but it's not deep," Will said, reapplying the tape.

"Tell me something, dear. Why did you get on that donkey?"

"I thought it would be fun, but my parents said no. Then my friends bet me that I couldn't ride it—and that only made me want to ride it more."

"Besides Leo getting hurt, did you—did you see anything out of the ordinary?"

Will shook his head and looked at the ground. "No."

"Will." Aunt Lucille put her hand on his sharp chin and lifted his gaze to hers. "Tell me."

"I think I'm tired. It was nothing."

"Tell Aunt Lucille what you saw. Don't be afraid, dear." She leaned close, and in her huskiest voice added, "I can help you."

"It was a shadow." Fear washed over Will's face. He ran his thumb along the jagged, tooth-marked brim of his pith helmet. "It was black, like a phantom—right next to me. Everything got icy cold."

Lucille placed a silken arm around the boy. "It was a spirit. You saw a dark spirit, Will. You've probably been seeing them for a long time, hmm?"

Will nodded. "How did you—"

"There is a reality all around us that most people can't see—but you can. It's a precious gift. I've only known one other person in my entire life who could see those things. He told me that everywhere we go, there are bright, good spirits and dark, malevolent ones." She could see the concern in his eyes. He looked as if he wanted to run away. "Oh, listen, whatever you do, you must not be afraid."

"If you saw this thing, you'd be scared too," Will said. "It was like a monster—a black hole—and it stretched all over the yard."

"When did it appear—exactly?" Aunt Lucille asked.

"Before I got on the donkey and right after Leo got hurt."

"So it appeared twice?" Aunt Lucille knit her eyebrows in concern.

"Uh-huh," Will responded. "They usually disappear, but this one stayed put."

"Will, our gifts are given to us for the good of others.

We are all set apart for some great work. This may be part of your work," Aunt Lucille said, rubbing his shoulder. "I promise to help you make sense of this gift, and you might even be able to help me, dear."

"What do you mean?"

Aunt Lucille hesitated. She tapped her hand on the pith helmet resting on Will's knees. "There is a book that your great-grandfather kept—"

In a rush, Deborah and Dan barged into the room still bickering about Will's punishment.

". . . then I'll give him chores to do around the house for three weeks," Deb told her husband.

"How does that teach him a lesson?" Dan demanded.

Will started to speak, but Aunt Lucille shushed him with a flutter of her hand. "Deborah, I have an idea. Why don't you let Will serve out his punishment with me?"

"N-n-n-no . . . he's not going to Peniel," Dan sputtered, shaking a finger in the air. "We've discussed it. He's not going there."

"Did I say he was going to Peniel?" Aunt Lucille said, rising to her feet with annoyance. She pulled the brocade collar of her silk jacket up around her neck, ignoring Dan. "I have been doing some volunteer gardening at the church. St. Thomas has that piece of land along the river with nothing on it—looks ghastly. Will can come plant the new trees I bought for the churchyard."

"Is this the help you were talking about?" Will whispered to her.

Aunt Lucille shot him a cold look and pressed on. "The planting will take at least two weeks. What do you say?"

Dan and Deborah turned to each other, and just as they opened their mouths to respond, Aunt Lucille clapped her hands. "It's decided, then. Father Cash will be so excited when I tell him we have another volunteer. Meet me at the church in the morning, Will. And bring your helmet—the sun can be brutal. Now, where exactly is Leo? I want to see his cast." With that, Aunt Lucille shook her strawberry-blond curls and sped toward the waiting room door as Deb trailed behind her.

Dan Wilder apprehensively approached his son, one hand firmly clutching the other. "Just do the garden work, and after a few weeks . . . assuming you do a good job, we'll reevaluate."

Will nodded in agreement. He placed the old pith helmet on his head, pulling the brim down over his eyes.

Dan stared at the hat in disgust. "Do you have to wear that . . . thing . . . indoors?" he mumbled.

Emergency workers pushed two stretchers down the hallway, past the waiting room window. One carried a catatonic man with wide eyes; the other, a squirming, dripping-wet middle-aged woman.

"This guy's vitals are not in normal reference range. He's unresponsive. Slow heart rate. He hasn't said a word," one of the paramedics informed the attending doctor. The man on the stretcher wore a damp captain's uniform and stared up at the ceiling, frozen, as if he were a mannequin.

The hefty woman on the other stretcher kicked her blood-streaked legs as she attempted to sit up. Shredded fabric dangled from the bottom of her purple dress.

"Something was in the water!" she screamed hysterically to the medics pushing her. "Don't tell me I was scratched by some sunken tree branches. I felt—claws! Look at my legs. Something is out there!"

Through the thick glass Will and his father could hear the muffled sound of the woman's voice, but neither of them could decipher her words.

CHAPTER 3

TWELVE TREES

The water gushing over the boulders at the falls created a soothing backdrop of sound that enveloped St. Thomas the Apostle Church. The building seemed to spring from the rocks alongside the Perilous River. One of the church's stone walls rose up from the water's edge, capped by a central spire. In its shadow, Will unhappily counted the trees leaning against the rear of the church, wishing he could be anywhere but there.

As the bells tolled, marking the end of the Monday morning Mass, Will saw a handful of people—no more than eight—walking toward their cars. Soon Aunt Lucille and a pink-faced, roly-poly priest in green vestments emerged from the rear door of the church. Aunt Lucille descended the stairs with her usual swift grace. She was wearing a long-sleeved wheat-colored silk outfit that didn't look anything like gardening attire. The jolly priest remained on the top step as if he were the pope preparing to address a crowd gathered below.

Perspiration dotted the bald priest's forehead, and he seemed out of breath. Waving a hand in the air, he blared, "Billy boy!" Will startled. "I want to thank you so much for volunteering to help out with the yard. Your aunt Lucille tells me you're in for the long haul. Is that right, Billy boy?"

"I guess so, Father," Will nervously said, faking a smile. "And my name is Will. . . ."

Father Ulan Cash scrunched the features of his basketball-shaped head into a mock grimace. "Is Billy sad today?" he bellowed in an absurd baby voice. "Don't be! Sun is shining and the day is new. Now look, Billy, I wish I could get out there and shovel some earth with you myself. But this is the only two weeks I'll get off till after Christmas. Gotta catch a flight to Minneapolis in a few hours." He panted as he continued. "But you won't be alone. Old Tobias Shen'll take care of you."

"Tobias?" Will shot a confused glance at Aunt Lucille.

"He's the groundskeeper around here—helps out in the church too. If you and your family came to Mass more often, you'd know Tobias. See, when you skip church, you miss out on so much! Haaaw-haaw-haaaw." He quickly recovered from the simulated laughter. "Tobias has been at this parish a lot longer than I have. From near the beginning, right, Lucille?"

Aunt Lucille nodded, turning a chilly eye on Will.

"Lucille and Tobias go way back. Anyway, he'll tell you where to plant the trees. He's doing Mass cleanup now, but he'll be along shortly. In the meantime, why don't you drag those saplings to the middle of the field so you'll be ready for his direction? Look, it's great seeing you, Billy. Come back and let's have a chat sometime, okay? Okay?"

"Sure, Father," Will said halfheartedly.

Father Cash gave a double-handed wave with his massive palms, flashed a yellowed smile toward Aunt Lucille, and disappeared into the church.

Will did as he was told. He bent over and clumsily hugged a tree twice his size. He squatted to hoist the thing into the air, but it was so heavy he couldn't really straighten up, so he waddled in a low crouch to the middle of the yard.

"Well done, Will. The shovels and hoes are in that storage shed behind the church," Aunt Lucille said, straightening the emerald-green necklace at her throat. "Call if you need anything. I'll be just a few minutes away." Aunt Lucille slid her purse strap toward her elbow as if she were about to leave.

Will unceremoniously opened his arms, depositing the tree on the spot where he stood.

"Uh, Aunt Lucille?" he said, removing his pith helmet and mopping his forehead with the back of his bandaged hand. "I thought *you* volunteered to do yard work and I was going to help you."

"You are helping me, dear. You're taking my place. This is a job for one man, not a man and an old woman. We learn more by doing than observing, Will. Sometimes it's better to be thrown into the middle of things. How would it look if I were out there in the blazing sun doing backbreaking yard work while a strapping young man like you stood around staring?"

"It'd look fine," Will countered.

"I think it would be embarrassing—for you, dear. . . . Besides, I know nothing about gardening. I made that up to get you out of sitting in that vile city hall for days. Do I look like a gardener? I have a museum to run, which I really must attend to." She glanced down at her watch. "Oooh. Tobias will give you instructions once he arrives."

"So I'm doing this alone?"

"That's usually the best way to experience a punishment. Now please keep the pith helmet on your head or you'll burn to a crisp, and stay away from that river. There was some nasty business downstream yesterday. Very nasty business, apparently. Whatever attacked those poor people is still out there, so you stay on dry land. Oh, and let me know if you *see* anything out of the ordinary." Her voice dropped to the basement, and with a wink she added, "You know what I mean."

"What if one of those shadowy things comes back? You can't leave me alone—"

"If you see anything, just tell Tobias. You can trust him, and he's quite capable. All you have to do is follow his directions. I'll check in with you later." She turned to leave.

"What about the book my great-grandfather kept? The one you started to tell me about at the hospital."

Aunt Lucille stopped walking and slowly turned her head toward Will. "Not now. Not yet. . . ." She hesitated as if she wanted to say something more. "There'll be time to talk about the book and your great-grandfather . . . later." She blew Will a kiss and headed for the parking lot.

Will petulantly popped the pith helmet onto his head. He couldn't believe that his favorite relative had condemned him to weeks of lonesome gardening servitude. Answering phones at city hall would have been a lot easier. He unhappily kicked his red sneakers into the dirt while hatefully eyeing the pile of trees waiting to be moved from the church. *I can't do this for weeks,* Will thought. *There's got to be a way to get off yard duty. Maybe I can make a deal with Tobias?*

Behind him, Will felt a strange presence. The fear straightened his spine. He shut his eyes, gathered some courage, and abruptly spun around. Standing no more than six feet away was a slight Chinese man in a gray workman's uniform. Deep, sun-carved lines surrounded his eyes and mouth. He had a full head of white hair and an expressionless round face.

"You move like a turtle in a snowstorm," he said, without so much as a hint of humor. Strands of his hair floated like mist in the humid wind as he stared at Will. "I am Tobias Shen. We will be working together." He carried a folding chair and an unvarnished walking stick.

"Did Lucille tell you to move the trees here?" Tobias's face was fixed as stone and unreadable.

"Uh, yes—I mean, Father Cash did."

"Well, what are you waiting for? Move the trees." Tobias gestured to the ground with his walking stick. *"Here."*

"All of them?"

Shen's faint eyebrows rose. "Let's make a deal. You move eleven of them here. I'll move the last one myself."

Will scratched his head. "If you tell me where you want them planted, I could drag each one to the right spot now."

"Trees are like people—they enjoy being close together. After you move all eleven here, we will discuss their placement."

"But that's double the work," Will complained. "Why don't we let the trees have their family time now, and later I can move them to their final resting places?"

"Shhhhhh." Tobias threw his walking stick to the ground. "Obedience requires following one direction at a time, Mr. Wilder. When you complete one task, then you receive the next task. Very simple." With a flick of his wrist he opened the folding chair and jammed its legs into the ground.

"So you want me to move all those trees to the middle of the yard, then move them again?"

"Good listening. Yes, Mr. Wilder. Stack eleven of them here, and I will move the twelfth myself. I came to assist you."

Will shuffled over to the back wall of the church, imagining Tobias Shen was following behind him. But the man with the downturned mouth remained standing by the folding chair, never taking his black eyes off Will.

"From over there you look just like your great-grandfather

Jacob Wilder," Tobias said, finally breaking into a smile, deep wrinkles running from his eyes. "Of course, he moved much faster than you. I knew him when I was a boy. Are you warm?" Shen squinted and looked heavenward. "It's very warm out here today. I need my hat. Continue moving trees." Like a toy soldier, Shen stiffly made his way down the path toward the gray stone rectory next to the church, as if his knees no longer functioned.

Will exhaled in protest, bitterly threw his arms around one of the trees leaning against the church, and wobbled out onto the field. From a distance, his unwieldy attempt to balance the huge tree resembled that of an ant trying to relocate a telephone pole. By the time he got to the middle of the yard, Shen had emerged from his house wearing a broad-brimmed straw hat. "Now we both have protection from sun," Shen said as he walked.

Attempting to lower the tree to the ground, Will lost control and somersaulted over the trunk onto the grass.

"Urgh," Will moaned, adjusting the helmet he was glad to be wearing.

Looking down at the boy, Shen clasped his strong, craggy, age-spotted hands in front of his body. "Even a turtle in a snowstorm must get off his back and keep moving. Up, up, up. Nine more trees, Mr. Wilder." Shen fell into the folding chair. "If your great-grandfather had moved like you, this town would still be a wilderness overrun by wild beasts."

"I know, I know," Will huffed, leaping to his feet.

"Tell me what you know."

"I know that my family founded Perilous Falls. My great-grandfather Jacob built the town. Then my grandfather Joseph and Aunt Lucille helped grow it. . . ."

"Jacob built this church right after World War II. Did you know that?"

"I guess not."

Shen pointed to the back wall of the church. "When you select your next tree, read the plaque on the cornerstone there. Go, go, go."

Will tilted the pith helmet back and followed orders. The bronze plaque had a small frieze of Jacob Wilder, who did share Will's crescent eyes, sharp cheekbones, and chin. The plaque read:

THIS CHURCH ERECTED JUNE 13, 1947,
BY JACOB WILDER
FOR THE PRESERVATION OF THE RELIC OF
ST. THOMAS THE APOSTLE,
A GIFT FROM ARCHBISHOP PIETRO TESAURI
OF LANCIANO-ORTONA, ITALY.
"FOR CHARITY DELIVERS FROM DEATH AND KEEPS ONE
FROM ENTERING THE DARKNESS."
TOBIT 4:10

Will embraced the next tree and teetered out into the field.

"Almost there," Shen cried out. "Now only eight more."

Will tossed the tree next to the others in the field.

Winded by the effort, he bent at the waist to catch his breath. Glancing up at Tobias, he asked, "What's this St. Thomas relic all about?"

"You don't know about the relic?"

"Nope."

"You have never seen the relic?" the old man asked with astonishment.

"Nope."

"Pity. It is the finger bone of St. Thomas. We keep it protected inside the church."

"Why does it need protection? Who'd want it?"

An exasperated Shen folded his arms and leaned back in the folding chair. "Do you know what many people believe keeps the river from flooding this town?"

Will shrugged and shook his head.

"The relic! The relic of St. Thomas! People pray to the saint, and his prayers have great power in heaven. Miracles wait on his intercession. Like a magnifying glass focuses sunlight, so the relic focuses faith."

"Hmm." Will smirked skeptically.

"Do you know who St. Thomas is?"

"An apostle who followed Jesus?"

Shen slapped his thighs and pursed his thin lips. "The great-grandson of the man who built this glorious shrine to Thomas knows nothing about the saint. If you don't know your past, you will never discover your future, young Wilder. St. Thomas was the doubting apostle—like others I know." He raised his eyebrows and got very still. "The only way he would believe the Savior had risen from the dead was to shove his hand into the Lord's side and his finger into the nail wounds of Christ."

"And that finger is in this church?" Will asked, sitting in the grass.

Tobias Shen wiggled forward in his chair, the promise of a smile on his lips. "The relic is in a special Keep designed by your great-grandfather. We display the finger bone once a year on the Feast Day of St. Thomas—coming soon—on July third. But at all other times, it is locked in the church Keep."

"Is that some kind of safe?"

"A very complicated safe. Very detailed—tricky to get into. Only the parish priest and a Wilder can—"

Will's head snapped to study Tobias's face.

The old man had clearly said more than he wished. He shut his hooded eyes and spoke carefully. "The Keep is ingenious and dangerous. There are special rules for getting into it. Not just anyone can go in there."

"But a Wilder can get in?" Will said, drumming his fingers on his knees.

"I suppose. Your great-grandfather wrote elaborate plans in a notebook. But I have never seen it. What matters is the relic is safe."

"And this relic can do what?"

"For centuries people have claimed miracles from just touching it: healings, protection, amazing things. Your great-grandfather Jacob used to say, 'The relic is a key that unlocks the faith.' The relic attracts holiness—and where holiness grows, evil is diminished. This is why we must protect the relic—all relics."

Will rolled his eyes. *Probably a legend,* he thought. *Or maybe not.* In the silence, his brain started working overtime. *I'm sure Dad doesn't believe any of this stuff—*

"Enough rest," Tobias Shen announced. "These trees still need moving, Mr. Wilder." Shen pulled a thin pipe from his front pocket and began to shove tobacco into the nozzle. He used it to point toward the tree pile. "Quick, quick, quick."

Will begrudgingly moved the remaining eight trees, taking short rests in between. All the while he began to think about the relic and how it might be able to deliver him from the punishment he so despised—assuming it was real and not some old lore concocted by his ancestor.

"All right, Mr. Shen. I did my part," Will said, fanning himself with his pith helmet. "Eleven trees piled, as ordered. Mr. Shen? Mr. Shen?"

Tobias Shen dozed in his folding chair, his head tilted to the side.

Will shifted his lips sideways with irritation. "Mr. Shen! You said if I moved eleven trees, you'd move the last one."

Mr. Shen woke with a jolt. "Oh, finished so soon?"

"Yes, sir. Now, about the last tree. There are no more over by the church."

"You are right." Tobias Shen reached down and picked up his rough walking stick. "Here is the last tree."

"That's a . . . a . . . AH-CHOO! It's a . . . AH-CHOO!"

"Your allergies are very bad, Mr. Wilder. Do trees not agree with you?" Shen queried.

"That's not a tree, it's . . . ah-ah-AH-CHOO!" A series of violent sneezes overtook Will. His eyes watering, he managed to say, "It's a stick. Not a tree. You said you were going to move the last tree."

"After you water the stick, feed it, give it love, it will become the last tree. Since the last will be first, you can plant it near the river there." Shen pointed to the very edge of the grass, where the land sloped down to the riverbank.

"You want me to plant a walking stick?" Will asked drily.

"I want you to be obedient." Shen stood, holding the gnarled staff. There was writing carved into the wood near the knobby top. "He who is obedient in little things will be obedient in big things, Mr. Wilder."

Will sullenly took the stick and a shovel and marched to the spot Shen had indicated, sneezing the whole time. Will had never seen letters like those engraved at the top of the staff:

הֵכֹ ֹהֵן אֲהָר ֹן.

Probably Chinese, Will thought, studying the writing for a minute.

"This is very hard work." Shen began to yawn. "It's nap time. Go ahead and plant the tree there. When you're finished, you may plant another opposite it, over here." Shen pointed to a place near the pathway to the rectory. He then acted out each step. "Dig the hole first, place the tree in, then cover the roots with dirt. It's all very simple. And don't go near the river."

As Shen tottered away, Will began to dig a hole for the walking cane, muttering complaints under his breath.

Inside the Wilder home at 490 Rapids Lane, Leo and Marin were in the family room watching cartoons when they first heard the bizarre sound.

Any time a Wilder child was ill, the family room was transformed into their personal sickroom. They were given control of the TV while Deb Wilder lavished him or her with soup and attention. Since Leo's catapult accident, the plaster cast covering his right arm had given him full control of the family room. And he used it.

King of the couch, Leo was in the middle of watching his seventh consecutive episode of *Breadbox Roundhead*, a mindless animated series set in an abandoned school cafeteria. Leo exploded with laughter as Breadbox tumbled from the countertop, shattering to pieces for the umpteenth time—exactly as he had in the six earlier episodes. Feeling restless during a blaring commercial break, Marin hopped up and cartwheeled in front of the flat screen. She momentarily blocked Leo's view.

"Could you sit down and stop flipping?" Leo said.

"I can flip anywhere I want to flip. I'm working out like

Mom," Marin responded, positioning herself for another cartwheel.

Leo removed a half-eaten bowl of popcorn from his lap, placing it on the coffee table before him. He pointed a threatening finger at his sister. "This can go one of two ways," he whispered. "Either you stop jumping in front of the TV, or I'm getting Dad."

"This is not your bedroom, Leo! We can all play here," Marin said. She proceeded to throw her hands to the floor and repeatedly flip in front of the screen.

"That's it. I've had it!" Leo exploded. He leapt to his feet and began chasing his sister in circles around the room, his sling barely holding the cast in place.

Marin jumped on top of a recliner. "Something is wrong with you. Mom said you were supposed to keep still, not run wild."

"Something is wrong with me? Something is wrong with *me*? I'm not the one who travels by cartwheel! When do you EVER sit still?" Leo was now yelling, furiously motioning with his healthy arm. "I try to watch a show in peace and quiet and you have to barge in and . . ." His mouth warped into a grimace. "Ayyyyyeeeeeeeee."

"What's wrong, Leo?"

"My shoulder. I hurt my shoulder." Leo backed into the couch, trying not to move the arm in the cast.

Dan Wilder raced into the room. "What—what's happening, Leo?"

"I think I hurt my shoulder. Marin was jumping in front

of the TV, and then she made me chase her around the room."

Marin lost it. "I did not! You chased me around the room!" Her waterworks started running. "Daddy, he chased me around the rooooooooom!"

Dan closed his eyes and folded his arms as if trying to calm himself. "Kids, I'm finishing up some very important work. Now please, Leo, sit there. Marin, you sit in the recliner by the window and just watch TV. Your brother's arm is hurting, and we have enough problems without fights. So just—just relax. Relax . . . and get along." He rubbed the back of his head and darted from the room.

After several minutes of taking in the mind-numbing antics of Breadbox Roundhead, Marin broke the silence. "We saw this episode last week, Leo. Can I do one cartwheel?"

"No."

"Come on. Just one. Pleeeeeeease."

"I said no."

THUNK.

The kids fell silent and looked up at the ceiling. Leo muted the TV.

THUNK. THUNK.

Something was hitting the roof.

"What is it, Leo?"

"Shut up. I can't hear if you're—"

THUNK. THUNK. THUNK.

Whatever it was, was landing in threes—and hitting the house with greater frequency.

THUNK. THUNK. THUNK.

"Is it acorns?" Marin asked.

"You think squirrels are throwing acorns three at a time? Or are they just falling off the trees three at a—"

THUNK. THUNK. THUNK.

Marin yelled for her father, who exploded into the room moments later. "Can't you all get along for ten minutes without—"

THUNK. THUNK. THUNK.

THUNK. THUNK. THUNK.

Marin's brown eyes were huge. "Daddy . . . what is that?" she whimpered.

Dan raised his chin to the ceiling and listened.

THUNK. THUNK. THUNK.

THUNK. THUNK. THUNK.

"Daddy, I'm scared," Marin said.

"Me too," Leo sputtered.

Never taking his eyes off the ceiling, Dan Wilder headed toward the front door. "You two stay here."

The sounds were even louder outside, and they were coming from the roof.

THUNK. THUNK. THUNK.

Dan went to the garage and fished out his long ladder, the one he used once a year to hang Christmas lights. He leaned it up against the side of the house. Through the family room window he could see Marin pressing her face against the glass and Leo watching him with rapt attention. As he climbed the aluminum ladder the sound grew more intense.

THUNK. THUNK. THUNK.

THUNK. THUNK. THUNK.

The objects were falling faster and faster and still in threes.

Dan raised his head over the edge of the roof to find his gutter filled with what he thought were dark rocks falling from the sky. He quickly checked Heinrich Crinshaw's house and glanced across the street. The things were only dropping onto his own home. Each one pounded the roof and then rolled into the gutter, a few spilling onto the ground.

THUNK. THUNK. THUNK.

When he dug his hand into the gutter, Dan realized these weren't rocks hitting his house, but slimy green clams, stinking fish bones, sticks, and crab shells.

"Where are they coming from?" Dan said to himself. He stared into the cloudless sky overhead. The shells and bones and barnacled bits of wood fell like hail—from out of nowhere. Panting, Dan climbed down the ladder and ran into the house. His face had turned an ashen white, and he started to sweat.

"What is it, Daddy?" Leo asked.

THUNK. THUNK. THUNK.

"It's . . . it's nothing. . . . Go into the kitchen, kids," Dan said.

Marin touched her father's arm. "It *is* acorns, isn't it, Daddy? Is it acorns?"

THUNK. THUNK. THUNK.

"No, honey. It's not." Dan gently pushed the children out of the den.

THUNK. THUNK. THUNK.

"Where is it coming from?" Leo asked.

"I don't know, son. I . . . I don't know."

CHAPTER 4

CAPTAIN NEP BALOR

By late afternoon on that Monday along the Perilous River, clouds had consumed the sun. With the back of a shovel, Will patted the soil around the newly planted walking stick behind St. Thomas Church. Then he felt it coming. His eyes rolled back in frustration as he helplessly endured another sneezing fit. The sneezes were so loud they competed with the sound of the water crashing over the falls.

During a brief lull between sneezes, Will jiggled the handle of the walking stick to make sure that it had been buried deep enough to withstand the elements. Before he had released the stick, another titanic sneeze shook him.

"Why are ye wasting yer time there? That'll never grow!" a voice, which seemed to come from the deep, thundered behind Will.

When he turned, the boy spotted an enormous silhouette

standing on the deck of a touring boat near the riverbank. The speaker's features were shadowed by a sooty red-and-blue canopy running the length of the vessel. On the side of the craft's glossy hull the name *Tiamat* was painted in tall gold letters.

"Was it yer idea, son, to plant a withered stick in the ground?" the gravelly, spittle-laden voice asked.

"No, sir. It wasn't my idea."

"Well, we'd like to meet the fool who thinks a stick could bloom along these waters. Ha, ha, ha." The enormous riverboat pilot wore a ratty olive-colored slicker. His long, limp gray hair could not be contained by the rain hat he wore. With its turned-up brim, it reminded Will of the fisherman's hat on those boxes of frozen fish his mom sometimes served for dinner. But it was the sheer size of the seaman that held Will's attention. The broad, hunched back of the boatman was like that of a charging bull.

Will couldn't stop staring. He had never seen anyone so mammoth. With one massive arm, the pilot easily picked up the anchor and tossed it over the side of the cruiser. Out of curiosity, Will took a few steps down the sandy riverbank for a better look.

"No, no, stay where ye are," the pilot called out, emerging from his boat. "We'll come yer way." He moved with a lumbering force and speed that Will found frightening—and a little awesome. "These waters are no place for a boy. Been riding the currents long as I can remember. Something terrible stirs out there, I tell yeh."

What could be more terrible than this? Will thought as he eyed the grotesque face before him.

The seafarer had a wide head like a toad, a greenish complexion, and bloated, purpled lips that ran the length of his face. Probably the ugliest thing about the stranger was his bulging eyes. They were spaced too far apart and looked off in different directions. The right, yellowed eye fixed on Will. The larger one on the left, with a milky green iris seemingly surrounded by blood, stared off into the distance. Up close, the boatman looked so horrible Will felt sorry for him. But the boy couldn't hide the hint of revulsion hanging on his face.

"Yer lookin' at our eye, aren't yeh? It don't hurt none. Had it for a long while. Thank ye for not screaming or making light of it." A callused, swollen eyelid snapped shut on the wounded eye. He pointed at the messy orb and tilted his head down to hide it from Will's view. "Can't really see out of that one. But it hasn't stopped us from conquering these waters. Capt'n Nep Balor we are—run the Modo Riverboat Company. Never seen ye here before."

"I'm Will," the boy said, folding his arms.

"Yeh will what?"

"No, my name is Will." He raised his voice in exasperation. "Will's my name."

"Ah. Begging yer pardon, Will. No offense meant. And what are ye doing here?"

"I'm helping out at the church. Planting some things for them." Will wriggled his nose, trying to withhold a sneeze.

"They've got yeh working, boy? My keepers do the same. We labor and sweat while they take their ease. But it ain't safe along these waters. They shouldn't leave ye out here alone. Ye are alone, aren't yeh?"

"Mr. Shen was here earlier."

"Shen? That miserable—" The Captain spit, his lips turning to a snarl. "He's a selfish one. Thinks only of himself. . . . Beware of him, lad."

"Why do you say that?"

"'Cause we known him for years." Nep Balor lifted a grime-streaked hand and held the left side of his face. He gritted his teeth for a moment, as if struck by some sudden pain. "Shen withholds that relic from the people who need it most. What good's it doing locked up in there? . . . Ahh, I shouldn't be burdening a child with all that."

"What do you know about the relic, Captain?"

Nep Balor rotated with hesitation back to Will. His malformed face softened, and he leaned close, a touch of lightness in his voice. "It has the power to heal. Seen it ourselves. So many of us could use it." He lowered his face to Will's level. "Look at our poor eye. Look at it. Sight wasn't always gone." The closed, oozing eye with the beet-red rims appeared to be infected. "Shen could have helped us, could have given us a touch of that relic. But he wants to keep all the power to himself. He's been hoarding it for years and years." The yellowed eye darted over the landscape. "Where is Shen now?"

"He's in his house, napping."

Balor turned his big head to the side and loosed a guttural snicker. "Course he is. Lazing the day away while ye waste yer time on a fool's errand. Burying a stick!" The nostrils of Nep Balor's flat nose flared in anger. "Shen's making a fool of yeh, Will! We've had cruel ones make sport of us every day of our existence. They use us like playthings. He orders ye to do something stupid, like planting a cane, and later he'll come with others to ridicule yeh. That's how they play it, son."

Will became suddenly concerned. Was Tobias Shen attempting to make a fool of him? Was he performing an idiotic task, only to be mocked for it later? Lost in his thoughts, Will's expression went blank. Then a look of hurt filled his eyes, which the Captain caught.

"Cruel is what he is, lad. Yer the one should be resting—not out here slaving for that scheming Shen."

"Why does Mr. Shen keep the relic from people who need it?"

"Never mind all that. It don't matter none." A sadness washed over Balor and he half turned, as if he were about to walk away.

"Wait! Maybe I could get the relic for you," Will said. The thought he'd been tossing around all day had suddenly slipped from his lips.

"How would ye get the relic?" The Captain rubbed his hands excitedly up and down the side of his slicker.

"I'm—I'm not sure," Will said, a tremble in his voice. "You think it could really heal somebody of something?" Will sneezed.

"Think it could heal *anything*."

"Like a broken arm or a shoulder?"

"An eye, an arm, a shoulder—anything. Might even cure sneezes." Captain Balor smiled, revealing a mouthful of uneven teeth like gray barnacles. "But Shen'll never let ye near it. What are ye thinking, lad?"

"Mr. Shen told me that a Wilder—that's my family name: Wilder—can get to the relic. My great-grandfather built the church."

The boatman's yellow eye widened, and the corners of his mouth turned up.

The worried voice of Tobias Shen intruded from the churchyard above. "Mr. Wilder? Mr. Wilder?"

In an unwieldy fashion, Captain Nep Balor sidestepped toward his boat. He displayed all the finesse of two grizzly bears trying to share a dinner jacket.

"Tell Shen nothing, Will. There is much ye don't know. Tomorrow when he goes in, we'll meet ye here—tell ye more. There's a secret way into that church, a way to reach the relic."

He bounded onto the deck of the boat and began to pull up anchor. "Stay on dry land, well away from these waters. Do ye hear us? Till tomorrow, then." The Captain tugged at the front of his rain hat in a type of salute and sped off in the boat.

Will, sweaty from the heat, slowly climbed the embankment back up to the yard. "Coming, Mr. Shen," he called out. Though Will's legs ached with each step, he could think only of the finger bone of St. Thomas. *If the relic can heal—it can fix Leo's arm and shoulder. Once Leo is better, my fieldhand days will be over. He'll be able to compete in the karate championships—and Florida, here we come! I've got to get my hands on that relic. . . .*

"One stick and one hole. After hours and hours you dug one hole and planted one stick?" Shen said, his hands on his hips. The old man's faint eyebrows drew close together. "You're a very lazy boy, Mr. Wilder. Run along home. The day is done. Tomorrow, bright and early, we'll meet here for more landscaping enjoyment. Go, go, go."

Will took off his pith helmet, twisting the pelican medallion on the front with his fingers. "Mr. Shen, after reading that plaque on the church, I'd like to study . . . you know, learn more about the church. Where would that notebook my great-grandfather wrote about it be?"

"Strange sudden curiosity." The groundskeeper did not move a muscle. His face betrayed no emotion as his eyes studied Will. "After you plant more trees tomorrow, we can discuss your great-grandfather's notebook," he said evenly.

Will put the pith helmet back on his head and started kicking at the ground. "That would be great, Mr. Shen, but . . . I'd really like to learn it from my great-grandfather. I never knew him, so reading his book would be kinda cool, ya know?"

"It's not here. I told you, I have never seen it. Good evening, Mr. Wilder. The angels go with you."

"You too, Mr. Shen."

He's holding back on me, Will thought as he waved goodbye to the old groundskeeper. Rather than going directly home via Falls Road, Will ran down a wooded path along the river, toward the center of town. Above the trees in the distance he could see the main tower of Peniel, faintly lit by the dying sunlight.

If that notebook is anywhere, Aunt Lucille will know where to find it, Will thought. Everything Jacob Wilder treasured was stored at Peniel; why not his notebook? Even though his father had discouraged him from going there, Will felt a quick visit couldn't do any harm.

The gravel path he walked upon sloped down along the river's edge. In his peripheral vision, Will saw something stir in the water. His heart began to race. *It's probably just a duck or a log floating downriver,* he reasoned. He determinedly kept his focus on the path ahead, but out of the corner of his eye, what he saw was unmistakable. A huge reptilian tail the size of a tree trunk emerged from the water. The pointed tip of the tail then hooked back on itself, touching the water's surface. When it made contact, bubbles welled up like lava.

Will turned his face to the river. The tail was nowhere to be seen, though steam was wafting over the agitated waters.

Had he imagined it? Was it another "spirit"?

In a gush, bloated and bug-eyed fish poured up from

the depths of the river. Hundreds of dead catfish, bass, and bluegills spun to the surface as if they were boiling in a huge kettle. Will crouched by the shoreline. He could feel the heat coming off the surface of the river. With the tip of his index finger he hesitantly dabbed the water.

"Ouch!" Will screeched, snatching his hand back quickly. He looked down at his freshly scalded skin. The pad of his finger had turned a bright red. Recalling Mr. Shen's, Captain Balor's, and Aunt Lucille's cautions, Will backed away from the water, then dashed toward Peniel with an urgency fueled by fear and excitement.

At Aunt Lucille's baby-blue mansion on the river, he took a sharp right into the backyard. Beyond the clearing flanked by great oaks, Will spotted the craggy rock face he meant to climb. He ran up the steep, winding path and was outside the gates of Peniel within minutes.

Will sheepishly approached the main entryway, having been told repeatedly by his father that he was never to go there alone. He paused for half a second. Then, placing two hands on the lanced dragon carved into the door, he pushed with all his strength. Save for some chanting voices in the distance, the outer library was quiet and dimly lit. A wall of books was held captive by a series of ornate brass grilles that continued up to the ceiling. Every so often a gold pelican, like the one on his pith helmet, appeared to be perched on the grating.

"Who's there?" a deep voice called out from the darkness at the end of the hall.

"Uh . . . is Lucille Wilder here?"

"Depends who's askin'?" the man said. Like an off-kilter spider, a twisted man strode into the candlelight, balanced on two wooden crutches. He had dark skin, a kind, puffy face, and long teeth that gleamed when he smiled, as he did then. With every step, he threw his turned-in, unresponsive right leg to the side. The slightly oversized brown tweed coat and salmon pants he wore gave him the appearance of a homeless professor. "What's goin' on, Will?"

"Oh, Mr. Bartimaeus. I was doing some work at the church and just thought I'd drop by. . . . It's been a long time."

"Will, you and ya aunt Lucille have a lot in common." Bartimaeus squinted and moved close. "Old Bart may not be able to see ya like I used to, but neither of ya can lie— least not without me hearing it. So how's the punishment going?"

"It's all right. I planted a stick today."

"Ha, ha, ha." Bartimaeus rumbled with laughter. "Tobias is a sly one. He never changes. So what brings ya in? It's getting kind of late. Shouldn't ya be home?"

In the corners of the room Will suddenly saw twinkling lights dancing in all directions. He repeatedly blinked to clear his vision, but the glittering lights remained there, hovering. "I had a question. Up at the church, Mr. Shen said there was a notebook my great-grandfather kept when he was building St. Thomas Church. I thought it'd be fun to take a look at it—since I'm spending so much time up there now."

"That I can help you with—since you're family and all. You can find Jacob's notebooks over there in section ten." Bartimaeus pointed a crutch to the bookcases behind Will. "Second bookshelf from the bottom. We keep all of his journals and personal writings there. I can't see worth a nickel anymore, but you can take a peek. Let me open the gate for ya—we don't let just anybody get in here." Bartimaeus reached into his hip pocket, produced a dull green copper key, and unlocked the gate.

Will pulled the thin brass gate wide. If the books had been birds, half the collection might have flown away. There were small journals and leather-bound books of all shapes and sizes.

"So, Will, the St. Thomas Church journal with the plans and all is a little green leather number. It should have a black ribbon holding it together," Bartimaeus said. He looked in the boy's direction, but from the way he squinted, Will sensed that he saw very little.

After scanning the second shelf from the bottom several times, Will finally lighted on the slim emerald-green book. He greedily snatched the volume, untied the black ribbon binding it, and started flipping through the pages.

"Hand it here," Bartimaeus said. The man held it very close to his eyes, then ran his hands along the sides of the book before returning it to Will. "So that's the one; the St. Thomas book. Jacob spent almost as much time building that church as he did building Peniel. While you take a gander at the notebook, I'll go fetch your aunt Lucille."

Bartimaeus took hold of the wooden crutches and propelled himself with some strength out of the library and into the main hall. He had long been Aunt Lucille's right-hand man at Peniel, a constant presence on the rare occasions when Will had visited. His voice reverberated off the high pitched stone ceiling of Bethel Hall's expanse. "Looo-ceeele. Where are ya?"

"No need to yell, Bart," Aunt Lucille said from behind one of the glass cases on the right side of the room.

Spinning around, Bartimaeus excitedly hobbled in her direction. "He's here! Will's out there," he said in a sharp whisper. "Tell him about the prophecy! It's not a mistake that he's come. When was the last time the boy set foot in here alone? Let him at least hold the book."

"He's not ready yet," Aunt Lucille said, her white-gloved hands delicately placing an ancient crimson-and-gold garment into the glass case. "He needs more time. He's so young."

"Ya father was young when he started. You were young. I was young. We were *all* young! You can't control this, Sarah Lucille."

"Perhaps not, but we can prepare him. And that's what I mean to do," Lucille said, calmly arranging the cloth in the case.

Bartimaeus slammed his crutches together in front of his body to get Lucille's attention. "We have been waiting for more than forty years for this moment, Lucille. There's not a day goes by that I don't think about that prophecy. He *must* be the one."

He continued in a perturbed whisper. "After that bit about the donkey and the blood, what does the prophecy say?" He closed his eyes and lifted his head to the ceiling. "'This shall be the sign that the battle is near and all must prepare.' *Prepare!* 'For in those days the beasts shall rise from the pit to test my people. Truth shall go farther away while falsehood and darkness draw near. The inhabitants of the land shall multiply evils and the *Sinestri* shall deceive many. But in those days of tribulation and darkness, I shall pour out my Spirit upon all flesh; sons and daughters shall dream vivid dreams and sing angelic songs; the young shall see visions; and their elders shall prophesy and make war on the foul beasts.'" Bartimaeus smiled widely and pounded out each word that followed. "'Behold, my chosen, the firstborn of the house of Wilder, will lay hands upon this *great book* and its seven locks shall be opened to him alone. . . .'"

"'This too shall be a sign,'" Aunt Lucille continued under her breath sadly. Her hands were still in the glass case, laying out the precious garment. She turned her full attention to the display. "I know the prophecy, Bart."

"So it's his destiny, Lucille. Those beasts are gonna rise one way or another. I think they're among us already. I can feel the *Darkness* all over."

Aunt Lucille frowned and bit her lip. Looking over

Bartimaeus's shoulder, she strained to produce a smile. "Will. Come in, dear," she called out.

In the soft golden haze of the seven burning candelabras, Will marveled at the displays filling the grand hall. He automatically removed his pith helmet, his eyes roving over a dusty skeleton laid out on a rectangular red cushion. Standing like a ghost under glass was a nun's brown habit, complete with a long veil and rosary beads about the waist. Then he happened upon an exhibit that caused him to run right up to the case.

"What is this, Aunt Lucille?" Will asked, pointing at a solid gold arm with two fingers extended toward the sky.

"That's on loan to us from the Metropolitan Museum of Art in New York. Only the gold sculpture is theirs. It's a reliquary—a housing for a sacred relic. Could be a bone, a lock of hair, clothing—anything associated with a saint. Look inside."

Two square holes on the side of the golden arm revealed a long blackened bone. "What is that?"

"It's the ulna—the forearm bone—of St. Peter the Apostle. The Met may have the reliquary, but we have the relic. It's a long story, but this is the first time those two pieces have been reunited in hundreds of years."

"I didn't know Perilous Falls had so many relics. St. Peter's arm is here; St. Thomas's finger is over at the church. You've got enough bones to build a new saint." Will let loose the honking laugh that he reserved for those special moments when he amused himself.

"Don't be flippant," Aunt Lucille warned, narrowing her eyes. "They're sacred touchstones. They're antennae of faith—magnets that draw belief and devotion from us. My father would say, 'A relic is a key to unlock our faith.' These relics are the remains of holy lives. Each and every bone or scrap of clothing is a physical connection to someone now in the presence of God."

"They have real power!" Bartimaeus bellowed, moving between the exhibit cases. "In the Old Testament, in the Second Book of Kings, some fellas were burying a man in the grave of the prophet Elisha. Well, the minute the body touched the bones of the prophet—POW! The man rose up from the dead! Then there was a woman who was bleeding; she barely touched the cloak of Jesus and—POW! Totally healed!"

"So this is all real? You believe this relic stuff?" Will asked.

"Seen it with ma own eyes, son," Bartimaeus said. "Course it's real. You think we'd be wasting our time up in here if this wasn't real?" He swatted a hand in front of his face as if trying to kill a fly. "These are not just old pieces of the past. In the right hands they're spiritual weapons. So they must be respected—and kept out of the wrong hands."

Aunt Lucille reverently removed the faded crimson-and-gold garment from the open case and presented it to Will. "Do you know what this is?"

"No idea."

"This is what remains of the prophet Elijah's mantle,

his cloak. History tells us it can control water and fire, and even allow the wearer to hear the voice of God."

Will went to touch the woven cloth.

"Uh-uh," Aunt Lucille said, pulling the garment away. "No touching."

"What about the St. Thomas relic?" Will asked, following her back to the open case. "What can it do?"

Bartimaeus jumped in. "You mean what can *he* do? St. Thomas was mighty close to Jesus, so he's permitted to do a lot. One of the things he can do is keep water from rising. See, he carried the faith to the East; went all the way to India. So while he was there, the apostle pulled this post out of the ground that couldn't be moved by any man or beast. The story goes that St. Thomas planted that post in another location—and on that very spot they built a big cathedral. Do ya know, even when the monsoons and the tsunamis came and the whole town flooded, not one drop got into the cathedral? People say St. Thomas held the waters back. Your great-grandfather certainly believed that."

Aunt Lucille locked the case containing Elijah's mantle and removed the cotton gloves from her hands. "Now you know why my father built a church to protect the relic. For nearly seventy years, the Perilous River has never breached its banks."

"The relic can heal people too, right?" Will asked.

"Yes—assuming the faith of the individual is strong." Aunt Lucille placed a hand on his shoulder. "I'm glad you're interested in your great-grandfather's work, Will. He spent his life assembling this collection, and it is *very* important, especially now."

Bartimaeus hobbled over. "He was even reading one of Jacob's notebooks earlier. Maybe we should show him that *other* book, Lucille. . . ."

"I—I have to get home for dinner, Mr. Bartimaeus," Will interjected rapidly, slapping a hand to his head. "If I don't go now my mom'll start worrying." He rapidly moved toward the exit, slipping the pith helmet on. "But this was fun. Don't worry about the bookcase—I locked it all up— and thanks for the tour. It was . . . it was fun. Bye."

"Come see us again, you hear?" Bartimaeus yelled.

"You're back at St. Thomas in the morning?" Aunt Lucille asked.

"Yes, ma'am."

"Keep away from those waters." Aunt Lucille waved as Will ducked out of Bethel Hall. She ran the backs of her fingers along her chin in silence. Her blue eyes shot over to Bartimaeus. "He snatched the notebook. You know that?"

Bartimaeus smirked. "So what if he did? He'll learn about his great-granddaddy. It also gives his aunt Lucille a reason to drag him back here and acquaint him with that *other* book." The old man shook his head and chuckled, ambling away. "Like my mama in New Orleans used to say, 'Bart's always got a plan.' . . . I know that's right."

As Aunt Lucille watched her friend lurch away on his crutches, her eyes filled with worry.

CHAPTER 5

TROUBLE IN THE DEN

Dinnertime was always a clamorous event at the Wilder house, and this night was no exception. The familiar shrieks of Leo and Marin, seated at the dining bench and jabbing each other with forks, greeted Will as he opened the front door.

"Mom, he keeps stabbing me!" Marin screamed from the kitchen. "Aaaah! Look at my hand. He cut my haaaand."

Leo hadn't, but it was a marvelous tactic to attract Mr. Wilder's attention. "Guys, please," Dan Wilder huffed. He sat rigidly in the kitchen dining nook, a slew of folders before him, the children seated across the table. Once they quieted, he turned to his wife.

"Anytime there is an incident in town, the mayor and the rest of the city council feel they have to do *something*. Doesn't matter what. Now Ava has scheduled a floor vote for Wednesday, and we don't even know what we're considering."

Deborah Wilder stood at the stainless steel stove, dishing out pasta and chicken. "How can you vote on a course of action when no one has a clear idea of what happened at the river?"

"That's exactly what I told Ava. All we know for sure is this: a fisherman's boat overturned, and he's gone missing. But the guy went out when it was still dark. He could have passed out, been drinking, got caught in the current—anything. It may not even be related to the tour boat accident—which is, admittedly, more concerning."

He flipped through one of the folders on the table. "This is from the tour boat accident report." Taking off his glasses, he read, "'Fifteen people injured with minor scrapes and bruises. One woman, Sonya Peterson, claims her legs were scratched by an animal' . . . blah, blah, blah. . . . 'The captain of the vessel, Seymour Grayson, remains in a coma-like condition. He cannot close his eyes nor communicate in any way. Captain Grayson has not moved since the boat capsized. Attending physicians have no explanation for his condition. The tour boat is believed to have been struck by an unidentified large animal or object.'" Dan closed the folder. "It's just unbelievable to me. They've trolled the river. There is nothing there."

"I still don't understand how the council can hold a vote without knowing all the facts. Or is that just politics?" Deborah said, placing steaming plates before Leo and Marin.

Will quietly stood in the doorway, absorbing as much of the conversation as he could.

"On the way out of the office, Sheriff Stout tells me a couple of swimmers—teenagers—were attacked this afternoon downriver." Dan gnawed on the temple of his glasses. "They're trying to keep it quiet. One of the kids is missing. The other swimmers say they saw something big in the water. They claim their friend was, uh . . . pulled underwater by a thing with arms. Like a croc or a gator."

"Do you think it could be alligators?" Deborah wondered.

"We've never had gators in the river. We're too far north. But here's the worst part." Dan lowered his voice and cupped his mouth so the younger kids couldn't hear. "Stout told me that along the shore they found bits of—" His eyes traveled beyond Deborah. "Eavesdropping isn't polite, son," Dan said, staring at Will.

Deborah threw an arm around Will and kissed him on the head. "How was your day, big guy?"

"Punishing," Will said, glaring at his father and taking a seat at the table.

"Well, I'm glad you're home," Dan said earnestly. He put his glasses on and turned back to Deborah. "Anyway, who knows what's in that water. And there is no way to offer real solutions if we don't know what we're dealing with."

"Just like the things that hit the roof today, Daddy?" Marin asked.

Dan Wilder's jaw muscles started to flex. "Th-th-that—that's different."

"What *things* hit the roof today?" Deborah asked Marin, delivering two more plates to the table.

"Me and Leo were watching TV and there was a thud, thud, thudding noise."

Will sat straight up in his seat, all ears.

"It sounded like rocks were hitting the house," Leo added. "They were coming down three at a time."

"Why don't we eat?" Dan said, placing his folders on the floor and grabbing his fork.

"Daddy went up on the roof and looked. But he wasn't for sure what it was," Marin volunteered.

Deborah studied Leo's and Marin's faces as she sat down at the end of the shellacked oak table. "What was it, Dan?"

He started eating and didn't look up. "I don't know."

Deborah and the children said grace. Dan continued eating.

After several minutes Will broke the silence. "So something hit the house, but you're not sure what it was? What'd you see, Dad?"

"How much gardening did you get done today, son?" Dan casually asked, eyeing Will.

"Dug a hole, buried a stick in the heat, and learned a little bit about the relic of St. Thomas."

"You didn't go near the river, did you?" Dan asked.

"The yard is right next to the river, but I didn't go swimming if that's what you mean."

"I'd keep away from the water, son. I think some fish or reptile population is out of control."

Deborah pushed the hair off her forehead, tucking it behind her right ear. "So, tell us about the relic. Did you see it?"

"Please, let's not encourage . . ." Dan grimaced and shoved a piece of chicken into his mouth. Each bite was like a protest against the current conversation.

"Don't mind him, Will. Tell the rest of us about the relic."

"I didn't see it, but I'd like to. Mr. Shen said it has miraculous powers."

Dan scowled at Deborah.

Will set his fork aside and got serious. "Do you think it's real, Mom?"

Deborah nodded. "I do. It has a fascinating history. I did a *Supernatural Secrets* episode on the relic years ago. People say that the relic and the intercession of St. Thomas keep the river in check. But it's not a good luck charm or anything. It's the faith of the people."

"Oh, I know, Aunt Lucille explained it to me. . . ." The stern look on Dan Wilder's face caused Will to stifle the rest.

Dan struck the table with his palm, shaking the dishes. "We are not going to talk about superstitious claptrap at this table," he said, seething. "Do you all understand?"

Deborah cooed, "He has a right to ask questions about the artifacts. Your grandfather spent his life preserving them."

There was a smoldering fire in Dan's eyes, which he trained on his wife. "I don't want him knowing all that foolishness, Deborah. 'A relic is a key to unlock our faith,'" he said sarcastically, before turning to Will. "I know what they're telling you. It's tall tales and legends." He tapped his finger on the table. "You be respectful of your aunt Lucille, but don't accept everything she says as the truth. The truth is what we can see and touch. That's real, Will. All the rest is make-believe—stories made up and passed on by people too afraid to accept reality. This is reality." He patted his hand on the tabletop. "This is reality. I can see it; I can feel it. Put your trust in what you can verify."

"But there are things we can't see and touch, like love and electricity and sound waves," Deborah told Will. "Just because you can't see or touch things doesn't mean they don't exist. Many people, including your mother, believe there is a world we can't see or touch but can feel at times. I have seen the effects of that world on too many lives. When I am in the middle of an interview and a person tells me they found hope when everything seemed lost, or that an inexplicable thing happened just when they needed it most, or how their son or daughter was healed when the doctors said it wasn't possible . . . I can't dismiss that as make-believe. Those people are witnesses to the power of belief—of the divine. And their experiences are just as valid and real as any physical encounter."

"Deborah, please. That's emotionalism." Dan petulantly stabbed at his food. "This is like having dinner at Oprah Winfrey's house."

THUNK. THUNK. THUNK.

The sounds were coming from somewhere down the

hall. No one at the table moved. The thunks swiftly became louder and more frequent. Whatever the source of the noise, it was not coming from outside, but from the direction of the den. The sound vibrated through the walls of the house. Will's breathing quickened. He moved to get up, but Dan pressed a hand on his shoulder, pushing him back into his seat.

"Stay there. All of you stay where you are," Dan ordered, moving down the hall toward the den.

"Mommy, I'm scared," Leo said in an undertone.

THUNK. THUNK. THUNK.

THUNK. THUNK. THUNK.

Swiveling in his chair, Will saw two shadows form in the upper corners of the wall opposite him. Suddenly, like spilled varnish, the shadows slid down the face of the wall and moved into the hallway, as if trailing after his father. Despite Deborah's objections, Will leapt from the table and chased the shadows toward the den.

Dan Wilder stood outside the open doors of the family room, his hands clutching the back of his neck, trembling. Will could see shells, fish bones, rocks, and dead beetles raining down in zigzag patterns all over the den. The sofa, the carpet—everything—was covered in slimy green river trash. A moldy stench filled the hall. *The bottom of the river is in our family room.* The stuff continued hailing down at weird angles.

"Why is this happening? Where is it coming from, Dad?" Will sputtered.

"The ceiling," Dan squeaked. When Will bent down, he could see the refuse materializing from the ceiling, leaving no holes. Dan slammed the den's double doors shut, as if blocking the horrible scene would somehow make it go away. But Will could still hear the terrible plopping and crackling of trash and dead things pelting their furniture inside. The sound seemed to intensify throughout the house.

The kids and Deborah could hear it as well. Marin unleashed a high-pitched scream that cut through Will's very being. When he looked back to the kitchen, a flood of twinkling lights, like those he had seen at Peniel, came rushing in his direction. He ducked as the mass of illumination flew down the hall and pushed past him and his father. The flickering lights passed through the seams in the double doors and vanished. Will ran to the doors and clutched the flat knobs.

"Don't, son," Dan warned. Will was scared, but not enough to keep him from seeing what was inside. He ripped the doors open.

The flickering lights were gently disintegrating into the windows and up the chimney, and there before him was an immaculate den. Not a hint of a bone or a shell or anything out of the ordinary remained. Will scurried behind the chairs and peeked in between the leather sofa and the wall for some evidence of what he had seen only moments before.

"Dad, you saw it, right?"

"Our imaginations are powerful things, Will."

"You saw it! You said it was coming from the ceiling."

"I don't see anything, son. Do you?" Dan walked back to the kitchen, smoothing the hair protruding from the side of his head. "It was probably a car backfiring," he told his pale children at the table. "Or . . . it could have been anything. Let's finish dinner."

He returned to his seat. The sweat around his forehead caught Deborah's attention.

"Are you all right?" she whispered.

"He saw the whole thing," Will yelled, pointing at his father. "There were shells and beetles and . . ."

"You're scaring everybody with your stories, Will. How about you call it a night and go to bed," Dan said.

"Why don't we talk about it tomorrow?" Deborah offered, taking Will's hand.

"I know what I saw and so do you," Will sputtered to his father, droplets forming in his eyes.

"Sit down and finish eating?" Deborah begged.

"I've lost my appetite," Will said, pouting. "I have some summer reading to do, and then I have to get up early to plant more *trees*." Will stormed out of the room, grabbing his pith helmet in one hand and his backpack in the other.

Charging up the stairs, Will overheard Leo and Marin questioning their father about the weird sounds they had all clearly heard. But Dan provided no direct explanation and suggested that an early bedtime was in order for them as well.

In his bedroom, Will pulled his great-grandfather's green

journal from his book bag, topped the bedpost with his pith helmet, and flopped onto the mattress. Under the sheets he devoured the pages of the little book with the help of a strategically positioned flashlight. Most of the notes contained lists of stones and metals used to construct various sections of St. Thomas Church. Between the pages there were invoices charged to Wilder Mining, the old family company that his great-grandfather had used to finance the building. It was hard for Will to decipher Jacob Wilder's tight scrawl or make sense of his sketches, but he determinedly plowed ahead, looking for something, anything, about the relic.

Finally, near the back of the book, he came across detailed notes about "the Undercroft," a subterranean series of chambers beneath the church that led to "the Keep." *The Keep! Just as Mr. Shen said.* Will studied the diagrams and notes, trying to visualize each of the rooms leading to the Keep. The only problem was: nowhere did the book show how to get into the Undercroft. Just as he began reading the final pages, sleep got the better of him. Will's face fell against the pages, and his flashlight tumbled off the bed. Soon his snores filled the room.

Outside, at 11:35 that night, Dan Wilder's slippers scraped across the driveway. Exiting his garage wearing a gray T-shirt and blue striped pajama bottoms, he carried an aluminum ladder and a flashlight. He propped the ladder against the side of the house, near the den. Quietly he climbed to check on the piles of shells and bones that had fallen from the sky earlier that day. He was sure he had seen them. He had scooped them from the gutter with his own hands—hadn't he? But a little verification never hurt anyone. Standing on a rung near the top of the ladder, he shone the flashlight on the roof. Nothing. He directed the beam of light down the gutter. It too was completely empty. Dan quickly descended, passing the light over the grass where he had seen the debris fall from the roofline. It was clear as well.

Assured that no proof existed to confirm the afternoon disturbance, he breathed easier for the first time that night. It must have been a hallucination, he tried to convince himself. He ignored his lingering anxiety and headed inside, checking the den one last time before going to bed.

Had Dan Wilder stayed outside and turned his flashlight a bit farther down the lawn toward Heinrich Crinshaw's house, he might have seen the mounds of wriggling river scraps that had pounded his roof and occupied his den. A long trail of bones, beetles, shells, and wood now jerked down the alley toward a street drain—returning to its source.

ANOTHER CRACKPOT SCHEME

The moment he leapt from his bunk bed that Tuesday morning, Will picked up his cell phone and scrolled through his contacts. When he found Andrew Stout's name, he pressed a button and up popped a digital picture of his hearty redheaded pal. Will texted him:

> **Can u meet at Bub's Treats and Sweets at 3? Sorry I can't bike today, but need your help.**

He texted a similar message to Simon Blabbingdale and Cami Meriwether. After a quick shower and a change of clothes, he collected his pith helmet and his book bag and headed downstairs.

"You're up bright and early," Deborah said, pouring cereal for the kids, still in her purple nightgown.

"Gotta go plant my trees." Will kissed his mother on the cheek.

"Do you want to talk about yesterday? What you saw? Did you see the old 'fuzzy' things?"

"No. Dad knows what I saw. Ask him."

Deborah exhaled. "I don't know what I'm going to do with the two of you. Dad left about ten minutes ago. I'm headed to Peniel later to scope out a new exhibit that I might feature on the TV show, so dinner could be a little late."

"Works for me, Mom. I'll see you later."

Deborah straightened his pith helmet and gave him a long hug.

Will grabbed a granola bar and was out the door, beginning the six-block trek to St. Thomas Church. It was one of those steamy days. Will could almost taste the moisture of the river in his mouth and feel it on his face. He was less than excited by the idea of doing hard labor in this weather for two weeks. But the thought of whittling the punishment down to a few days didn't seem so bad. During the walk, his phone blinged three times.

Andrew and Simon texted that they would see him at the ice cream parlor that afternoon. Cami was more cagey:

Since it's summer, I know u don't want homework assist. Y all the mystery? What do u need help with?

Will typed with one hand as he walked:

Come at 3 and find out!

Like the others, Cami relented and finally agreed to meet him at Bub's:

As long as the ice cream is on u!

Will laughed, dropping the phone into his backpack.

Tobias Shen was already hard at work in the St. Thomas churchyard by the time Will reached the end of Falls Road. The stubby man was dragging the last of the trees into place for planting.

Shen laughed when he caught sight of Will. Pointing to the lopsided stick protruding from the earth, he said, "If you're going to bury a stick, at least bury it straight so people don't think you're crazy." Brushing his hands together, the old man continued to snicker to himself.

Will's good mood evaporated. Was Mr. Shen calling him crazy? Shen was doing exactly what the Captain had warned Will about: demanding that he perform a ridiculous chore, then mocking him for it later! For a moment Will's face flushed with anger.

"Why are you so sour? I did half the job, Mr. Wilder," Shen said, indicating the trees scattered around the yard. "Though I saved the best part for you. Dig, dig, dig. When you finish digging holes, I'll come help hoist the trees."

Will squinted at the old man. He desperately wanted to tell Shen that he could plant his own stick next time—plant a whole yard full of sticks. But he held his tongue, calmed by the thought that this would soon be over once he had the relic. "Yes, sir," he said.

"Ahhh. This is progress," Shen announced, a satisfied smile on his face. "Obedience, Mr. Wilder, is the beginning of true growth. Dig, dig, dig, and keep your distance from the river. Death runs through those waters."

"I saw some dead fish when I was going home yesterday," Will said, picking up the shovel.

"Nature is in rebellion. The river is *verrrry* dangerous now." He pointed a wrinkled finger at Will for emphasis. "I'll go clean the church—the visiting priest made a mess in the sacristy. When you finish digging your holes, we'll plant together, yes?"

"Sure," Will said, jamming the blade of the shovel into the turf.

"Very good, Mr. Wilder. We also can speak of your great-grandfather when I return." Shen shuffled up the path to the church, his legs moving stiffly.

Will did as he was told. Within minutes his allergies ambushed him. He muffled the sneezes with one of the eight tissues he had shoved in his pocket that morning just in case. As he lifted the dirt from the ground, he kept an anxious eye on the river, hoping Captain Balor would appear.

Sweat dripped from beneath his pith helmet as the hours passed. Will's thoughts turned resentful. Why was he baking in the sun while Mr. Shen got to enjoy the cool of the church? Why wasn't Leo being punished? After all, Leo had given Will permission to ride the donkey so he could test the catapult. And what about Simon and Andrew? They had bet him that he wouldn't do it. They were all partly responsible. Now while Will dug holes in the blazing sun, Leo was enjoying himself at home watching TV in the air-conditioning; his friends were out playing; Aunt Lucille, who was responsible for this gardening expedition, was kicking back at Peniel; and his dad was cool as a cucumber at city hall. Will violently jammed the blade of the shovel into the earth with his heel.

"Will! Will, lad, where are ye?" a voice urgently called from the riverside.

Will threw down the shovel and scampered to the edge of the yard. He glanced down the slope that led to the river. There on the gravelly shore stood Captain Nep Balor, his toadlike face filled with excitement. His massive hand yanked at the air, gesturing for Will to come his way.

"Down here. Come quickly. Just stay clear of the water," the Captain said, in a futile attempt to keep his voice down. Balor trudged to the point where the church's stone foundation met the river.

Will hesitated for a moment, checking over his shoulder to be sure Mr. Shen was nowhere in sight. He took a breath and bounded down to the shoreline, following the Captain's lead. From behind, the Captain's slicker undulated oddly, one side awkwardly heaving up, then the other. If Will hadn't known better, he might have thought three men were wrestling beneath Captain Balor's raincoat as he moved.

Balor wheeled around at the corner of the church's foundation.

"Ye've given us such joy, Will," the Captain said, yanking his rain hat from his head and tilting his face to the left. "By tomorrow we'll be seeing out of our eye. What a gift ye've offered us, lad." Despite the Captain's enormous size, he seemed like a little kid struggling to find words of gratitude.

"I was worried you weren't coming," Will said, panting from the run.

"Ye never have to worry about Nep Balor. We keep our promises, Will." He spoke quickly, wiping the clotted spittle from the corner of his mouth. "Time is short. Listen well, lad. Tomorrow, ye come right here at nine a.m. sharp. It'll be low tide."

"But I'll be working in the churchyard at that time. Mr. Shen might—"

"Yeh leave Shen to us," Captain Balor said, his purple lips turning down. "We'll figure a way to draw him from here—distract him. Where's Shen now? Cooling himself, if I had to guess."

"He said he was doing some work in the church."

"Of course, keeping himself comfortable while others suffer is that lout's full-time occupation. Some guardian he is! Never mind him—you just make it yer business to be here at nine a.m. tomorrow. With the tide low, we'll be able to take ye round to the mouth of the Undercroft. It's right round there, where the church wall meets the river. It's too high to enter now—but tomorrow morning the water'll be low. That's the only time it'll be safe to get into the church."

"I have my grandfather's notes, so I—I *think* I can get to the relic."

"Don't think, lad. Do! Ye'll have only one chance to get in. One! Bring some of yer pals along. Ye may need them to run up ahead and reveal the traps and such to yeh."

"That was my plan," said Will, happy that he now had a clear path to the Undercroft. "Do you think it's safe for my friends? Could they get hurt?" he asked.

"Depends on yer friends. Any of us could get hurt, but we have to take the chance." He trained his yellowed eye on Will. "People like Shen, they're never going to help us. We have to help ourselves—and stick together. Who else is here for yeh now, Will?"

"Nobody. They don't even care." To his right the dark currents of the river churned, and a water moccasin slithered beneath the surface near the shore. "Captain Balor, have you ever seen something—something scary—and the next thing you know, it's not there?"

"Ah, our minds—even the waters—deceive us all the time. What things ye been seeing, Will?"

"Yesterday I thought I saw a giant tail coming out of the river. The fish were boiled alive. Killed everything."

Captain Balor shook his immense head slowly. "We told

ye these waters were filled with dangers. Look at what happened to that swimmer the other day, and the fisherman. Awful! Creatures ripped them poor souls to bits. . . ."

Will was breathing hard. "Weird stuff has been happening. Things started hitting my house yesterday. There were bones and shells and junk all over our den. Inside our house! My dad and I saw it. Course now he's pretending he didn't see anything."

"That's a disgrace." Captain Balor flattened his greasy hair and put on his rain hat. "When a man lies to his own boy, he ain't fit to be called 'father.' But leave those feelings aside for now. Focus on what ye can touch. What ye can verify."

Will's eyes grew wide. "That's just what my dad says: 'Put your trust in what you can verify.'"

"Well, he may be right about that. Unlike all the empty promises yeh hear, all the blather, yeh need to get yer hands on something real. That relic is real. Ye can hold it. Possess it. And just think of the great things ye'll be able to do once it's yours."

Will sneezed. "I'm not ah-ah-AH-CHOO! I'm not sure I can get all the way to the Keep. The chambers are complicated—AH-CHOO! I've been reading my great-grandfather's notebook. It's a series of riddles—AH-CHOO! There's a challenge in each chamber."

"Ye can do it, lad. Think of this eye and what that relic will mean to us. We'll be able to see again, Will." Balor's drooping left eyelid started to rise. A quick glimpse of the foul bloodied eye caused Will to look away. "Think of yer poor brother's arm."

Will nodded in agreement. To end his punishment, to heal Leo's arm, to restore the Florida trip, and to help Captain Balor—he had to get the relic.

The Captain's lips parted into a smile, revealing his dull gray teeth. "We knew we could count on ye, son." His voice dropped into a soothing key. "We only ask that ye touch the relic to our eye once ye grab it. That's all we want. Now get back up there before Shen starts asking questions. Till the morning, then. Don't tell anyone we talked, right, lad?"

"Right," Will said. He waved to the Captain and ran up the embankment. As he climbed the levee a thought occurred to him. Will turned. "Captain, how did you know about my brother's arm? I didn't tell you. . . ."

The bare riverbank lay before him. Captain Balor was gone. Will looked down the shoreline and into the river. There was no trace of the Captain, only the clouds casting their heavy shadows on the water. Will shivered and ran up to St. Thomas Church.

Tobias Shen was kneeling in the first pew of the darkened church when Will pried open the rear doors. A shaft of sunlight invaded the building, reaching clear across the center aisle and falling on Shen's shoulders.

"Finished digging yourself into holes?" Shen asked, without looking back. "Have you completed your work?"

"I dug a few holes and replanted your walking stick."

"Not my stick. Your tree!"

"I have to go meet some friends," Will said in a hush, holding the heavy door. "I'll see you in the morning, I guess."

"Come in. Close the door." Shen's strong, low voice ricocheted off the high plastered ceiling.

"My friends are waiting for me. I have to leave, Mr. Shen."

"Shh-shh-shh. . . . You have to be quiet."

Will laced his fingers behind his neck and stood in the middle aisle. He so wanted to flee.

Tobias Shen's head turned like that of a great gray owl. "Kneel."

Will reluctantly stepped into the last row of the church and dropped onto the kneeler. "What are we doing?"

"Waiting for instructions."

"But I have to meet my friends."

"Shh-shh-shh. You can't hear instructions if you're talking. Obedience, Mr. Wilder, requires listening. And listening requires silence. Shut the mouth and the heart opens." The old man rose from his place and walked toward the rear of the church. When he got close to Will, he placed a firm hand on the boy's shoulder. "You will hear in silence what a multitude of words will never give you. Your great-grandfather found wisdom here. Be still and listen."

Tobias Shen walked to the door of the church. "After you listen, water your walking stick tree. The most fragile often need the most care." Shen exited the church, leaving Will alone.

Kneeling in the back pew, Will didn't have the slightest idea what he was supposed to be listening for or what "instructions" he was to receive. Though basking in the silence did calm him, banishing jealous thoughts of Leo and dispelling the anger he felt toward his father. Sitting back in the wooden pew, he gazed at the statues in the niches on either side of the church. He marveled that his great-grandfather had built something so beautiful and so peaceful.

Catching sight of the small golden door to the right of the altar, Will's mind flipped back to the illustration he had seen in Jacob's notebook. He fished the notebook from his backpack. Near the end of the green book was a sketch of a short golden door. According to the notes, the door led directly to the Keep. Will jumped to his feet, raced to the front of the church, and opened the marble gate separating the pews from the high altar. In the sanctuary, he squatted down near the polished door. The lettering at the center read:

SANCTI THOMAE APOSTOLI

Behind this door was the Keep and the relic he longed to touch. Will had to find out whether it was real or not, whether it could do anything. It was worth the risk. He yanked at the door's single ring on the off chance that it might give and eliminate the need for him to meet with the Captain in the morning. Three locks held it firmly in place. There was only one way he was going to get that relic—by entering through the Undercroft. Kneeling before the door, in the quiet, he considered the idea of just asking Tobias

Shen to show him the relic. Maybe he could bring Leo to the church, even invite Captain Balor in too? But Mr. Shen would probably say no. The Captain did tell him that Shen kept the relic from those who needed it most. *Can't chance it,* Will thought. Staring at the golden door, he resolved to find his way to the Keep, no matter what.

Looking at his watch, he realized he had only ten minutes to meet his friends across town at Bub's Treats and Sweets. He vaulted over the altar rail, dashed up the aisle, and went out the back doors. After quickly throwing a bucket of water over the buried stick in the yard, he headed downtown.

It was slightly overcast on the run to Bub's. Tearing down Falls Road, Will hooked a left at Perilous Falls Elementary and ran straight up Main Street. Towering oak trees shaded the wide walkways. With its quaint turn-of-the-century-styled storefronts, downtown was Will's favorite part of Perilous Falls. He dashed by the stately city hall with its Grecian columns and steep manicured lawn, knowing that his father was probably inside stuck in a meeting or flattening the back of his hair at his drafting table.

On the next block, a succession of familiar hanging signs dangled overhead: Milk and Honey's Bistro, Dagon's Hair Cuttery, Bobbit's Bestiary, Evening Wear by Eve, Bonaventure's Used Books. This was home to Will, and everything seemed in its place.

He sprinted until he came to a corner where a small crowd had gathered. A mangled bicycle in the middle of the

sidewalk blocked his path. Pushing past some gawking la-
dies with shopping bags, Will realized what had drawn the
onlookers. An older man in biking shorts lay at the edge of
the street. He was agitated and twitchy. A younger woman
in spandex with short brown hair held the man's wounded
head in her hands. Just a few feet away a car with a dented
bumper was still running.

"Ma'am, the ambulance is close by," a short police officer
next to Will quietly told the woman.

"Daddy, they'll be here in a minute," she assured the man
with the bleeding head. "Hang on."

Will could feel a giant sneeze building. He rubbed his
nose, trying to stifle the explosion. But the tickling sensation would not go away.

"AH-AH-CHOO!" The noise caused members of the
crowd and the policeman to stare at him. But Will was too
busy staring at something else. Coming out of the street, he
saw a dozen shadowy arms and hands—claws—reaching,
grasping for the injured man.

A pudgy bald guy in a button-down shirt and gray pants
stepped forward. He knelt next to the man in the street.
"May I say a prayer for you, sir?" he asked.

The daughter's face hardened and her eyes narrowed.
"No, thank you."

"It'll only take a minute," the pudgy man said. "Just a
quick prayer?"

The old man moaned, kicking his legs wildly.

"We're dealing with an emergency here," the daughter

said to the bald man. "Unless you're a doctor, please go away."

Will, in a frightened trance, heard none of what was said. He was too transfixed by the scores of smoky claws rising from the street, inching ever closer to the old man. He alone could see them. But what could he do?

"Get away! Get away!" Will screamed without thinking. He was embarrassed the moment the words escaped his lips. The whole crowd turned their eyes on him again.

"It's okay, kid," the policeman said, squeezing Will's arm. He then turned his attention to the pudgy man kneeling in the street. "The boy's right, sir. You need to step away."

As the bald man struggled to his feet, Will searched for the shadowy hands. They were all gone. They had vanished as quickly as they had come.

"Everybody should move along. You too, son," the cop instructed.

Crossing the street, Will looked back to make sure the shadows had not returned. He saw only the now peaceful old man staring in his direction, waving a weary hand. Though he waved back, Will didn't know what to make of it. The shadows seemed to be appearing more frequently, but why?

Trying to shake the experience, he jogged away quickly. According to his watch, Will was already seven minutes late. Cami would be furious. With no more time for shadow thoughts, he double-timed it the rest of the way.

Given the dogs, cats, and birds swarming outside of Bub's Treats and Sweets, it could have been a pet store. The managers regularly laid milk and food out for visiting pets, and the sweet-smelling trash bins in the alley always attracted a haze of flies and bees. Critter traffic aside, Will and his friends thought it the best ice cream and candy shop in town. And it was.

Through Bub's big front window, Will could see Simon, Cami, and Andrew sitting at a small metal table next to the chrome-covered soda bar and swivel stools. Simon's face was blocked by a thick paperback book he was devouring. Andrew nearly broke his straw diligently scraping the inside of one of the two sundae glasses before him.

Cami raised a thin hand and made eye contact with Will the moment he entered the glossy whitewashed space. Her chestnut brown hair was pulled back into a familiar ponytail—as familiar to Will as the raised eyebrows and knowing look on her face.

"So what's this about, William? I've got a sundae riding on your answer," Cami said, her green eyes never leaving his. Pleasantries had never been her strong suit. She warily studied Will's expression the way a sparrow might study an approaching tabby.

"Andrew thinks you need help doing chores at home. Simon thinks you're planning to hold up the Morning Star Bank." As she spoke the skin around her mouth protruded slightly to accommodate the braces covering her teeth. "But the fact that you couldn't tell us what you're planning leads me to believe that it's another classic crackpot William scheme. And by the way, you're eight minutes late." She took a slow sip from the straw in her milk shake without touching it with her hands.

Throughout the entire speech, Simon continued reading.

Andrew buried his nose in a tall soda glass, gulping down its contents. When he was finished, he carefully positioned the glass beside the empty before him. "Me and you can take care of any chores, you know. We really don't need them." He indicated Cami and Simon with his eyes, wiping milk from his upper lip with the back of his ruddy hand. "I mean, she's a girl, and he has the strength of half a girl. For a few bucks, I'll always help you out," he joked.

Simon lowered his bulky copy of *The History of the Decline and Fall of the Roman Empire.* Still shaking a bit from the ice cream sugar rush, he straightened his rectangular black-framed glasses and addressed Will. "If you need to do anything more than punch a hole in a wall, Cami and I have more than enough spare brain cells to compensate for Andrew's deficit." His high nasally voice could have cut through the front glass.

Andrew's face flushed. He reached his long arm across the table and swatted Simon on the top of his curly head.

"Don't touch me!" Simon squealed, drawing some of the patrons' eyes. He defensively shook his paperback at Andrew. "One more time and you can tutor yourself in the fall. Without me, you'll be back in elementary school!"

Andrew started to move toward Simon.

"Easy, big guy," Cami said, patting Andrew on his broad shoulder. He was a good six inches taller than any of the boys in their class, including the two at the table. The red blotches on Andrew's cheeks gradually faded as he settled back into his chair.

"All right. Answers, William," Cami demanded. "My brother's bus is pulling up any minute and I promised my mom I'd take him home." Cami's brother suffered from Duchenne muscular dystrophy, and he had recently begun using a wheelchair.

"Okay, okay. I'll cut to the chase." Will yanked the lacquered green notebook from his book bag and tossed it onto the table. "Do you know what that is?"

"Lists of the people who used to be your friends until you withheld information?" Cami said drily.

Simon blinked and took a stab. "The codes to the safe at the Morning Star Bank?"

Andrew rolled his eyes and reared back in his chair. "Just spill it, Will-man," he said, shaking his big head.

"These are the detailed plans of the Undercroft—the chambers beneath St. Thomas Church." Looks of confusion surrounded him, so Will briefed his tablemates on the relic and what it could do. "If we can get our hands on the relic, it might cure Leo's arm, end my punishment, and *our trip to Florida would be back on.*"

"What do you mean, 'if *we* can get our hands on the relic'? What do you need us for?" Simon asked.

"Backup. You each have your own specialty: Simon, you have the brains, Andrew has the strength, and Cami has incredible instincts. And since my great-grandfather built the church, I've got to be there. We'll sneak in through the Undercroft of the church and together I think we can get in and get out."

Cami sat back in her chair, unmoved by the pitch. "So you want to break into a church?"

"My family built the church. It's not a break-in. It's like going into your house through the garage door. We're not taking the relic. We're just borrowing it. The minute Leo touches it, we'll put it right back."

"Can't you get somebody's permission to just borrow the relic?" Cami inquired.

"It's not a library. They don't let people leave with this thing," Will said, flipping through the pages of the notebook until he found the diagram of the Undercroft. "There are three chambers under the church. Each room has a riddle that we must solve to move into the next chamber. After we pass into this third room, we reach the Keep. That's where the relic is stored."

Simon piped up. "I love riddles. I just finished a book of Old English riddles. Tell me what they are. I'll bet I can solve them right now."

Will shut the green notebook and returned it to his book bag.

"I'll show you everything once we are in the Undercroft.

There could be a few booby traps, but most of them are detailed in the book. We can probably get around them." Will locked eyes with each of them. "So who's with me?"

The boys were fascinated. Andrew glanced over to Cami, whose ponytail was flicking side to side as she shook her head.

"You shouldn't do this. It's too dangerous."

"C'mon, Cami. We need you. It'll be an adventure," Will pleaded.

But Cami had already seen her brother's bus pulling up outside the window. A ramp was unfolding from its back. "I have to go," she said, getting up. "You shouldn't go near that relic. Did you ever think that your great-grandfather went through the trouble of building this 'Keep' to keep the relic where it is? Watch your back—and your front," she told Will. "Bye, guys." Cami grabbed her red vinyl purse from the back of her chair. Adjusting the belt of her shorts, she said, "Simon, ice cream's on you. Told you it was another crackpot scheme." With that, she ran out to meet her brother.

Simon and Andrew checked each other's faces as if silently asking, *Should we do this?* Will could see their hesitation.

"Andrew, let's remember: you got me into this mess. I got on the donkey because you made a bet with me." Will laid on the guilt.

"Actually, launching your brother in the catapult was the problem," Simon observed. "And that's on you."

"Me? Simon, you bet me a souvenir to gallop that old donkey. You know it's true. The donkey threw me, and I accidentally hit the catapult lever."

The two boys stewed in a guilty silence.

"Leo would be fine today if it weren't for the two of you," Will charged. Then he closed the deal. "If you want to go on the trip to Florida, you'll help me get the relic. If not, we can all stay here . . . all summer long. It's up to you."

"All right, all right. I'm in." Andrew smiled in his goofy way, punching Will a bit too hard in the arm.

"May I study the notebook tonight?" Simon asked, eyeing the book bag.

"Nope. Are you in or not? You can study it all you want tomorrow."

Simon took another sip of his milk shake. "I'll be there. What time do we meet?"

A huge black cat with tangled fur and sparkling green eyes nuzzled Will's leg. He jumped at its touch.

"Oh, Miss Jackie, always trying to get away," said a rotund waitress with a thick drawl, appearing next to the table. She wore a large frilly white apron and a doily in her cherry-red bouffant. With one quick scoop, she caught the cat in her meaty arm. "Miss Jackie is an active one. Don't mind her none. Can I get you boys anythin' else? We got some yummy blackberry pie out back."

"No thanks," Will said briskly.

"Well, y'all get back to your business. My name's Miss

Ravinia if y'all need anything." The cat hissed and cut its eyes at Will as it was carried away.

"Tomorrow morning be at the shoreline near the church at nine a.m. sharp. You should both bring some rope, flashlights, and maybe your scout knives. It'll be an adventure. With the notebook, how hard can it be?"

Outside, Cami rolled her brother Max's wheelchair toward their home a few blocks away. His matted brown hair was evidence that he had fallen asleep during the bus ride from camp. Now fully awake, the boy excitedly thrashed his head from side to side. He often did this when he had something to say. In addition to his muscular dystrophy, Max had mild autism, which inhibited his speech. As she pushed him Cami patiently listened for the words she knew were coming. So many times she had seen other children make fun of the nine-year-old boy's disability. They were blind to his sweetness, his gentleness, his understanding. They only saw the immobile right arm and the withered limbs, a kid in a wheelchair who at times struggled for breath. Cami saw much more. She knew the real Max Meriwether, and she loved him. She rolled her brother in and out of the shadows stretching from the oaks overhead.

"Dream. I had a bad dream," Max almost sang in a flat tone, tapping his left hand on the wheelchair arm.

"What kind of dream?" Cami asked, playing along. "Were there hobbits?" Max had repeatedly watched the animated *Hobbit* movie and often talked of hobbits.

"No hobbits. It was a bad dream! I fell into water. Down, down I went . . . and the bad one took the sparkly gold treasure. The bad one took it."

Cami ran around the front of the wheelchair and bent down to Max's level.

"Where was the gold treasure, Max?"

He shook his head, clenching his teeth. "In the gray castle. The sparkly gold treasure was in the gray castle. But the bad one took it and I fell underwater."

"Who is the bad one, Max?"

His watering eyes locked on hers. He shook his head as if afraid to speak. Then, in panic, he cried, "*Sinestri. Sinestri. All the voices say 'Sinestri.'*"

CHAPTER 7

ENTERING THE UNDERCROFT

Wednesday morning Will filled his book bag with some rope from the garage, a water bottle, his crank flashlight, a Swiss Army knife, a small ax, and his great-grandfather's green notebook—which was placed in a ziplock bag and shoved into a side compartment. He was hunched over the bag when Leo, arm still in a sling, padded into Will's bedroom.

"What are you packing for?" Leo asked.

Will startled at his brother's sudden appearance. "Just some stuff I need for today. You know, for gardening."

"You need a flashlight and a rope to garden? What are you doing, Will?"

"Nothing," he said aggressively. "I'm gardening. It's a punishment for hurting my little brother, remember?"

"It's a lot more fun than what we're doing. Marin and I

have to go to the museum to look at some new exhibit with Mom later." Leo closed the door, blocking his brother's exit. His eyes glistened neon blue behind his wire-frame glasses. "I have a question. What did you see in the den the other night?"

"I'm not sure. Some kind of junk falling from the ceiling, but when we went back in it was totally gone."

"Where did it come from?" Leo asked.

"I don't know! It dropped into the den like rain. I saw it," Will said, closing his book bag and checking the alarm clock. It was 8:32.

"Mom and Dad say we shouldn't be worried and that maybe you imagined it." Leo twisted the sleeve of his blue pajamas. "I heard the stuff hitting the house when we were watching TV before you came home. I heard it falling in the den too. I'm worried, Will." Leo threw his cast-free arm around his brother, locking him in a bear hug.

"I have to go, but don't worry. Everything's going to be fine. And I'll bet by the end of the day you won't even have to wear that cast anymore."

Leo released Will. His brow wrinkled. "How is that going to happen?"

"I have a plan. You'll find out later. Just keep your mouth shut, and don't tell Mom and Dad about what I have in the bag, okay?"

Leo nodded and let Will open the door.

In the kitchen, Deborah sat at the table, finishing up a plate of eggs while Dan intently stared at the small TV hanging under the cabinets. Even without makeup, Deborah glowed in the morning. She pushed the bangs from her eyes to get a clear view of Will.

"I'm off for another fun day of manual labor," Will announced sarcastically.

"Come here," his mother said, embracing him. "It won't be too much longer. Just think of the good you're doing."

"Shh. Be quiet," Dan snapped, without taking his eyes off the television. He turned up the volume.

"We are just learning of this tragic accident. Let's go live to Herb Lassiter, who is at the Perilous River. Herb?"

As if caught in a tractor beam by the television, Deborah rose from the table, pulling her terry cloth robe together. "Herb covers homicides at the station—crimes, not accidents. This won't be good."

On the screen, a middle-aged man with a bushy mustache and wispy, slicked-back hair clutched his microphone solemnly. "Bob, it is a sad scene, unlike any I have witnessed in my twenty-five-year career. An early morning fishing trip, a chance to enjoy the outdoors with friends, has turned deadly for at least two young campers. Members of the Wheelie Camp Club, a summer camp for physically challenged youth, went to Gareb Pier this morning for an outing. Shortly after casting their lines in the river—the unexpected occurred."

A shaken camp counselor, a dripping-wet teenage girl with hair pasted to her forehead, appeared on-screen.

"I don't know what caused it. We were out on the pier

and it felt like a big submarine or something hit it. We couldn't see anything. There was a boom and everybody fell into the water. The pier just, like, collapsed. Most of our campers are wheelchair-bound, and it was just John and me, and we didn't know what was going on." The girl collapsed into tears.

Herb Lassiter, looking grave, was back on-screen. "Nearly all the campers are now accounted for. As we reported earlier, at least two have been declared dead. Authorities are not identifying the victims or giving us any details about the cause of those deaths. Lots to unravel here in the hours ahead. A couple of the campers I spoke with before they were ushered away by police told me that they were attacked by what they called 'gator creatures.' They used the word 'creatures.' Neither the sheriff nor Mayor Ava Lynch's office will comment at this time. This is the third tragedy of this type in the past week on the Perilous River. The families of the victims are demanding answers and a response from city hall. We'll bring you the latest as we learn it. Reporting from what was Gareb Pier, I'm Herb Lassiter."

Dan Wilder grabbed his black suit jacket off the back of a kitchen chair and stumbled toward the door, visibly shaken. "Don't—don't go to the churchyard today, Will. Your punishment can start again tomorrow."

Will reached for his book bag. "I promised Mr. Shen I would be there. I'll be way upriver from the pier."

"Just—just—stay away from the water," Dan cautioned,

heading for the garage door. He stopped at the threshold, doubled back into the kitchen, and gave Deb a peck on the cheek. "I have to get to work. This is unbelievable."

Will had already smashed his pith helmet on his head and had one foot out the front door. "Bye, Dad. Later, Mom," he said, bolting.

It was 8:50 by the time a breathless Will reached the yard at St. Thomas. Things couldn't have been more tranquil. The unplanted trees lay scattered around the clearing, with only Mr. Shen's walking stick standing at attention. Will anxiously ran to the edge of the lawn and peered down the sloping riverbank. No sign of Captain Balor or Mr. Shen.

He jogged up to the church to check if Shen was there. Empty. Will knocked on the door of the small stone rectory where the old man lived. No answer. At any moment his friends and the Captain were due to arrive. If Shen caught them, they'd never make it into the Undercroft and the entire mission would be over before it began.

Will decided to busy himself by watering the stick, then by digging a hole in the yard. Appearing to be following orders was always a good strategy. No sooner had he driven the shovel into the ground than he felt an ominous presence behind him. Will grabbed the spade with two hands, raised it, and turned quickly.

In a flash, Tobias Shen smacked each of Will's hands so rapidly that the shovel flew across the yard.

"Jumpy, Mr. Wilder." Tobias Shen stood before Will like

a stone statue in his billowy gray uniform. "What troubles you?"

Will could not believe that Shen had so easily disarmed him. "How'd you do that?"

"By following instructions; day by day listening carefully to older and wiser people."

"Yeah, but you barely touched my hands," Will said, still surprised by the sudden kung fu display.

Shen wrinkled his nose. "All things come with obedience. One thing mastered, then another. Now you can master burying trees, please. I have something I must do."

Unexpectedly, Will blurted, "Let me come with you. Are you going to the pier?"

Shen paused and seemed to consider the request. "Dig, dig, dig, Mr. Wilder. Fulfilling our duties protects us. Chasing excitement leads to bad ends." Shen hastily moved toward the thicket of trees that led downriver.

"Where are you going?" Will yelled.

"Down the path I must travel. I'll return shortly. Dig! Dig!"

As soon as Shen had vanished into the trees, Will walked over to the shovel. He stared down at it for several minutes. Why was he always the one left behind, the one punished with manual labor, the one whose questions no one would answer? *I'll show them. When I get the relic, they'll see what I can do. Why should Mr. Shen be the only one to touch it, the only one to use its power?* He angrily kicked the shovel down the riverbank. It slid along the gravel and into the riled waters. All Will wanted was a little adventure and a chance to make things right on his own terms. What was wrong with that?

The smack of a speedboat beating its way through the choppy river water pulled Will from his thoughts. Captain Balor was coming! The boy ran to the edge of the yard, searching the river. His shoulders slumped as he recognized the approaching pale blue boat with gleaming brass railings. It was the *Stella Maris,* Aunt Lucille's prized vessel, slicing the waves at breathtaking speed. "Will, dear, I wanted to be sure you were safe," Lucille called out from behind the wheel of the boat, holding a teacup in her left hand. She was going so fast she had to cut the wheel to the left, creating a massive wave to slow down.

"You're in a hurry," Will said.

"I am. Are you all right?" she asked, taking a quick sip from her cup. "You're not seeing anything strange, are you? Shadows?"

"Nope. Just trees and sticks." Will pointed over his shoulder with a thumb.

"Good. You should come to Peniel this afternoon. It's time I showed you the book—the one that belonged to your great-grandfather. I'll come back for you later," Lucille said as the boat engine purred.

Will nodded and nervously looked down the shore, certain that it must be nearly nine o'clock.

"What happened downriver is not natural, Will. None of these incidents were accidental. Bartimaeus and I are going to investigate." She spoke anxiously, tugging at the top of her teal silk jacket with a high collar—the way a military man might just before entering the field of battle. "You stay on high land. Did Tobias already leave?"

Will told her he had. Aunt Lucille threw him a kiss, took another sip from her cup, and sped downriver in moments.

Now Will was torn. Aunt Lucille had ordered him to stay on high land, but if he didn't go near the river he would miss his only chance to get the relic—a chance to heal his brother. . . .

On each side of him, tall shadows like specters suddenly materialized. He felt cold all over. Escaping the shadows, he plunged down the riverbank. He ran toward the point where the church's foundation touched the water. Looking over his shoulder as he ran, Will could see the dark forms pursuing him. When he faced forward, he ran smack into the Captain.

Nep Balor stood calf-deep in the muck of the river beside the church. He glared at Will. "Our time is short, lad." Though wearing his old slicker and hat, the Captain seemed taller and wider than before. Or maybe he only looked that way because Will was standing so close.

Balor's yellowed eye scanned the boy's face. "We must move before the tide rises." The Captain spun around and started walking along the wall of the church facing the river. "Well, are yeh coming?"

Will checked to make sure that the shadows were not still pursuing him. They had vanished. "What if Mr. Shen comes back? Or my aunt Lucille?" Will stood his ground on the gravel near the corner of the building.

"They'll be occupied for some time. Passed that accident downriver this morning—horrible, horrible things there. We'd best be getting yeh into that church. Don't want ye in these waters for any longer than ye need be."

"What happened to those kids downriver, Captain?"

"There's no time for ye questions!" Balor roared, sounding as if three people were speaking from within him at once. "Do ye want the relic or not? We're risking our own hide here as well!"

"I shouldn't go in the water."

Rage filled Captain Balor's open eye. He clenched his massive fists, and his mouth gaped wide as if he were about to yell. Then he shut his purple lips, swallowing his anger. Wading through the marsh toward Will, he gently rasped, "Ye don't have to fear, boy. We know these waters. Get on our back—walk ye to the Undercroft ourself. *Time is short!*"

Captain Balor turned his back to Will and lowered his enormous frame. Without turning, he said, "A little while now and ye'll have what Shen's been keeping from yeh. Ye'll know what yer aunt Lucille won't tell yeh. Think of the look on yer father's face when yer brother's arm is healed—totally healed. And our eye, Will." The Captain swiveled his head to the left, projecting the bulging, pus-sticky eye right into the boy's face. "I'll be able to see again, lad. Oh, what a moment. But we must be quick. Grab on!"

Will impetuously threw his arms over the Captain's

shoulders, pressing his face against the dirty slicker. He rose six feet in the air. At this proximity, Balor smelled like rancid fish bait. As they moved, Will's chest was pulverized by the ridges of back muscle writhing beneath the Captain's slicker. The pounding of the muscles all but knocked the wind from his chest. Several times his pith helmet nearly fell into the muck. Within moments they arrived at a rounded, stone-edged opening on the church wall. Its interior was covered in green slime reaching to the ceiling. Water obviously filled the cavern daily.

Balor walked up a slight incline and lowered Will to the spongy ground.

"This is it," the Captain said.

"This is the Undercroft?"

"It's the entrance to the Undercroft. Where's yer flashlight?"

Will fumbled in his backpack until he found it. The light revealed a rusted wrought-iron gate running from the ground to the ceiling. A thick dimpled chain with two locks held the gate shut.

"How are we going to get in?" Will asked.

Balor ran a pointy gray tongue along his jagged teeth. "We're not going in. *Yer* going in. Let me help yeh with the gate. Stand back." The Captain approached the forbidding wrought iron. He clenched his fists and took a long drag of air. Lunging, he grabbed the chains with both hands. "Aaaaarrrr!" he bellowed. The Captain pulled with all his might. His great arms shuddered and his back buckled as if it were about to rip apart. Will noticed smoke coming from the chains.

"Are you okay, Captain?"

He answered with an anguished cry of pain but did not release the irons. "Aaaaaaarrrr!"

The loud snap of the links filled the cavern. Broken bits of chain fell to the floor. The Captain's knees went weak, and his great bulk crumbled and slunk toward the water's edge. He thrust both his hands into the river.

"Captain?"

"Be fine in a minute, Will," he wheezed, exhausted.

"Can't you come in with my friends and me?"

"No, lad, we daren't go any farther. Yer the Wilder, not me. But we'll be waitin' here when ye come out." He turned a teary, pitiful yellow eye to the boy. "Counting on yeh, lad. Counting on yeh."

Outside, Will could hear Andrew and Simon yelling his name.

"Can you help me open the gate? It looks pretty heavy."

"Can't do it, Will," he panted. "Ye boys will have the strength for it. Just be sure to bring us the relic when ye come out. Only need one touch of it—and oh, the wonders we'll see."

"It's a deal, Captain."

Balor offered a weary smile, touching the brim of his rain hat in a tired salute.

Will stuck his head outside the murky rounded opening to find his friends. Andrew and Simon were already wading through the marsh.

"Who were you talking to?" Simon asked, his sports-goggle glasses making him look like a nerdy space alien.

"Captain Balor," Will said nonchalantly, gesturing with an open palm toward the Undercroft entrance. "Come on, I'll introduce you."

Andrew and Simon exchanged concerned looks. "Captain *who*?" Andrew asked, stepping into the mouth of the tunnel.

Will flipped his head right and left and back again. "He was right here. He popped the chain on the gate open for us."

Simon shone his flashlight on the shards of rusted links littering the floor. "And your 'Captain' did this with his bare hands?"

"Yes. He's really strong. He was just here," Will said, still looking for Balor. "Captain?"

"Are we going to stand around looking for your imaginary friend, or are we going in? I don't got all day," Andrew complained.

"We're going. We're going," Will assured them, pulling the green notebook from his book bag. He opened the book and told Simon to shine a light on the first pages describing the Undercroft. Simon leaned in close to inspect the notebook as the river's waters began to lap into the Undercroft entrance.

"The first chamber looks pretty easy. It's just a drainage pit," Will said, moving a finger over the page. "There is a stone incline on the right and another on the left side of the room. You see this writing over here? My great-grandfather says there is only 'one way to rise from the waters.' That would be the incline—I think."

Simon pointed at the pencil-drawn lines in the illustration running upward along the wall, next to the stone ramp. "What is that?"

Will pushed his pith helmet back and stared hard at the notebook. "Probably just a stray line or a decoration."

"It's on the opposite wall too," Simon said, pointing to the angled thick line traveling up the wall above the incline on an adjacent sketch.

Will slammed the book shut. "We'll figure it out when we get inside. There's also some scribbling about St. Paul that I don't quite get."

Andrew was already pulling at the wrought-iron gate. It was stuck in the mud and refused to give. "How are we going to open this thing?" Andrew asked.

"Together," Will said, sealing the notebook in the ziplock bag.

He, Simon, and Andrew heaved on the old gate with little success. After about ten minutes of sustained effort, the gate began to inch open by degrees.

"We're getting there," Will yelled.

"The only place I'm getting is to the chiropractor," Simon carped, grabbing his lower back.

After much more tugging, they had created a twelve-inch opening. Simon easily slipped through the gap. So did Will and his pith helmet. Andrew got half his chest through but couldn't move any farther. And the water was rising.

"Simon, you've got to help me push the gate open," Will demanded.

"He's stronger than we are. Let him pull the gate and we'll wait for him inside."

"When I get in there," Andrew seethed through gritted teeth, "you'll wish you'd stayed home, bug eyes."

"Leave him," Simon said.

"We can't leave him. Get over here," Will said, ramming the gate with his shoulder.

Simon reluctantly joined in, positioning himself on the other side of Will to avoid Andrew's reach. The river water began to cover their feet. Low tide was over.

"Wiggle the gate back and forth," Will ordered. The water helped to loosen the soil holding the gate in place.

But Andrew was not happy. Strawberry blotches broke out on his cheeks, and his features twisted. "You're going to break my ribs."

After repeatedly wiggling the gate, it finally sprang open. They pushed it so wide that the bottom jammed in the mud of the entryway. Freed from the metal grip, Andrew staggered toward the boys.

"If you'd lay off those burgers, you might be able to pass through a perfectly ample opening," Simon teased.

Andrew swatted the goggle-faced, thin boy with the back

of his hand. "If you'd keep that trap shut, you might have more friends."

"Guys, guys. Focus on the adventure." Will turned and shone his flashlight down the pitch-black tunnel before them. "The first chamber is this way." Will tapped the top of the pith helmet with his palm and started moving forward.

"Are you going to wear that old helmet the whole time?" Simon asked.

"Always," Will said without turning.

"Should we close the gate?" Andrew yelled ahead to him.

"Nah," Will's voice echoed from inside the tunnel. "Leave it."

Simon and Andrew shrugged and followed his silhouette into the darkness.

In the river, two gray-green scaled creatures slithered toward the entryway of the Undercroft. Their reptilian bodies stretched on for twelve feet. Two pairs of rounded yellow eyes sat unblinking atop the surface of the rising water. Once the creatures reached the water's edge, they remained perfectly still, drifting, floating, waiting for the tide to take them where they had been commanded to go.

CHAPTER 8

BOTTOM DWELLERS AND DEEP WATER

"Can you slow this thing down, Loo-ceele?" Bartimaeus hollered from the passenger seat of the *Stella Maris*. "Going this fast makes my head all cloudy."

Lucille Wilder's boat tore through the waters at a furious clip. She clutched the steering wheel with both hands as if racing for her very life. Trees and occasional homes blurred by on the right side of the boat. On the left, Wormwood, a dark forest the locals called the Rooky Wood, hid any signs of life. "We have to get there to see what we're dealing with, Bart. We may already be too late. They may have scattered."

"What are you talkin' about, Lucille? Don't matter when you get there. The devil is the devil is the devil. He may change his shape, but the stink and the death are always the same. So what are we rushing for?" Bart wore sunglasses and leaned back in his white upholstered seat. In his mismatched brown tweed jacket and bright green pants he looked like a passenger on a hobo pleasure cruise.

"Those children and the swimmer were attacked by something supernatural, Bart. Gareb Pier was structurally sound—it doesn't just fall into the river one day. Ships don't simply overturn. There is an intelligence at play here. What is lurking out there?" She turned her squinty blue eyes to Bartimaeus, who seemed to be drowsing. Lucille kicked the side of his seat, giving him a start. "Well? What is out there? Focus! I need your help."

"You're driving so fast it's a wonder my poor brain ain't scrambled by now. Focus? You focus on applying the brake," Bartimaeus said, jabbing a finger in her direction. "Don't tell me about focus—I focus just fine. I was the one who told you I felt the creep of something dark the other day. 'Give Will that book of prophecy,' I said. But no . . . 'He's not ready yet.' Don't be lecturing me about focus. My focus is always where it should be—right on target. Uh-oh." He fell silent and frantically reached down for one of his crutches on the deck.

Lucille slowed the boat's speed. "What's wrong, Bart?"

"Oooooh, something's near, Lucille. Something is very, very near. Give me my other crutch." Lucille handed it to him. Bartimaeus moved to the back of the boat, balancing his forearms on the crutches, his open palms facing the water. It was as if he were trying to feel the air itself. Aunt Lucille stood directly behind him.

His eyes closed behind the dark glasses, and Bartimaeus groaned, a pained expression covering his face. He shook his head as if saying no. Then, in a husky whisper, he warned, "They're circling us, Lucille. They're right round this boat. Three—uh, I'm wrong—six, maybe."

"Six *what*?" Aunt Lucille pushed her loose silk sleeves to her elbows. "What are they?"

"Hmm. Thought your daddy got rid of 'em all. But I think they're back." His voice dropped into its deepest register. "*Fomorii*. It's the Bottom Dwellers. I've never seen them so big and powerful. The blood of the innocent hangs on their lips—and they know we're here." Before he could say another word, green claws dug into the railings of the *Stella Maris*.

The clatter of the creature scaling the back of the boat caused both Bartimaeus and Aunt Lucille to seek shelter in the center of the vessel. The monster's claws crushed the brass rails as it pulled itself up. Others could be heard pounding against the sides of the *Stella Maris* beneath the water, tossing the boat to and fro.

The green beast with the pointy face of a dragon and round fish eyes expelled a guttural hiss. It opened its protruding mouth, not unlike that of an alligator, and exposed three rows of serrated teeth. Only it was double the size of an alligator, with the lethal advantage of long legs and a razor-tipped tail.

"I can't see too hot with these corneas, but I *know* that thing is ugly," Bartimaeus whispered.

Lucille moved Bartimaeus behind her. She stretched her arms out, placing her index fingers and thumbs together to form a triangle.

The creature threw its front legs over the railing and began to flail, attempting to propel itself onto the deck.

Lucille closed her eyes and pulled her hands toward her chest. Then, extending her arms, a fiery ray of red-and-white light shot from the triangle of her digits. The twelve-foot-long beast was thrown backward over the water and dissolved into a foul gray ash.

"Remind me to call you when my furnace light goes out," Bartimaeus laughed. Suddenly he bent his head down and went into the deep voice he used when relaying one of his visions. "So, we got more coming. You take the two on the port side. I'll wallop the one on the starboard." He spun around, a crutch over his head.

Aunt Lucille inhaled and directed the light shooting from her fingers to the left side of the boat. She could hear the awful scratching of Bottom Dwellers climbing the *Stella Maris*. Just as the first claws of the two slithering savages presented themselves, Lucille projected her red-and-white ray. The eyes of the beasts bugged out as they were thrown into the air and reduced to an ashy mist. Behind her, Bartimaeus faced another creature already over the railing, its blood-coated mouth wide, ready to lunge.

Old Bartimaeus swung his crutch like a baseball bat. He cracked the monster squarely in the lower jaw, dislocating it. Wailing in anguish, it gouged the glossy white wood beneath the railing with its talons. Aunt Lucille calmly turned and projected her hands to finish the creature off.

"Oh, no, you don't. He's mine," Bartimaeus said, slamming his crutch into the creature's sleek skull. After one more strike to the front of the snout, the thing lifelessly slumped over the railing. "That's what you get when you mess with a boy from the Lafitte Projects. We better get moving. So I'll hold them off, and you do your speedboat routine."

Aunt Lucille hustled to the steering wheel and gunned the engine. Bartimaeus used a crutch to pry the monster into the churning waters of the Perilous River. He then hobbled over to Lucille.

"Now, I know you're gonna be angry. But we got no time for pride." He reached into a cloth satchel he had hidden under his tweed coat. "I knew ya wouldn't listen, but you know old Bart. So I used my emergency key." From out of the satchel he pulled the olive-colored Book of Prophecy. The metal filigree adorning the cover twinkled in the sunlight.

"Why did you bring that here? Those Bottom Dwellers will kill us for it."

"I had no choice. The boy needs to hold this book *now*. It's time, Sarah Lucille. You can't stop this. He's all that stands between us and the *Darkness*. Now take it to him."

Aunt Lucille flared her nostrils in anger. Her hands trembled as she gripped the steering wheel. "How dare you. You should have left that at Peniel. It's not safe out here. It wasn't yours to take, Bart." She wanted to cry.

In that moment, her fears for the future collided with her concerns for Will. She anguished over the burden that

she would be laying upon the shoulders of a boy—a child—
and an unpredictable child at that. But deep down she knew
Will's fate was bound up with that of Perilous Falls and perhaps the fates of others far beyond the town's borders. She
understood what she had to do.

"I know it's not my responsibility." Bartimaeus dropped
one arm out of his tweed jacket and lifted the strap of the
satchel over his head. He gently placed it around Lucille's
neck. "It's your responsibility. So take it to the boy. We have
no choice, Lucille."

She laid a hand over the cloth satchel. Through the fabric she fingered the chunky locks along the edge of the book
she had spent her life protecting. This was her life's mission: to fulfill the prophecy, to protect her family, and to
realize her father's vision. Relinquishing the book would
surely usher in the final act she knew she could influence
but not ultimately control.

Bartimaeus's voice again fell into that deep monotone,
as if he were in a trance. "Take me to Dismal Shoals. Then
get the boy. You're gonna need him."

"Why Dismal Shoals? It's a *Hell Mouth*. It's too dangerous, Bart."

"It's all dangerous." He smiled, returning from his mo-
mentary vision. "The Bottom Dwellers are nesting in the
Shoals, and so is whatever's controlling them. I won't go
inside the old temple, but I'll need to get a fix on what's in
there."

Aunt Lucille said nothing. She jammed the boat's throttle, and the *Stella Maris* steamed forward with great speed. Around the slight bend in the river, they could see the remains of Gareb Pier, its fragments bobbing atop the water like abandoned rafts. Along the shore, rescue crews finished their work. Wheelchair-bound teens were wrapped in towels or caught in the embrace of grateful parents. Reporters stood at a distance under the watchful eyes of deputy sheriffs who had blocked off all traffic along the road leading to the river's edge.

Nearing Dismal Shoals, the boat's passage was stalled by huge rocks protruding from the river. Aunt Lucille slowed the boat's advance. It was not only the rocks that caused her delay, but the mangled bodies of the Bottom Dwellers she saw upon them. More surprising was the frantic movement on a large stone in the middle of the river, just in front of the *Stella Maris*'s bow.

A man in a gray uniform, with unrelenting speed, smashed the *Fomorii* one after another as they rose from the water around him. He hurled them to nearby rocks or plunged them into the waters with only a stick and his keen instincts. Twisting the long pole in his hands, a winded Tobias Shen dropped two Bottom Dwellers on either side of him.

Lucille instructed Bart to hold the wheel. She moved to the bow of the boat and unleashed the powerful red-and-white ray from her hands. It exploded on the waters surrounding the rock Tobias Shen stood astride. She swept the ray back and forth like a searchlight, destroying all the creatures in its path. Ash bubbled up from the water like magma. The gobs of molten black matter were pulled downstream by the current.

Tobias Shen, stoop-shouldered and exhausted, leaned on the long pole, drenched in purple liquid. He breathed deeply for the first time since he had arrived. "You're good friends. But you're very, very sloooow."

No more Bottom Dwellers floated to the surface, and their strange hisses had faded from the river. "I think we got 'em all," Bartimaeus barked out to Shen.

"I certainly hope so," the white-haired man said, surveying the twisted carcasses of *Fomorii* piled on the rocks surrounding him.

Aunt Lucille slowly accelerated the boat's engine, sailing the *Stella Maris* near the rock Tobias Shen dominated. With his blood-soaked stick, he could have been one of the bronze war memorial figures in the park.

Bartimaeus sat in the copilot's chair, drained from the excitement of the last few minutes. He closed his eyes tightly and once again extended his hands as if trying to feel for something just out of reach. "Yeah, I think we got 'em all." Then he rose to his feet. "There's something else! Something dark and strong. It's not the Bottom Dwellers. What do you see, Lucille?"

Her eyes ran along the surface of the river to the bank and over to Tobias on the rock. "Nothing out of the ordinary. It's all very quiet."

At that moment the water violently rippled. Suddenly the lifeless Bottom Dwellers on one of the rocks near Tobias slipped into the river. The reptilian bodies piled on another rock followed suit. One by one the boulders were cleared of dead *Fomorii*, shoved into the river by an unseen agent. Like a spectator at a hyperactive tennis match, Shen turned his head back and forth as he tried to track the dropping Bottom Dwellers. Sensing danger, he raised his bloodstained pole. But before he could fully extend it above his head, Shen was lifted into the air by his left foot. His stick tumbled into the river. Suspended upside down over the water, Shen was completely immobile save for his head. The next thing he knew, he was flying toward the shore. Yowling as he drifted, Shen disappeared around a bend in the river.

"So, what in the blazes happened?" Bartimaeus asked.

"I don't know," Lucille said with a tremble in her voice. "He flipped upside down and just floated away. The *Fomorii* remains are gone as well."

"Go to Dismal Shoals," Bartimaeus instructed. "Whatever nabbed Tobias is sure to take him there."

Beneath St. Thomas Church, the boys stepped out of the darkened tunnel and into the first chamber of the Undercroft. From the weak light seeping in from high above, it was hard to get a sense of the immense square room. In the damp stone ceiling, four shafts directed dingy sunlight into the fifty-foot-high chamber. The light barely illuminated the steep inclines along the side walls. They were treacherous-looking ramps—more like slides, Will thought—made of unsupported stone blocks jutting from the rough walls. The problem was that both inclines led up to a flat stone wall. There were no doors or openings of any kind in the chamber except for the tunnel behind them.

"Do you think maybe we should read your green book now?" Simon asked. "Or do you want to just guess at our next step here?"

Will fished out the ziplock bag containing his great-grandfather's notebook. Having flipped open to the page bearing the sketch of the first chamber, he presented the book to Simon with reluctance. "Be careful with this." He pointed to the writing at the top of the page as he handed it off. "My great-grandfather calls this room the St. Paul Chamber."

"Considering the number of times St. Paul was imprisoned, that may not be a good sign." Simon pushed his sports goggles up the bridge of his thin nose and squinted at the scribble. "This is interesting."

The boys moved behind Simon's shoulders, trying to read the text.

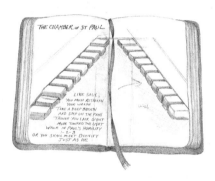

"Do you all mind backing off? You're standing in my light," Simon protested, even though he was holding an LED penlight. Once they moved away, he read rapidly in his high-pitched squeal:

THE CHAMBER OF ST. PAUL
Like Saul, you must restrain your wrath.
Take a deep breath and step on the path.
Though you lack sight,
move toward the light.
Walk in Paul's humility,
1-2-3,
or you shall meet eternity
just as he.

"I'm lost. Who's Saul?" Andrew sighed. "I thought you said this was St. Paul's room?"

"Wasn't 'Saul' Paul's name before God knocked him off his horse and made him blind?" Will asked Simon.

"That's correct. Saul persecuted Jesus's followers, but after he was blinded by a bright light, he converted to Christianity and became the apostle Paul. That's the way I learned it in Sunday school, anyway." Simon returned to the writing near the bottom of the page. "I get the 'take a deep breath and step on the path' part—which I guess means we should step on one of those inclines. But where is the light we're supposed to move toward? Is it that light from the ceiling?"

Without hesitating, Will flicked the brim of his pith helmet, shifting it upward away from his hazel eyes. His pupils shot from the stone incline on the right to the one on the left side of the chamber. Impulsively, he marched to the very edge of the ramp on the right. "Here goes nothing." With that, Will inhaled, placing both his feet on the first sloping stone block—not at all sure that he had chosen the right ramp.

The grinding of stone and the clinking of chains reverberated through the chamber, creating an awful clatter. Simon and Andrew startled at the sound. Will never flinched, but continued looking upward. At the very top of the incline, a piece of the solid wall slid away, revealing an arched opening. Bright light shone from within.

"Let there be light. I guess that's what we're supposed to move toward," Will announced as he lifted his leg to walk up the incline.

Simon ran forward and grabbed him by the arm. "Don't move. Do you see that cutout in the stone there?"

Will glanced up to his right. Just above his eye level there was a four-inch slit running all the way up the wall.

"The book says, 'Walk in Paul's humility, one-two-three, or you shall meet eternity just as he.'" Simon was still holding Will's arm. "How do you walk in the humility of Paul?"

"Better question: How did Paul 'meet eternity'? How did he die?" Will asked.

"I was thinking the same thing," Andrew added.

"Oh, I'm sure that's what you were thinking . . . ," Simon said, glancing back at Andrew. "Paul was beheaded. They cut his head off in Rome. The legend is that Paul's head bounced three times. On each spot where it bounced, a spring of water shot up."

"So if I don't 'walk in humility,' I could drown or lose my head! Great," Will said, scratching his neck. "How do I walk in Paul's humility?"

The three boys exchanged looks. Finally Andrew spoke up. "Don't look at me. I've never seen nobody walk in humility."

Will fell to his knees. "This is humble, right?" He started moving up the incline, onto the next stone block.

"The instructions actually say to *walk* in humility," Simon lectured, reading from the notebook, his voice going higher with each word. "It doesn't say crawl, Will. It says *walk*."

Ignoring the advice, Will continued to make his way up the stone ramp, one kneecap at a time. At nearly the halfway point, he stopped. "There is a number one on this next stone," he shouted down to his friends. "What do you think I should do?"

"Don't step to the left," Andrew snickered.

Simon's eyes turned to slits. "Your comic asides are not helping." He then directed his comments to Will. "I suggest you stay low as you move to the number one stone. Is there a two and a three?"

Ahead of him, Will could see the other blocks with

numbers carved onto their faces. Each numbered block was separated by an unmarked one.

"I'm blaming you if I get my head sliced off, Simon," he shouted as he crawled onto the number 1 block.

Will felt the stone quake the instant he touched it, a whirring noise sounding overhead. Above him a pair of swordlike blades spun out of the slit in the wall and retracted three times. Sweat covered Will's forehead. Still on his knees, he instinctively leapt forward onto the next stone—an unmarked one—and not a moment too soon. Within seconds, water poured from the wall over the number 1 block he had just vacated.

"Look out!" Will warned the boys below. He could feel the wall rumbling to his right.

The number 1 stone was thrown across the room by a gush of water, smashing it to the floor. A torrent now spewed from the hole in the wall where the stone had been and pooled below. *I won't be going back that way,* Will thought, glancing at the broken path behind him. The boys hadn't much time, and Will knew it.

"You two are going to have to go up the ramp on the other side of the chamber. Stay low and move fast," Will instructed.

Simon and Andrew did not need an invitation. They fell on all fours and teetered on the first block of the incline opposite Will. There was just enough room on the stone's surface for the two of them. The clatter of chains and an awful grinding echoed from above. At the top of their ramp, another opening presented itself, blinding them with light. The water was rising fast.

Andrew glanced up at the long, steep climb ahead of them. "If we don't get moving, we won't make it. Come on, four eyes." Andrew linked arms with Simon in case the boy lost his balance. "I got you."

Simon was panting. "I can't stand heights—I can't breathe when I'm off the floor." The boy was puffing out his cheeks, inhaling and exhaling air with great effort.

"You're going up a stone slide. You ain't having a baby!" Andrew said.

But Simon did not take the bait. He ignored the comment and continued to huff and puff, moving cautiously up the incline.

Across the chamber, Will made the decision to speed-crawl to the top of his ramp. "You guys keep moving. Once I reach the opening, I'll be able to help you." He hustled onto the number 2 block, triggering the appearance of a new set of blades overhead. He quickly pounced on the number 3 stone and neared the opening. In a matter of seconds, both the number 2 and 3 blocks had been pushed to the floor by a pair of geysers springing from the wall. Only these sprays of water were so powerful, they reached clear across to Andrew and Simon's incline.

"I can't do this. I'm slipping," Simon whined, sliding backward on the wet stones.

"Hold on. I got you," Andrew assured him. The bigger boy tried to drag his scrawny sidekick forward. A steady stream of water cascaded toward them, and they were still several stones away from the numbered blocks in the middle of the ramp.

At the summit of the opposite incline, Will tumbled through the opening. His pith helmet rolled onto the tiled floor inside. When he looked up, he found himself in a bright, expansive chamber.

"Guys, I made it. I made it!" Will cried jubilantly, taking a quick peek at the next room. The new chamber was at least a hundred feet tall. Facing him, on the other side of the room, a wall of fire illuminated the space. He realized this was the source of the bright light he had seen from inside the first chamber. The only break in the wall of fire was a wide black metal door at the center.

On Will's right and left, huge grim stone statues lined the walls. Many of their faces were hidden under hoods or wrapped in rocky veils. The visible faces wore pained expressions turned to the sky. *I guess this is not the party room?* Will surmised. He reached around for the green notebook in his backpack and then remembered that Simon still had it.

A high-pitched yowl drifted in from the first chamber. It was Simon!

Will pulled a coiled rope from his backpack and fleetly tied a bowline knot at its end, just as he had been taught in Boy Scouts. "That's pretty badge-worthy," he told himself, tying off the knot. He snatched his pith helmet from the floor and raced toward the opening at the top of Simon and Andrew's incline.

In the first chamber, gushing water from across the way pounded his friends, making it hard for them to advance up the ramp. Will threw his rope to Andrew, who now held Simon by the collar of his drenched orange shirt. In a full panic attack, Simon wailed and begged to remain where he was. This was not an option. The pair was only one stone away from the numbered blocks, and Will knew from experience they had to keep moving—and fast.

"Tie the rope around Simon and I'll pull him in," Will instructed Andrew. While the large boy struggled to get the rope around his uncooperative climbing partner, Will tied his end of the rope to the leg of the nearest statue in the second chamber. Once he had doubled the knot, he looked up at the mammoth hooded figure. "Whatever you do, don't make any sudden moves," Will said.

Simon's shrieks echoed from the first chamber again.

"He's freaking. I can't get him to stop," Andrew complained.

"Just get that rope around him. Once you touch the first numbered block, you've got to move quickly. The stones will start flying fast." Will then turned his attention to the bleating member of the team. "Simon, calm down! You have my great-grandfather's notebook, and if you fall . . . I'm going to kill you! We need that book."

The deflated Simon sobered up. "I can't make it. I'm feeling nauseous."

Andrew threw an arm around Simon's back. "We're going now. Control yourself and don't barf on me."

Before Simon could offer any resistance, Andrew pulled him toward the number 1 stone, then on to the unmarked one. The razorlike blades scissored over their heads. A blast of water shot out of the wall inches from where they knelt. As expected, the stone behind them went flying.

The whole time, Will clung to the rope, steadying Simon.

"I'm not going any farther. Leave me here," Simon huffed.

"I'd love to leave you here. But if I keep climbin', there won't be a 'here' for you to stand on. You'll be down there." Andrew tilted his head to the right.

Looking over the edge, Simon saw brown water rising and—out of the corner of his eye—something gliding in the drink. "What is that?" He pointed toward the completely submerged tunnel they had used to enter the chamber. A pair of rounded yellow eyes and a long snout floated atop the water's surface.

"I don't know what it is—and I don't want to find out. Do you?" Andrew said.

Simon crouched low and waddled ahead with new determination. Andrew followed his lead, affecting his own munchkin shuffle.

"Watch your head," Simon said, stepping onto the number 2 block. Andrew just barely ducked the second set of crisscrossing blades, quickly toddling onto the next unmarked stone. Simon wasn't quite fast enough.

"Dan, honey, we need to talk," Mayor Ava Lynch brayed from the other end of city hall's executive corridor. With every step her heels dug into the gray marble of the second-floor hallway. The woman with taut, glistening skin and a sculpted plume of black hair advanced at amazing speed.

Dan Wilder knew what she wanted. He fumbled his key into the lock on the door bearing his name—desperately trying to get inside before she reached him. "Ava, I have an important call now. But I'll come down and see you before the vote," he said, faking a smile.

"Dan. Dan! I need to speak with you *now*, sugar."

Her booming voice was muffled by the closing office door, which he locked. Within the walls of his well-ordered corner refuge, Dan was safe. The colored pencils arranged by hue in their segregated cups, the draft paper stacked in neat rows above his slanted worktable, the bare oak desk holding nothing but a phone restored his calm. This was his retreat, his perfectly appointed hideout from the world, immune to the madness outside. He leaned back on the thick wooden door and heaved a sigh of relief.

"Dan. Dan." The mayor's voice got progressively louder outside. "We got the autopsies back from the coroner's office on the two kids who died at the river today. Dan, I need a moment."

"I can't now, Ava," Dan Wilder yelled. He had just heard from Sheriff Willy Stout, Andrew's father, about the odd deaths at the river. Bruises on the victims' legs and arms held "reptilian-like" impressions, but the thing that most rattled Dan, the information that had sent him trembling into his office, was the revelation that the victims had been choked to death. Their mouths and lungs were filled with what Sheriff Stout called "river trash."

"Never seen nothing like this. Without knowing better, you'd think the bed of the river just appeared in the coroner's office," Stout told him. "Chunks of green mud, snails, shells—algae-covered river trash—all shoved in their little mouths. No animal could have done this. Makes no sense. . . ."

Dan stumbled toward his desk, trying to forget his conversation with the sheriff and to expel the memory of the refuse he had seen fall onto the roof of his home, and into his den. He dropped his keys onto the desktop and headed toward the red stuffed leather chair, its back turned to him. As he spun the chair around, his face went white. There on the seat was a reeking pile of green bones, shells, and river muck. The stench of the rotten debris filled the office. More of it was piled beneath his desk—writhing, heaping mounds of the putrid waste. It was actually throbbing—moving.

There was a rap on the door. "Dan! Open up. I can't wait till later. We need to speak now," the mayor said again.

Dan ripped off his glasses, wiping the sweat from his eyes. Placing the spectacles back on his face, he took a deep breath and began flattening his hair in the mirror on the wall. His mouth was dry and he couldn't swallow.

"Coming. One minute," he croaked. He stole a glance at his chair before going to the door. The pile of river trash was still there. And on the floor, the shells and mud and broken bones were slowly advancing toward him. He was not imagining this. With one awkward movement, he pulled open the door and slid into the hallway, quickly slamming it behind him.

"We should talk in your office," Mayor Lynch said. "What's wrong with you, Danny?"

"Nothing's wrong. I'm perfectly fine." Dan's wide eyes and slight tremble told a different story.

"The autopsies came back on those two kids. Very strange deaths. I want you to be on the oversight investigative task force."

"Can't do that. I—I—I'm very . . . uh, really . . . busy." He rubbed his lips together as if trying to stall a cry. "No, I wouldn't be good at that sort of thing."

Mayor Lynch folded her arms, lowered her chin, and looked down her chiseled nose at Dan. "I didn't ask if you'd be good. I said I want you to be on that investigative task force."

"Why? Why me?" He anxiously ran his hands up and down his pant legs.

"Because you'll do a thorough job and you're a Wilder. You'd bring a sense of credibility to our work. . . . Did you know your aunt Lucille was down on the river near the crime scene today?"

"Lucille? She was? I—I haven't spoken with her."

The mayor turned on her heels and began to walk away. "I'll see you for the vote, sugar."

Dan leaned back on his office door but couldn't bring himself to reach for the handle.

Leo Wilder stared absently at the ancient crimson-and-gold fabric in the open display case at Peniel. Standing beside him in Bethel Hall, his mother focused her television camera on the garment. Peering through the viewfinder, she gave Leo explicit directions.

"Okay, gently close the glass door on the case. . . . Now open it slowly. Good. Stay right there. Don't move. I'm going in for the close-up."

Deborah kept her eye plastered to the viewfinder, barely breathing. She was all business. Deb was a perfectionist who insisted on shooting and editing everything herself. Which explained why her TV show aired not only in Perilous Falls, but all over the country. Leo tapped the cast on his arm, seemingly trying to relieve an insistent itch.

"Mom, can we go yet?" Marin asked for the fifth time that hour, flopping her head side to side nearby. The little girl started spinning in a circle, as tired children are wont to do when they are bored.

"Marin, as soon as Mommy gets this shot, we can go. But I need you to be a good girl and read your book or look at the pretty things in the cases," Deborah said, her eye still fixed on the viewfinder. "Just don't touch anything, sweetie. Hands behind your back, okay?"

Marin placed her hands behind her back but continued to spin in a circle, bumping nearly every other case as she whirled about the Gothic hall. A pair of strong arms suddenly surrounded her. The girl gasped.

"If you're not very careful, you could fall and hurt yourself. It's important to listen to your mummy." The owner of the defined biceps holding Marin was in his midtwenties and spoke in a high English accent. He had a breathy, soothing voice that calmed Marin instantly. Or perhaps it was his blue eyes and chiseled face that held her attention.

"I'm sorry. She didn't touch anything." Deborah Wilder crossed the room in an instant.

"No worries at all. We wouldn't want your aunt Lucille to get angry with us," the man said playfully, releasing Marin, who ran into Deborah's arms. He wore a woolen tailored vest, gray pants, and an eggplant-colored tie. "I'm Valens Ricard. I've been working with Lucille and Bartimaeus for a few months. They told me you'd be coming. Shooting Elijah's mantle, are you?"

Deborah found herself staring at his royal-blue eyes. "Yes, I'm shooting the mantle. For my show."

Valens was already heading toward Leo and the open display case. "You're a wonderful presenter. I watch *Supernatural Secrets* every week, Mrs. Wilder. And this must be Leo." He mussed Leo's brown hair, which the boy clearly detested, given his scowl. "Do you know about the mantle?"

Leo shook his head, huge eyes blinking behind his glasses.

"Well, in the Second Book of Kings—it's in the Old Testament—there is a perfectly wonderful story about that very mantle. It was the prophet Elijah's cloak. And when Elijah went up to heaven, another prophet, Elisha, picked up the cloak, folded it, and struck the River Jordan. What do you think happened?"

"The cloak got wet?" Leo answered.

"Very perceptive." Valens looked over at Deborah with a jaunty smirk. "I'm sure it did get wet. But it also miraculously split the waters of the river and allowed Elisha to walk clear across. It has other powers too."

Leo was now even more transfixed by the cloth. Marin and Deborah were transfixed by Valens.

"I'm very sorry to interrupt. I heard voices and thought I would come up and say hello. I do truly enjoy your show, Mrs. Wilder." Valens extended a long hand, which Deborah happily accepted.

"What do you say to Mr. Valens, kids?"

"Thanks for the history lesson," Leo said.

"You're pretty," Marin giggled.

"He's handsome, Marin. Not pretty. I mean . . . you use the term 'handsome' with men. At least some men. The pretty ones." Blushing, Deborah hurriedly returned to her camera. "Thank you for being so kind, and I'll make sure Marin doesn't break anything."

"Till next time, then." Valens gave a little bow and vanished into the entry hall just as Deborah's cell phone rang. It was Aunt Lucille.

"Deborah, you haven't heard from Will, have you?"

"No. Is something wrong?"

"With the tragedies on the river, I just want to make sure he's safe."

"Have you called Mr. Shen at the church?"

Aunt Lucille hesitated. "Tobias was . . . detained. He was way downriver. I'm in the boat just now. After I make a quick drop-off, I'll go check on Will. I'm sure he's still planting trees at the church."

"Let me know when you get there. I'm taking my last shots of the mantle, and then we'll come meet you at St. Thomas."

"Perfect, dear. I'll call you soon."

Deborah clicked off the cell phone, adjusted her camera lens, and worriedly tried to capture the last shots she needed for her story. Leo pressed his face against the side of the open glass case, his big blue eyes studying every weave of the miraculous ancient cloth within.

In the Undercroft, Andrew leapt onto the solid unmarked stone. But Simon lingered on the block marked 2. A rush of water now covered his feet.

"Aaah!" Simon screamed as he and the stone were ejected from the wall. The block splashed into the pool below, leaving a second gaping hole in the incline. Simon was thrown out into the middle of the chamber, and then, because of the rope tied around his chest, he swung toward the wall directly below Will. Drenched and petrified, Simon dangled like a dazed spider from the cord in Will's hands.

"Owwwww. That hurt!" Simon screeched. "My shoulder is aching. I'll feel that one in the morning."

"Andrew, you're going to have to come up here and help me pull Simon in," Will calmly ordered, struggling with the rope.

Andrew crouched on an unmarked block, his back against the rough tan wall. "If I come to you, the next stone—number three—will go flying and might hit the other end of your yo-yo." He brushed his wet red hair away from his eyes.

"That could be a problem," Will muttered to himself.

From below, Simon's shrill voice rose up. "There is something moving in the water. And in case you don't realize it, *the water is rising.* Pull me up now! Pull me up!" Simon reached into his backpack as he spoke. Past the green notebook he found an inhaler, which he pressed to his mouth and dragged on for several seconds.

Andrew began to stand on the stone block. He told Will to back up. As a linebacker on his football team, he had rushed the line since he was ten. This time he planned on rushing the opening at the top of the incline—without touching the number 3 block. He assumed a three-pointed crouch. With water peppering the side of his face and cascading down the stones in front of him, Andrew focused all his attention on the opening ahead.

"Keep your head down, moron," Simon directed from below. "If you lose that pea brain of yours, I am not going diving for it."

"Shut it, Simon." With that, Andrew lunged for the brightly lit opening before him.

CHAPTER 9

THE FIERY TRIAL

Andrew Stout's dive toward the opening atop the incline was off by a few inches. He cleared the number 3 stone. Unfortunately, his size nine and a half shoe did not.

"Will!" Andrew screamed as his foot slipped on the wet stones. Flat on his face, he slid backward down the slick surface. Fearing that he'd fall off the incline completely, he pressed the balls of his feet into the stone—any stone—trying to get some traction. His foot finally found it on the number 3 block.

"Oh no. I didn't mean to do that," Andrew said in a panic, feeling the stone trembling beneath his arched toes. He desperately dug his fingers into the space between the blocks in front of him, clawing his way forward. As water shot from the wall, the numbered stone flew behind him.

Andrew grabbed the only sure thing within reach: the taut rope holding Simon.

"You're going to drag us both into the water, big boy," Simon screamed from below, the number 3 stone whizzing by his head.

Ignoring Simon's bleatings, Andrew shinnied up the rope and joined Will, climbing into the bright entryway of the second chamber.

"Glad you avoided that last stone," Will said sarcastically, still holding the rope with two hands.

"If it's all the same to you," Andrew said, grasping the line, "I got enough criticism from the mouth at the end of this string without you chiming in." He irritably yanked on the rope.

Within minutes the two boys had hoisted a rattled Simon into the second chamber.

"See, we all made it. Not bad, guys," Will said, clapping his damp friends on the back. His excitement was not contagious.

"My shoulder is aching, and I know I have rope burns under my arms," Simon groaned, massaging his armpits.

"How many more of these chambers do we have to pass through?" Andrew asked, untying the rope from the statue's leg.

"Just two more," Will said. "This second chamber and the third. Then we reach the Keep with the relic." Gazing beyond his friends, Will's eyes sparkled. "Look at this chamber!"

The wall of fire on the other side of the enormous cavern warmed the boys, who were amazed by the sheer size and opulence of the place. Will thought it looked like some sort of shrine. He now realized that the floor was tiled with mosaic images of saints—some showing only their faces, others featuring their heads and shoulders. Bits of brightly colored glass and gemstones embedded in the tiles shimmered in the firelight. To the right and the left, twelve large statues of dreary saints, many wearing veils and hoods, faced each other: six statues on one side of the room, six on the other.

"Whoever they are, they're not a happy bunch," Andrew commented, ogling the statues. "Did their friends just croak or something? Your great-grandfather probably calls this one the Chamber of Sad Sacks."

High overhead, a thick stone balcony encircled the room about ten feet beneath the ceiling. Will studied the chamber intently, his fingers intertwined behind his back. He noticed that the balconies above the right and left sides of the room were missing a few stones. *Those ledges look like the mouth of a kid waiting for the tooth fairy,* Will thought.

"Adventure calls, gentlemen. Another chamber, another challenge," he announced.

"I'm kind of challenged out," Andrew said, wringing the water from his pant leg.

"I refuse to proceed unless I go first," Simon demanded. "I will not be left swinging from a rope again, victim to your foolishness, Will—or to that big galoot's incompetence!"

Paying no attention to Simon's blizzard of complaints,

Will calmly walked behind the chattering boy, unzipped his backpack, and retrieved the ziplock bag containing Jacob Wilder's green notebook. Turning to the appropriate page, Will tried to read the instructions. "If you can stop griping for a minute, here's our next clue."

TRIAL OF THE SAINTS
We stand on the shoulders of the saints
to escape the consuming flame.
For by fire will the Lord render judgment,
and many shall be slain.
Enter by the narrow gate,
for the wide gate brings death and pain.

"There's only one gate, and that's the one in the middle of the fire wall. We have to walk toward it." Simon pointed to the flame-free, wide black metal door straight ahead. "Look at the tiles on the floor. What does it say about the saints?"

"'We stand on the shoulders of the saints to escape the consuming flame,'" Will read.

"Easy. I've got it. We can only step on the tiles that show the shoulders of the saints."

Will patted Simon on the back. "Pretty good thinking. So what are you waiting for? I thought you wanted to go first."

Simon tugged at the rope still tied round his torso. "Hold this, just in case my calculations are off." He tossed the end of the rope to Will.

Simon checked the strap on his sports goggles and tentatively extended his foot to touch the nearest tile featuring a saint's head and shoulders. When nothing bad happened, Simon shifted his whole weight onto the first tile. So far, so good. With all the flair of a goose waddling on hot asphalt, Simon hopscotched from saint's shoulder to saint's shoulder, closing in on the black metal door.

Andrew, leaning on one of the big statues along the wall, seemed perplexed. "You know, that door is kinda wide, isn't it? What's the book say about the gate?"

Simon had already made his way halfway across the floor. He shot a hateful look in Andrew's direction.

"It says, 'Enter by the *narrow* gate, for the wide gate brings death and pain,'" Will read from the green notebook. "But it's the only gate!"

"I'm just sayin' it looks wide to me." Andrew shrugged his broad shoulders. "But if he wants to keep hoppin' around, let him hop to the wide gate. What do I care?"

Simon spun to face Andrew. "Forgive us, Dr. Jones, but if we rely on your genius to crack the code of the Undercroft, we'll be down here permanentl—" The tile beneath him suddenly broke in two, dropping Simon through the floor. Will grasped the rope just as Simon's head slipped out of sight.

"Hold on, Simon!" Will shouted.

Andrew scrambled to get hold of the wriggling rope as well. Together, the boys hauled Simon back up through the broken tile floor.

"It stinks. There's some kind of grease down there," Simon squealed as he was dragged sideways across the mosaic tiles. His shorts and bird legs were covered in a slick brown substance. Leaning against the left-hand wall of the room, Will and Andrew pulled Simon all the way to their position.

One by one, the tiles near the break in the floor began crumbling away. The mosaics fell into what appeared to be a pool of brown oil, which grew larger by the moment.

Will ran toward the hooded statue farthest from the flaming wall. "You were on the wrong saint's shoulders, Simon!" He began climbing the arms of the stone figure like a chimpanzee. "*These* are the saint's shoulders we're supposed to be on! Andrew, let Simon climb your back—onto this ugly guy next to me."

The statue next to Will portrayed a short, chunky monk with a bald head and a gloomy countenance.

"Why do I get the ugliest statue here?" Simon huffed.

"Because you're the ugliest kid here. Get up," Andrew said, shoving Simon onto the statue.

By the time Simon mounted the stone arm of the fat monk, the mosaic tiles were furiously splatting into the oil pit below. Tile by tile, the floor collapsed.

Andrew immediately scaled the statue next to Simon's.

Will hugged the stone head before him while reading from the green notebook. "'We stand on the shoulders of the saints to escape the consuming flame. For by fire will the Lord render judgment.' Why do I have a strange feeling it's going to get hot in here?"

Vibrations shook the statues holding the boys. Will slipped the green notebook into his backpack. Simon began moaning in terror, frantically tying the rope attached to his waist around the fat monk's carved head. Andrew found himself teetering atop a slender stone nun. After several awkward attempts to embrace her thin noggin, he opted to straddle her neck like a huge baby riding on its mother's shoulders.

"Sister better hold up!" Andrew shouted.

All at once every statue in the room—those on the boys' side and their companions across the way—began rising. They moved at the same steady speed, pushed upward by thick metal columns that shot up beneath each statue. The last tiles around the edges of the chamber floor tumbled into the lake of oil below. As the statues neared the ceiling, Will looked up, fearing that he and his saint would smash into the jutting ledge of the balcony above.

"We're all going to die," Simon wailed. "I'll be pulverized on the ceiling, then drowned in oil, and finally burned to a crisp. My parents won't even know where to find my torched remains."

"You're not going to be pulverized," Will said. "Look up." Above the statues were cutouts in the overhang, which would permit the stone shoulders to pass through freely.

"Let me adjust my statement," Simon went on. "I'll be drowned in oil and burned to a crisp, but not pulverized."

"For the first time today, he might be right," Andrew said, pointing below.

A thin stream of liquid spouted from the wall of fire. Within seconds the liquid ignited, becoming a flaming fountain headed straight toward the pool of oil.

The statues slowly passed through the missing blocks of the stone balcony. "C'mon, c'mon," Andrew kept repeating as the statues finally came to a halt.

Will leapt off his hooded friar and helped Simon untangle himself from the fat monk's stone head. "Get against the wall," Will told the others. Simon began to complain. But Will placed his hand over the boy's mouth. "Save it for after the cookout." He pushed Simon against the chamber wall and positioned himself next to his friend. Andrew pressed his face against the wall, giving the room his back.

They heard a rumbling *WHOOSH* below.

"Don't move," Will said, a knowing smile on his face. "One 'consuming flame' coming up." He used his pith helmet to protect his face from the inferno.

A sheet of raging fire appeared directly in front of the boys. Simon screamed, his hands shielding his face.

Though the fire was two feet away, Will could feel the intense heat not only on his neck and arms, but through his sneakers. The sizzling stone ledge beneath them was all that preserved the boys from the flame's destructive touch. Within a few moments it was over. The fire hovered on the surface of the pool below but had lost its ability to reach the ceiling.

"My rump's well done," Andrew said, rubbing his backside.

"No matter how it's cooked, it should be sent back to the kitchen immediately!" Simon said, lowering his hands from his face. Andrew and Will instantly began laughing at him. "What? What's so funny?"

Following the fire blast, Simon's cheeks and hands were slightly charred. When he lowered his fingers, white marks like war paint were torched onto the sides of his face where his thumbs had been. "I want to know what you are laughing at!"

"Never mind," Will said, trying to restrain his smile. "We have to keep moving." He looked to his friends for agreement and pulled the notebook from his backpack with a mischievous excitement. "Which way? Which way?"

"We don't know where we are going. How can we know the way?" Andrew offered.

Will gently punched Andrew on the shoulder. "We'll find the way, big guy. You already figured out the most important part of the challenge: avoid the wide gate. Now all we have to do is find the narrow one." Will glanced at the notebook and slammed it shut. "How hard can that be?"

Flicking his helmet back, Will peered down the length of the balcony they stood upon. It took a sharp right turn above the wall of fire. There Will could see two openings— both of them pretty narrow. Without a word he walked past Andrew and Simon, leapt over the stone heads blocking his path, and approached the openings.

"We'd better follow him before things start flying again." Andrew nudged the catatonic Simon and shuffled after Will.

Simon, in a bit of a daze, reluctantly gathered up the excess rope dangling from his waist and followed the others.

"This could be a problem," Will said, standing in front of the two slim black tunnels in the wall before him. He inched his fingers under his helmet, scratching his head. "They're both narrow gates. They're identical."

Simon took the end of his rope and measured the widths of the openings. "I'm afraid they are exactly the same size. So maybe we can go through both of them." Simon dropped his rope to the ground. Andrew quickly scooped it up.

"I wouldn't let your wick droop over the edge," Andrew advised, looking down at the wall of fire beneath them. "With that oil on you, you'll light up like a skinny hurricane lamp."

Simon did not protest for once, but offered a grudging smile of thanks.

Will busily ran the beam of his flashlight into one of the slim openings and then moved on to the other. "I see," he murmured. He showed the boys the difference between the two passages. Both went on for about eight feet, but the "gate" to the left had smooth interior walls and plenty of room. The one to the right was jagged, with bits of stone sticking out all along the passageway. "We'll have to squeeze down this one. With the rocks and stuff on the wall, it seems like the most 'narrow gate.'"

He replaced his flashlight, removed his helmet, and shimmied into the opening sideways.

Simon cut Andrew off at the entry, hustling to follow

Will. "I'd better go first, Slim Jim. When you get stuck in there, I don't want to be behind you." He disappeared into the dark hole.

Vapor wafting up from the pool below caught Andrew's attention. A tide of water had spilled in from the first chamber, extinguishing what was left of the flaming pool.

Andrew decided not to wait around to see how high the water would rise. He pushed out all the air in his lungs, sucked in his stomach, then crammed his bulk into the sliver of an opening, hoping he would make it to the other side.

Below, two Bottom Dwellers stealthily swam into the second chamber. Their cold eyes, just above the surface of the oil-laced water, searched for any movement—for the slightest sign of life.

"Sheriff Stout, we thank you for your report. But I find it hard to believe that there are—what did you call them?— 'reptilian, gatorlike creatures' in the Perilous River," Heinrich Crinshaw mockingly read from papers on the mahogany dais of the city council chambers. He sat in the center position, the chairman's spot, his beady eyes trained on the sheriff standing before him.

"The members of this council might have a problem swallowing your contention that our fair town is being terrorized not by alligators—but by, uh . . ."—he again flipped through the report for dramatic effect—"'creatures!' One of your deputies even calls them 'unknown river *monsters*' in this exhaustive report. Do you really stand by these descriptions, sir?"

Sheriff Willy Stout stood silent and sweating like a bald polar bear marooned on an island in the Caribbean. After more than twenty minutes of interrogation by the city council, he couldn't think of anything more to say. Clutching his green-brimmed officer's hat to his chest, the sheriff simply nodded.

Chairman Crinshaw released a pinched, staccato laugh. Other council members soon followed suit. "Are we to interpret your silence as confirming the contents of this report? These fairy tales? Are we to tell the victims' families that 'river monsters' attacked their children and 'gatorlike creatures' are on the loose?"

Dan Wilder, sitting at the end of the raised dais, pressed his forehead into the heels of his hands.

"I move that we reject the sheriff's ludicrous report," Crinshaw suggested in a croaky monotone, "and authorize our own *credible* investigation."

From the end of the table, without looking up, Dan Wilder spoke. "Mr. Chairman, I think Sheriff Stout has reported—is reporting—the facts as he and his team found them. None of this is inconsistent with the media reports or the evidence. Is it, Willy?"

The sheriff sheepishly shook his head. "No, sir."

There were murmurs and concerned looks all along the dais.

A solitary fingernail, hard as a pickax, struck the council's tabletop until there was silence. "I wish to offer some guidance, Mr. Chairman," a female voice blared from the other end of the dais. It was Mayor Ava Lynch, who was herself one of the six city council members. "Speaking on behalf of the concerned citizens of Perilous Falls, I move that we accept the sheriff's report, which we will seal from probing eyes. At the same time, we have been informed that certain individuals, not in the sheriff's report, were spotted near the *crime scenes*—I mean accidents—on the Perilous River. Since the sheriff has obviously not pursued every lead, I should like the city council to authorize an independent, three-person investigative task force. It will pursue any and all persons near the crime scenes so that we may come to a full understanding of exactly what occurred on the river, and who or what is responsible. I nominate myself, the chairman, and Dan Wilder to the task force. Any objections?"

Dan shoved a hand into the air. "I object. I am not an investigator. . . . Neither are you, Mr. Chairman . . . nor you, Ms. Mayor. We—we—we should leave this to the authorities—"

"Hearing no further objections . . . Thank you, Dan," Heinrich Crinshaw pronounced, pounding the gavel before him with authority. "I move that we accept the mayor's thoughtful proposal."

After a quick vote of five to one, the task force was approved and the council members scattered.

Mayor Lynch triumphantly marched up behind Dan, placing two hands on his shoulders. "Why don't you, Heinrich, and I confer in my office, sugar? We owe it to our citizens to start this investigation right away. I have lots of leads for us. See you upstairs." The mayor patted Dan's tense shoulders and trotted away.

CHAPTER 10

THE RELIC

Will squirmed free of the rocky tunnel, the "narrow gate," exiting into a darkened space. The moment his foot touched the platform at the end of the passageway, torches in the columns along the walls of the third chamber ignited. It was a good thing too. Had Will taken four or five more steps, he would have plunged seventy feet straight down to the black polished floor of the narrow room below.

To Will this last chamber looked like a tricked-out empty swimming pool. From the platform where he stood, two curved stone staircases reached down to a granite surface. The chamber walls were granite too. The other side of the chamber looked vastly different.

Directly across from Will, a thin set of stairs led up from the bottom of the granite well to a pair of life-sized white statues. The statues stood on half a black disk, the other half of which bent upward to provide a backdrop. To Will's eye, the carved figures appeared to be standing on a severely burned, open taco shell. A gleaming gold grate, like a wall, surrounded the rear edges of the "taco shell" but proceeded no farther—leaving the statue display completely unprotected.

Alone for the moment, Will considered the design of the room. He had been so focused on solving the riddle of each chamber and advancing to the next challenge that he'd barely allowed himself time to absorb any of his journey: the elaborate chambers Jacob Wilder had constructed to protect one old bone; the dangers and booby traps in each room that only a Wilder could navigate. *With all this protection,* Will reasoned, *the relic must have miraculous powers. Maybe it* can *heal those who touch it. Maybe it* does *hold the floodwater back and . . . The relic!* He needed to get that relic.

He forced himself to stop gawking at the exotic room and ripped open his great-grandfather's notebook just as Simon came plowing out of the tunnel. Will grabbed his hyper friend by the shirttail before he could run off the edge of the platform. "Take it easy, Flash," he advised, without glancing up from the notebook.

"Your relic must be over there," Simon exploded, pointing at the gold grille on the other side of the chamber. He then jutted his head forward. "Is that a statue of Jesus and St. Thomas? Oh, that must be the moment where Thomas was told to stick his hand in Jesus's side and feel His nail wounds—to prove that He had risen from the dead."

"Thanks for the Sunday school lesson," Will droned, intently studying the notebook.

Andrew painfully removed himself from the jagged passageway. His arms were scratched and bruised from the journey. "What did I miss?"

"Nothing," Will assured him. "Here's what the notebook says about this last chamber."

DIDYMUS'S WAY
One alone may climb the stair to reach
the saint's remains.
To pass this way, beware, you'll need faith
as well as brains;
Thomas could be moved,
and indeed he still can be.
What direction did the saint proceed
having seen the Risen One from Galilee?

"Who is Diddy-muss?" Andrew asked. "Sounds like an old rapper or something."

"Didymus was another name for Thomas, moron," Simon explained. "It's Greek for 'twin.'"

Will started moving down the stairs to the granite floor on the lower level. The boys followed him down. "I'm going over to the statues. You guys better hang back. 'One alone may climb the stair,'" he read from the notebook.

Simon and Andrew grumbled about being left behind.

"I should go up. I know more about this than you do," Simon protested, reaching the shiny black floor.

"But I'm the Wilder," Will said defensively. He gazed up at the two statues from the lower level as if possessed. "Stay here. I'll need your help." Will scrambled up the narrow staircase to the lifelike images, which were about two yards apart.

The figure of Christ held his robe open, exposing a chest wound; the palm of his left hand extended toward the other statue. Deep holes in the marble marked the palm and the chest of the image. The other figure was presumably St. Thomas. He too had a beard, long hair, and flowing robes. The chiseled Thomas pointed a single marble finger toward Jesus, his head leaning back in awe.

Will checked the floor. The Christ figure was firmly attached to the black granite base. But the Thomas statue slid along a metal track that stretched from the Christ image to the granite disk's edge. Where he stood a compass had been etched into the polished base, complete with gold arrows marking north, south, east, and west. Will pushed his weight against the back of the Thomas statue and it lurched forward.

"Okay, guys," Will called down, "this one must be Thomas—and since he's on a track, he can 'be moved.' The question is: Where?" Will leaned over the ledge, awaiting a response from the boys below. Receiving only blank stares, he sought answers in Jacob Wilder's scrawlings. "'What direction did the saint proceed, having seen the Risen One from Galilee?'"

"Proceed? Who proceeds?" Andrew fussed.

"Driven people proceed," Simon lectured. "Apostles proceed. I proceed. People of limited brain capacity—whom I won't mention—probably just 'go.' They go to the bathroom, go to fast-food joints, and occasionally go to juvenile detention facilities, but everyone else 'proceeds.'"

Andrew lunged for him, but Simon ducked and darted away. "I will proceed over here."

"That might be the last time you *proceed*—ever," Andrew threatened.

"Guys, focus," Will urged from above. "'Having seen the Risen One from Galilee,' did St. Thomas 'proceed' to touch Jesus's wounds? Is that what he did?"

"I already told you. Jesus instructed Thomas to inspect His wounds. So maybe you'd better push the Thomas statue toward the Jesus one," Simon said.

Will took a deep breath and nudged the Thomas statue forward, pushing it with both hands from behind. The pointed marble finger closed in on the other statue. As the sculpture moved along the track, Will wondered aloud: "Andrew might be onto something. The notebook asks, 'What direction did the saint proceed . . . ?' It doesn't ask what he *did*, but where he proceeded. . . ."

St. Thomas's marble finger then made contact with the hole in the open palm of the Christ statue. It was a perfect fit.

A groaning creak echoed through the chamber. Will's

head snapped toward the opposite wall, his eyes searching out the location of the sound.

It was coming from the lower level, between the stone staircases. As if in slow motion, the black metal door behind Simon and Andrew—the one leading to the previous chamber—cracked open. A cascade of foul water and oil spilled in from the door's edges. Water pooled on the granite, rising quickly.

"Get up the stairs!" Will yelled to his friends. Andrew and Simon charged up the single, narrow staircase nearest Will. With each step, the stairs disintegrated under their feet like a sandcastle swamped by the surf. Soon the whole staircase had melted before their eyes.

"This can't be happening," Simon said.

On the platform above, Will instinctively yanked the St. Thomas statue away from the Christ figure. A possible solution to the riddle occurred to him. *Thomas stuck his fingers into the wounds of Jesus to make certain that Jesus* was *the "Risen One from Galilee"! But where did he "proceed" after confirming that he had seen "the Risen One"?*

Mayhem broke out on the floor below. The stinking, oil-laden water from the previous chamber gushed in. With the dissolving of the narrow staircase and the water already up to their knees, Andrew and Simon raced back toward the only things above the waterline: the curved stairways they had taken down to the lower level.

Simon began wimpering, on the verge of tears. Andrew

stayed close, pushing him up the stairs. "Just keep moving. We'll be okay. At least we'll be dry."

"We're going backward. We shouldn't be going backward," Simon moaned. "How will we reach Will? How will we get out of here? Will? Will!"

Will paid the boys no attention as he tugged at the arm of the St. Thomas statue and began to spin it around.

"Guys, I've solved it. Mr. Bartimaeus told me that Thomas went to India after seeing 'the Risen One.' He went east." Will consulted the compass on the marble at his feet. East was the direction opposite the Christ figure. "He 'proceeded' east. This has to be right."

"We are marooned in this pit, Will. We don't really care what direction your statue is pointed," Simon raged. "It is your responsibility to get us out of here. Are you even listening?"

Murky water now covered the first seven steps of the staircase the boys had climbed, and it continued advancing toward their platform up top.

Across the way, Will finally redirected the Thomas statue toward the east. A loud click sounded the moment it was in position. Before Will knew what was happening, the entire black disk supporting him and the statues rotated 180 degrees, propelling him out of the chamber. Holding fast to the marble arm of St. Thomas, he found himself on the other side of the gold grille. He had finally reached the Keep! Facing him, on a high filigreed gold stand, was the object of his desire: the relic of St. Thomas.

Will leapt in the air and even did a little jig. He took his pith helmet off and gave it a kiss.

"We did it, Great-Grandfather." He then pressed his face between the gold bars of the grate, seeking out his distressed friends. "Guys, we did it. The relic . . . St. Thomas's finger. It's here."

"Use it to zap us to your side, would ya?" Andrew asked.

Simon was sucking on his inhaler, and he didn't look happy. The water level in their chamber rose by the second, gradually filling the granite pool.

"I'll get you guys out of there soon," Will said. "If I spin the St. Thomas statue around, the granite platform will probably swivel back. Then you can swim over and join me in here. Okay?"

Will began tugging on the St. Thomas statue again. As he rotated the figure, the disk beneath him trembled. Before it moved, he jumped off, landing on all fours near the relic. The statues disappeared from sight, spinning away on the black granite base. In their place stood a flat semicircle slab engraved with the words "Blessed are they that have not seen, and yet have believed." Will utterly ignored the writing.

He ran to the bars of the grate again, issuing orders to his friends. "When the water rises a little higher, swim over and turn the statue right—toward the east. I won't be gone long. I promise," Will said, retreating into the Keep.

"What if the water starts burning again? Or if the statue refuses to move?" Simon screamed over the water separating them.

Andrew grabbed Simon's shoulder and gave it a shake. "Will you relax, you little twerp?" he cried over the rushing water. "Have I let anything happen to you so far?"

As rattled as Simon was, he believed the big lug and even relaxed a bit.

In the Keep, Will ogled the eighteen-inch-high reliquary containing the finger of St. Thomas. A central base, like the bottom of a chalice, supported a clear rock-crystal tube through which Will could see the saint's distressed finger bone. Atop the transparent crystal, a dome of rounded gold was capped by a small cross, finishing the reliquary.

Twinkling white lights suddenly appeared in the corners of the small room. Will blinked a few times, trying to clear his eyes, but the lights seemed to pulsate with intensity, remaining on the edges of his vision. Will decided to ignore the light show and riffled through Jacob Wilder's green notebook until he came to a sketch of the Keep. It read simply:

THE KEEP
Locks three.
One key.
Faith shows the way; then you may flee.

Will strode over to the small golden door on the far side of the Keep—the same door he had seen from inside St. Thomas Church. Three locks held it shut. At the center of the gleaming door was a single, tiny keyhole. And next to the door, a cutout in the wall like an inset bookshelf held twelve delicately carved keys.

Which key will get me out of here? "One key." But which one?

Will studied the keys: one longer, another shorter, one slightly fatter. Their teeth seemed to be almost identical—any one a possible fit.

With Leo Wilder's assistance, his mother boxed up her camera and lighting equipment in the main hall at Peniel. Having collected footage of Elijah's mantle, Deborah attempted to corral her children. All the while, she punched up Aunt Lucille's number on her cell phone.

"Lucille, I'm almost finished here. I should be at St. Thomas's in the next fifteen minutes or so," she said into the phone. "Did you locate Will?"

"I'm still on my way to the church. The river is a mess today—we'll probably arrive at nearly the same time," Aunt Lucille squawked through a static-filled connection. "I didn't mean to alarm you earlier, dear. If Will is planting, I'm *sure* he's okay."

"When has Will ever done what he was told to do, Lucille?"

"With a shovel and a few trees, how much trouble can he get into? He's fine, Deb."

"I guess you're right. I'm packing up my stuff. We'll meet you at the church soon. And I have to ask you about this

Valens. What a sweet guy . . ." Deborah fell silent upon seeing a worried Cami Meriwether wander into Bethel Hall. "Lucille, I had better go." She hit the "end call" button.

"Cami, what's wrong, honey?" Deborah Wilder asked.

Cami Meriwether had a dazed expression on her face. She tugged at her ponytail and looked away. "I should have called you yesterday, Mrs. Wilder. I've been trying to call Will all afternoon, but he's not picking up his phone."

"What's the problem? What's going on?" Now Deborah looked worried as well.

"Since yesterday, my brother, Max, has been repeating something."

"What, Cami? What is he repeating?"

The girl shook her hands at her sides as if trying to release her guilt and spill the goods. She spoke in a rush. "He had a dream. And he told me yesterday that in his dream he fell into the water and that a sparkly gold treasure was taken from a gray castle. Well . . . Will told me that he was planning to break into St. Thomas Church to borrow the relic—the one I guess his great-grandfather put there."

Deborah Wilder's mouth gaped in shock. "You're kidding me!"

"No, ma'am, I'm not. He and Simon and Andrew were meeting at the church this morning. I wouldn't go with them."

"Why didn't you call me?"

"I just thought it was one of Will's harebrained schemes. I actually forgot all about it. But when the pier collapsed this morning, Max and a bunch of the kids from his camp fell into the water—just like he had said. Max is fine. They got him out quickly and took him to the hospital. He's okay, but it made me think about what he had said . . . about his dream."

"What else did he say?" Deborah asked.

Leo came around the mantle's display case to listen more closely. Even Marin stopped twirling and offered her full attention.

"Max said the bad one took the gold treasure," Cami confessed. "He called the bad one *Sinestri*. Does that mean anything?"

Deborah tried to process what Cami was saying. "*Sines* . . . what? No, I've never heard of that. Are you saying Will is a bad one? Is that what you're saying?"

"I don't know. I've been turning what Max said over and over. I told Will not to go after the relic. But he said he had to."

Deborah pulled out her cell phone again. After unsuccessfully trying to reach Will, she connected with Aunt Lucille, relaying everything Cami had told her.

"The *Sinestri*? I must meet this boy Max," Aunt Lucille said urgently. "He said the *Sinestri* took the gold treasure?"

"Yes. What is this Sines-tee? You know who these Sines-tees are?"

"Go to St. Thomas's straightaway. If the *Sinestri* get the relic or Will, all will be lost."

"Lucille! What do you mean, all will be lost? Who are they? Tell me! Is Will in danger?"

"We . . . My father spent his life fighting the *Sinestri*. We assumed they were vanquished, but they have returned. They'll do anything to get the relic of St. Thomas."

"The relic Will is trying to steal? The one he might already have?" Deborah turned to her children. "Leo, take that lighting case. Marin, in the car, honey. Lucille, I'll see you at the church."

"Deborah, you must be very careful. . . ."

Deborah ended the call. She thanked Cami for coming and brushed past the girl in a hurry, with Marin close behind.

Cami looked very lonely in the vast hall. She folded her arms as if trying to warm herself after a cold blast. Leo grabbed the lighting case and started dragging it out of the museum. Near the exit he stopped, put the case down, and shifted his glasses on his nose. He calmly walked back to the exhibit holding Elijah's mantle. With Cami watching, he removed the ancient mantle from the glass display, folded it in two, and placed it inside the sling, beneath his cast.

"I may need it," he told Cami, placing a finger to his lips. "Shhhhh."

Cami knowingly nodded. "You're just like your brother."

Marin stomped back into Bethel Hall. She pulled on Leo's cast. "Come on, you. Mom is waiting."

Leo picked up the lighting case again and made his way out of the hall. A tingling warmth ran through his right arm.

"Locks three. One key. Faith shows the way; then you may flee."

Will dwelled on his great-grandfather's words. But they failed to shed any light on which particular key he needed to escape the Keep. He intently inspected the twelve keys in the cutout next to the door—worried that selecting the wrong one might spring a trap or permanently lock him in. Some of the keys had figures engraved upon them. Others were stamped with minuscule crosses or Latin words he couldn't understand.

"Faith shows the way; then you may flee."

But how does faith show the way? Which is the key of faith?

Will whirled around in frustration, furiously throwing his pith helmet to the ground.

"Which is the key of faith?"

He kicked the hat in anger, sending it spinning into the inscribed black granite slab on the other side of the room.

The domed reliquary carrying St. Thomas's finger stood between Will and the engraved stone. Light came into his eyes as he slowly read the words of the inscription: "Blessed are they that have not seen, and yet have believed."

A tingling sensation started in his lower back, ran up his spine, and caused him to shudder. So many people believed in the power of this saint's prayers even though they had never seen Thomas's relic or touched it, he thought. Maybe the power of the Almighty could move through an old bone—or even through younger ones. He was filled with a new confidence. Focusing on the reliquary in the foreground, Aunt Lucille's words came rushing back to him:

"My father would say, 'A relic is a key to unlock our faith.'"

And Mr. Shen told me, "The relic is a key that unlocks the faith."

Even dad said it was a key. It's the relic! This is why only a Wilder can reach the relic and escape from the Undercroft. Only a Wilder would know that the relic is the key.

Will scooped up his pith helmet and plopped it on his head. With two hands he grabbed the base of the reliquary. It was heavier than he'd imagined. Looking through the golden bars of the grate to the flooded chamber that held his friends, he called out, "I'll be back. Remember, start swimming as soon as the water gets a little higher. You know what to do."

Simon responded, but Will was already advancing on the small golden door with the three locks. He pointed the tiny gold cross atop the reliquary toward the single keyhole in the door. It slid in with ease. He firmly turned it to the left.

SHLANK. SHLANK. SHLANK. One by one the locks disengaged. Will separated the reliquary from the door. It instantly swung open.

Ducking low, clutching the reliquary, Will scooted through the diminutive doorway and out into St. Thomas Church.

AH-CHOO! The acoustics of the old church amplified the loud sneezes that ambushed him all at once. Will thought it might have been a reaction to the dust of the Keep or the fumes of the oily water in the other chamber. As annoying as the sneezes were, they did not slow him down.

Outside, dark clouds rolled into Perilous Falls, and the river turned black. Choppy waves, as if stirred by some unseen hand, beat against the riverbanks. Even the waters seemed to be trying to escape the thing rising from its depths.

CHAPTER 11

THE EVIL EYE

Drizzle fell like tears from the heavens, staining all of Perilous Falls. Ignoring the mist, Will sprinted out of the church and headed home with the relic. He made it to the curb of Falls Road when a voice stopped him in his tracks.

"Wilder. Will Wilder, I thought we had a deal, lad?"

The voice seemed to come from all sides, as if a hundred megaphones were hiding in the trees. It was Captain Nep Balor. Will grimaced. He had forgotten all about the Captain. He knew Balor would want to see the relic before he took it to Leo—that had been their deal, after all.

"Over at the river's edge," Nep Balor's voice boomed.

For a moment, Will considered running home, letting Leo touch the relic, and then showing it to the Captain on his way back to the church. What difference did it make if the Captain saw the relic now or later?

"Will, the eye stings, lad. Are ye going to leave us blind forever? We showed ye the entryway to the Undercroft. We brought ye there safely. We got ye in." There was a cry in Balor's ravaged voice. "Don't let us down like the others, boy. Please, Will."

Will shoved his lips off to the side, undecided about whether to run home or to the river.

"Will, please. Just to see the relic would be enough."

The Captain's pleadings were a powerful lure. It would take only a minute to press the relic to Captain Balor's eye, Will thought, and then he'd be home in a flash. The boy changed direction and ran to the empty field next to the church. Clutching the domed gold reliquary with two hands, he stopped at the edge of the field, just beyond the stick he had planted. Looking down the slope to the river's edge, he spotted the Captain.

"That's a good lad. Knew yeh'd honor yer word, boy." Captain Balor stood in the water, which had risen higher than Will had ever seen it before.

AH-CHOO! Will's sneezes intensified.

"Ye'll catch yer death in this weather if yer not careful. That must be the relic." Captain Balor's good eye glistened at the sight. His gray tongue licked at his swollen purple lips.

Whether it was the fog along the water or the misting rain, Will found it hard to see the Captain clearly. He blinked repeatedly and rubbed a wrist over his eyes, hoping to clear his vision. Balor appeared to be twice his former size. The Captain bucked back and forth as if writhing in some sort of pain, though his face betrayed nothing. The grimy raincoat covering his massive frame wriggled about. *Is Captain Balor's body shaking like that? Maybe the wind is moving the coat?* Will couldn't be sure. He squinted, straining for an unclouded view of the Captain.

"Well, let us see it, lad. We'd like a closer look at the bone."

Will raised the reliquary in front of him, holding his position atop the embankment.

The Captain smiled, his body continuing to quake violently. "Oooh, that be it. May we touch it now, Will?"

AH-CHOO! A cold, stabbing fear ran through Will's body. He didn't want to move. He didn't want to speak. He wished only to be home or even back in the church.

"We had a deal, lad. Can't even see the thing from there. Bring it closer." Captain Balor's voice sounded different. It was higher, even shrill. "I thought we promised to help one another. Have we ever failed yeh? Why are ye failing us now?" Balor's voice then rumbled in a low belch. "Bring the bone closer."

A stench like the two-day-old tuna sandwich Will once found in his locker wafted up. AH-CHOO!

"I'm feeling kinda bad, Captain. AH-CHOO! Let me run home and see my brother—dry off—and then I'll come back and meet you here."

"How can ye go home after what yeh done? Yeh defied yer aunt Lucille, lied to yer parents, stole from Shen and the church." Balor shook his head sadly. "They wouldn't want to see a boy like ye. They're probably at home right now—the lot of them—doting on your *brother.* They're not giving yeh one thought, Will. Who's been yer *real* friend in good times and bad?" The Captain pointed to himself.

The words stung Will. But seeing the water rising around Balor, his mind leapt to Simon and Andrew still trapped in the Undercroft. "I have to get back to my friends in the church. They need my help."

"*They* need yer help? I need yer help! Did yer little pals show ye the way to the Undercroft? Did they know to enter at low tide? Did they distract Shen for yeh? We did that. We're yer only friend, Will." Balor opened his palms, raising them to the boy like a beggar. "A touch of the bone to this poor eye—that we might see again. Is that too much to ask?"

AH-CHOO! AH-CHOO! Something deep within Will told him to stay where he was, to not descend down to the murky shallows Captain Balor occupied.

"Yer just like the others. Just like Lucille, the priest, and that greedy Shen." Captain Balor's shoulders heaved up and down. It looked as if twelve people were holding a hula hoop contest under his coat. He seemed to be sobbing. "Ye care for no one but yerself. We should never have trusted yeh—NEVER."

Will felt guilty. Against his better instincts, still sneezing, he started down the hillside toward Captain Balor and the water's edge. He slipped on the muddy incline, his backpack and rear sliding into the muck. He strained to find his footing, all the while holding the reliquary in the air with one hand.

"Forget all about us. Break yer word! Break yer deal!" Captain Balor barked through tears, odd voices escaping his lips. "Who cares about an old blind riverboat pilot?" A beefy gray hand rose to cover his face.

Will contritely approached Captain Nep Balor. The choppy waves excitedly lapped up toward the boy, as if they were pleased to see him. The sky overhead turned a deep charcoal.

Will hesitated once he reached the shoreline, only a few feet from Balor. The closer he got, the harder it was for him to see the Captain. It made no sense to Will. It was as if he were walking into a dense, dark fog. AH-CHOO! AH-CHOO! The sneezes came faster and faster. And the stench made him want to gag.

"Ye best be getting indoors. These wild waters ain't for everybody. They're alluring at first. But once ye put yer toe in, yer liable to get swept under. We've seen it happen many times, we have. Poor souls." The dingy raincoat continued to undulate madly. "So may we touch the precious relic yer dear great-granddaddy *hoarded* for so many years?"

Will held the reliquary in one hand down at his side, defiantly. "My great-grandfather only built the church to protect it."

"He stole it! He was a thief from the beginning. He took it from—" The Captain suddenly sucked his bloated lower lip into his mouth. The diseased, tightly shut left eye twitched. When he spoke again, his voice dripped with sweetness and high tones. "Jacob Wilder did keep the relic safe, didn't he? For that we are thankful. We mustn't be ungrateful. Now let us touch it, lad." The Captain extended an algae-covered cage in his direction. It reminded Will of an oversized crab trap. Attached to a metal rod, the mouth of the cage could be opened or closed by the Captain with a flick of his fingers. The cage's jaws yawned, hungry for the reliquary.

"That wasn't our deal," Will said, holding the golden artifact behind his back.

"Ye said that we could touch it! Can't very well touch the thing from afar." Balor shook the cage emphatically.

"I agreed to touch the relic *to your eye,* Captain. I didn't say you could hold it."

A blackness washed over the Captain's gaping eyeball. "How are we to press the relic to our poor wounded eye without holding it? Give it here!" Again he snapped open the metal cage.

"I'll hold the relic." Will set his jaw. "You lean down and press your eye to it. Do you even believe that the relic can heal you?"

Captain Balor's body gyrated as if he were suffering some tremor—very likely caused by the seething anger that was evident on his face. "Is this how the little Wilder would like to make good on his promise? Will must hold the relic! Come closer then."

Will lifted the reliquary directly in front of his body with both hands. Captain Balor leaned in. When he was inches from the relic, Balor shifted his face to the left. The sick swollen eye, pus leaking from its rim, snapped open. A horrible beet-red orb with a green pupil bore down on Will. Its mere glance made him dizzy. He staggered backward, nausea rising up from the pit of his stomach. As Will fought to maintain his balance, a gray mass—a tentacle—smacked him hard across the jaw. The relic fell to the ground, as did Will.

His head was spinning. He couldn't move. Only the hard rain pelting his face brought him back to consciousness.

SNAP. Balor's cage slammed shut next to Will. When it rose, the reliquary was trapped within. The boy drove his elbows into the gravelly shoreline and struggled to lift his chest off the ground. He couldn't let the relic get away—he couldn't lose it. He tried to shake off the dizziness and face Captain Balor.

"Why are you doing this? I thought you were my friend."

"*'I thought you were my friend,'*" the Captain mockingly screeched. And though he spoke, Balor's lips were perfectly still. At least, Will thought they were still. The fog was so dense, the rain so constant, it was hard for Will to be sure of anything. "We were never yer friend. We're sworn enemies and ever 'twill be," the Captain continued. Both his eyes, one yellow, one red, cruelly glared at Will.

Captain Balor triumphantly shook the caged relic high in the air. "Now it is ours. The bone Jacob Wilder thought would restrain our power—the thing he imagined would enslave us—is now *ours!*" Balor's rain hat blew off, revealing a series of horned nubs protruding from his greasy hair. His body frantically convulsed, the quivering raincoat stretching at the seams. Great bulges, like the snouts of mad animals, pushed out from all sides of the slicker. Then the dirty green fabric split open in six places. From each hole craned a different monstrous face—a chaos of horns, bared teeth, and flaring nostrils—each moving toward Will.

Am I dreaming? Is this another "spirit"?

AH-CHOO! AHH-CHOOO! AHHH-CHOOOOOO! Will's vision dimmed even more.

"Sneeze yer head off—just like yer great-grandfather! He too couldn't help sneezin' whenever we appeared. We hope yer sinuses are ready for this. Take a good look, laddie!"

The shredded coat flipped away in the windstorm. Through the haze only Captain Balor's toadlike face and terrible eyes were recognizable at first. Then Will saw the thing that caused him to scream as he had never screamed before. It sapped the air from his lungs. Balor's head now bobbed upon a lengthy serpent's neck, wide and reptilian. Gray scales covered his hulking chest. Massive arms and a set of tentacles jutted out from his sides. From Balor's back, six writhing necks sprang forward, as thick as the one at the center, each bearing a distinct face of hatred.

Will now understood why that raincoat never seemed big enough for the Captain. He was carrying a lot of passengers under there.

A barnacled, decomposing face attached to one of Balor's

snaky necks shot forward. It had no eyes, just dark black holes. The face blocked Will's field of vision entirely.

"Perilous Falls will be ours once more," the barnacled one rasped. "The *Sinestri* are rising, *Wilder*! The Brethren will fall."

"I don't know who the Brethren are. What are you talking about? Captain Balor, I need the relic back," Will shouted.

"He wants the relic back, *Captain*. Haaaaaaaaaaaa," the barnacled face wheezed, recoiling with a wicked smile.

The soil under Will quaked. River water overtook his feet.

"Yer aunt Lucille can explain who the Brethren are. She's a lifelong member," Balor said, craning his head forward. He was almost transparent now. "Unfortunately, ye won't be able to ask her yerself—or do much of anything else. But ye'll still have yer *sight*—little *SEER*." Balor pried one of Will's eyes open with slimy fingerlike appendages.

"What? I can barely see you now . . . get your hand off me!" Will tried to escape Balor's touch, but a heavy tentacle pinned him to the gravel.

"Maybe yer losing yer gift, *Seer*. When yer heart is clouded, so is yer vision. . . . What a pity the Brethren will be blind again." Balor's diseased eye was shut tight, his breath like stagnant water.

"We have a special goin'-away present for ye, lad. The whole town's aflutter about what became of those poor souls we didn't rip to pieces or drag to the river's depths— the ones staring at hospital ceilings like they're in a coma, uttering nary a word." Balor's freezing spittle hit Will in the face. "In moments ye'll understand what happened to them all. But ye'll be just as speechless as they are. Thank yeh for the relic, Will. Yer family will be very proud."

"Leave me alone. I did what you asked. . . . Nooooooo!"

Balor moved his sickly, distended red eyeball directly in front of Will's vulnerable pupil. The creature held the boy's lids open, forcing him to take in the full horror of that wicked red gaze. Will's body went rigid, his eyes blank.

Thick black clouds blotted out the last remnants of the sun, and the levees quaked.

Beneath Balor two monstrous sea serpents rose from the waters, easily lifting the coiled, seven-headed creature above the tempestuous tide. Downriver the menagerie coasted, Balor waving the caged relic of St. Thomas about like a scepter at a coronation ball.

"The water's high enough. It's time to swim to the other side," Andrew exclaimed. The oily water in the third chamber of the Undercroft had nearly reached the top of their platform.

Simon squatted at the very edge of the filthy pool. He fixed his eyes on the white marble statues across the way. "Tie my rope around your arm in case I have trouble. It's a very short swim. It's a very short swim. It's a very short swim," he repeated, trying to convince himself. The jittery boy sucked deeply on his inhaler, adjusted the strap of his prescription sports goggles, and turned to Andrew.

"Okay, okay. I believe I'm ready. Let's go in together. It's a very short swim. It's a very short swim. . . ."

The two boys lowered themselves into the water, connected by the rope, and swam toward the statues of St. Thomas and Jesus. Andrew moved quickly with a wide stroke. Simon paddled with all the power of a Chihuahua in a lake of molasses.

His red head barely coming up for air, Andrew dragged Simon farther than the scrawny boy could have ever advanced on his own. After a few moments, Simon gave up all effort and floated, allowing Andrew to motor him the rest of the way.

Andrew had had enough of the drag. In the middle of the pool, he stopped swimming and turned to his friend. "Uh, Deadweight! Am I your tugboat now? You can't swim?"

"You're doing such an exemplary job that I felt my paddling would slow you down," Simon clarified, doing a slight dog paddle to keep his head above water. "We're almost there. Keep going."

Andrew smacked the surface of the water with open palms. "What do you mean, keep going? How'd I become your transportation? You keep going! I'm gonna sit here like an old lady on an air mattress while you pull me to the other side."

Through his fogged sports goggles, Simon stared past Andrew. His eyebrows hitched up somewhere near his hairline. His voice rose into the soprano range. "There's a . . . There's a . . . It's a very short swim, it's a very short swim, it's a very short swim. . . ." He frantically ripped the goggles off his face, dipping them in the water.

"This rope runs two ways, you know," Andrew continued, pulling the rope at his arm. "You can drag me across as easily as I can drag you."

His goggles clear and back on his eyes, Simon was speechless. He pointed beyond Andrew, lips moving but nothing coming out.

"Yes, that's the direction we need to go. Right over there. Start pulling your load," Andrew chided. "To quote somebody I know, 'It's a very short swim. It's a very short swim.'" Andrew was enjoying himself.

There was no response from Simon. He only continued pointing over Andrew's head—panic-stricken and bug-eyed.

"Scared of a little work? I'm not moving one inch," Andrew casually insisted. "We can stay here all day. I'm not your water slave or something. . . . What are you pointing at?" Andrew looked over his shoulder. Shivers ran up his back. "Holy crab butts!"

Climbing onto the black disk, one claw already on the foot of the St. Thomas statue, a Bottom Dweller slithered out of the pool. Its dragon face turned toward the boys, dead yellow eyes trained on them like prey.

"Swim back to where we were," Andrew whispered. "Don't freak, Simon. You freak, we die."

Simon nodded that he had heard. Andrew didn't wait for an answer. He dragged Simon by his pointing arm back to their original location, toward the two tunnels that led to the second chamber.

Andrew could feel Simon hyperventilating. "He's way across the water, Simon. Don't freak out."

"You're wrong, lummox," Simon squeaked.

Andrew looked back to confirm that the Bottom Dweller was still on the black marble disk on the other side of the pool. The thing had wrapped itself around the statue of Jesus and was clawing away at its marble head.

Arriving at the stone platform, Andrew lifted Simon up out of the pool. Simon's eyes were still wide and filled with fear behind his sports goggles.

"Relax. We're safe. The gator thing is all the way over there."

"I know. But . . . but . . ." Simon quivered, aiming a shaky finger over Andrew's left shoulder. "There's another one!"

A long prehistoric nose cut through the water's surface, headed straight toward the boys. It opened its long mouth, hissing at them, three rows of serrated teeth glinting in the light.

After dropping Bartimaeus at Dismal Shoals, Aunt Lucille had difficultly steering the *Stella Maris*. Each time she thought she had found a smooth path, the river's erratic waves pounded the side of the boat, throwing her off course. She finally managed to dock the vessel along the shoreline near St. Thomas Church. The water was so high she disembarked directly onto the muddy hill leading up to the churchyard.

Pulling her light blue rain hat over her face, she scaled the sloping embankment, yelling Will's name. Her tall rubber boots sank into the soft mud.

She searched everywhere. He wasn't in the field, he wasn't at Shen's house, and he wasn't in the church. Standing inside the vestibule watching the storm rage did not give her hope. Rain bulleted the ground, falling in great dollops. Wind tortured the trees, snapping branches and hurling them into the river.

Concerned that Will might have slipped into the waters, Aunt Lucille raced back to the boat. Just as she prepared to leap onto the starboard side, out of the corner of her eye she spied a mass along the river's edge. It was Will. The water covered his chest. He lay perfectly still in the gravel, his pith helmet half under his head but no longer on it.

"Oh, dear Lord!" Aunt Lucille flew to his side. She placed a hand near his throat. He was warm to the touch, for which she was thankful. She pulled him to higher ground and searched for marks, cuts, blood—some explanation for his state. She didn't even notice at first that his eyes were half open and unmoving.

"Will! Will! Answer me!" she demanded, shaking him, but there was no response. She thought of yelling for help, but in the torrential downpour who would hear her?

Aunt Lucille got behind the boy and sat him up. She placed Jacob Wilder's old pith helmet on top of her own rain hat and looped her arms under Will's. "Here we go, dearie. Let's get you out of this deluge."

She dragged Will up the embankment to the yard, his heels leaving deep ridges in the mud. Approaching the church doors, they were caught by the headlights of a vehicle speeding down Falls Road. The driver of the blue minivan slammed on the breaks, but Lucille did not wait for help. She continued hauling Will toward the church.

"What happened? What's wrong with Will?" Deborah Wilder screamed at the top of her lungs, evacuating the minivan, her hair and stylish black-and-white dress drenched by the downpour. "Lucille! What's happened to him?"

Aunt Lucille dragged Will inside the church and lowered him to the stone floor. "I don't know what's happened, Deborah. I just found him alongside the river." She pulled off her light blue raincoat, revealing the fabric satchel slung over her shoulder with the Book of Prophecy that Bartimaeus had given her. Lucille balled the coat into a makeshift pillow for Will. "He's not responding, but his eyes are open."

She knelt next to the boy, leaning in to his face. "It's very odd. He's breathing, but . . ."

Deborah fell to her knees. "Will, it's Mom! Talk to me, son!"

"Deb, I've tried all of that. He is not responding. I'm calling for help." She pulled out her cell phone and started dialing.

Deborah Wilder jiggled Will's arms, trying to wake him. "Will. Come on, baby. Talk to Mama. Talk to me." She grew more frantic, shaking his shoulders. Will's unfocused eyes stared blankly, his lips still.

Marin and Leo, wet and disoriented, wandered in through the church's main doors. "Mama, is Will okey-dokey?" Marin asked, wiping the rain from her forehead.

Aunt Lucille put an arm around the two children and closed the heavy wooden doors behind them, shutting out the rain. "As soon as we figure out what happened to your brother, he'll be fine." She pressed the cell phone to her ear but gave up seconds later. "Wonderful. All the circuits are busy. Could be the weather. We should drive him to the hospital."

"There are downed trees all over town. We won't make it to the hospital. I almost killed us driving over here," Deborah sobbed at Will's side. "Where was he, Lucille? Why was he alone?"

"I found him at the edge of the river. He was lying on his back, just like that. We should be thankful. He could have—"

"Where was Mr. Shen?" Deborah asked accusatorily.

"When the pier collapsed, Tobias went downriver to help the victims. Now he's . . . missing."

"The man who was supposed to be watching my son is missing? This is crazy. Crazy!"

"I wish I had a proper explanation for you, Deborah. . . ."

"He looks like the victims they fished out of the river the other day. He's just blank, Lucille. Look at his face."

Aunt Lucille and Deborah continued to bicker over Will's condition, but Leo didn't hear a word the grown-ups were saying. The younger Wilder boy silently knelt beside Will's head. Leo waved a pudgy hand in front of Will's eyes. There was not even so much as a flicker of recognition. Will's mouth was slack and his coloring pale. Leo had an inspired idea. He leaned close to Will's ear. "I'm going to try something," he whispered.

Maybe it was crazy, but if it could help his brother, it was worth the attempt. Leo could see the adults were still arguing among themselves, and there was no use asking them for permission. So Leo decided to just act on his inspiration and see what happened.

CHAPTER 12

ELIJAH'S MANTLE

Leo pulled Elijah's mantle from inside his sling, carefully unfolding the fabric. He laid it over Will's face, the golden weave of the old cloth glimmering as he adjusted it.

Aunt Lucille was the first to notice what he had done. "Leo, where did you get that?"

With complete calm, Leo looked up at her through his rain-flecked, wire-rimmed glasses. "They say this mantle can do miracles. Let's see if it can."

"Take that off him!" Deborah exploded. She started to rip the mantle away from her son's face.

Leo clutched his mother's wrist. "Please, Mom." He was so intent, so sure that the mantle might do some good, that Deborah released the garment and allowed him to continue.

Leo placed his plump hands on either side of the delicate

crimson-and-gold material draping his brother's head. "Wake up. Please let him wake up." Leo closed his eyes and lowered his head as if his simple pleading alone had the power to return Will to consciousness.

There was a stark stillness in the air. Marin, not wanting to be left out, bent down and imitated Leo. The little girl laid a hand on Will's hair. "Wake up, sleepyhead," she whispered. "Time to rise and shine with the angels."

Aunt Lucille's face contorted in pain as she watched the scene. From the tears coating them, her blue eyes appeared gray. The children's hands remained in place, hoping against hope that they could revive their brother. As the minutes passed, Deborah Wilder covered her mouth to contain her sobbing.

There was no movement from Will, nor a sound.

With the mantle covering his face, he appeared dead to Lucille. In her mind's eye she saw her father, a miserable stained cloth covering his dead body. Over the years she had lost so many she loved to the *Sinestri*—to the *Darkness*. Now her last hope, the one she had waited for, the one she had prayed for, was practically gone as well.

AH-CHOO! The gauzy material covering Will's face pulsated upward.

AH-CHOO! Like a tiny crimson-and-gold ghost, the fabric of the mantle popped up again.

"Yes, yes—I'll do it," Will said clearly.

Leo's blue eyes were the size of quarters, and Marin mouthed a "Wow-zee."

Deborah yanked the fabric away from Will's face. "Will? Can you hear us?"

He blinked repeatedly and met his mother's gaze, then Aunt Lucille's.

"I'm sorry, Mom," Will said hoarsely, grasping his mother's hand. He was shivering. "Aunt Lucille, I'm so sorry."

"Will, dear, the important thing is you're all right." Aunt Lucille's elation crowded out the tears produced just moments earlier. "Thank God."

Deborah Wilder planted kiss after kiss on her oldest boy's head.

"I'm so sorry for what I did," Will said.

"Don't apologize, honey. Your brother's arm is getting better. Accidents happen all the time," Deborah said.

"You don't understand!" Will tried to sit up. "I'm not talking about Leo's arm. I did something I shouldn't have done. I did it for a good reason, but I guess . . . it was wrong."

Deborah embraced him. "Cami told me you tried to break into the church. I don't want you to worry about it now. You're safe. We're going straight home when this weather blows over and—"

Aunt Lucille placed a hand on Deborah's shoulder, quieting her. "Where's the relic, Will?"

Will's cheeks reddened. "The relic. I had it—"

All expression fled from Aunt Lucille's face. "Where is it? You didn't remove it from the Keep, did you?"

"I was going to bring it to Leo, to heal his arm. But the Captain—Captain Balor—"

"Where is the relic now?" Lucille crouched down, moving Deborah aside. She took Will by the arms, her voice shaky. "Where is the relic? This is not a game, Will."

"The Captain knocked me over. He took it."

"Don't lie. You must have *brought* it to him! You're the only one who could have reached the Keep—using my father's notebook!" She jumped up, clapping her hands together vehemently. "Awwww, Will. We've got to get it back. Who is this Captain? Where did he go? Where did this Captain GO?"

Will confessed everything: how he had plotted to steal the relic, made a deal with Captain Balor, solved the riddles of the chambers using the notebook—how the Captain had met him at the river, transformed into a demon, paralyzed him with that "oozing eye," and snatched the St. Thomas relic. Aunt Lucille stroked her knuckles beneath her chin, listening to all Will had seen and done.

When he had finished, after a few seconds of silence, Deb Wilder turned away from her son, whispering to Aunt Lucille, "Do you think he's hallucinating? I wonder if he was struck on the head by a tree limb or something."

"I wish it were that simple, dear." Lucille looked Deb straight in the eye. "It's all true. Everything he's said is true."

Deborah flashed her hundred-kilowatt TV smile. "You believe that demon creatures are running around the river, stealing relics from little boys? Come on, Lucille."

Lucille raised a single porcelain finger, tapping it down with each syllable. "Every word is true. The things he sees are real. You must trust me now, Deborah. Will has a gift. I am going to need his help to save Perilous Falls—and perhaps the world."

"You're not making sense. He doesn't listen to anyone. Look at the trouble he's already caused."

"Perhaps it was supposed to happen this way. All of it. Mistakes are at times the doorway of destiny."

Leo picked up the pith helmet and returned it to Will. He threw both arms, even the one in the cast, around his brother. "I knew it would work," he said, looking up at Will. "I knew the mantle would wake you up."

"You're a good brother, Leo. Better be careful with that arm."

"My arm's all healed. Look!" Leo raised and lowered his right arm with ease. "The mantle probably did that too."

Will couldn't believe what he was seeing. But before he could ask Leo another question, the raised voices of his mother and Aunt Lucille intruded. The two women were eye to eye, their argument getting ugly. Will wriggled free of his brother's grasp and went over to them.

"There isn't much time, Deborah!" Aunt Lucille insisted, her strawberry-blond curls shaking indignantly. "We need to go now."

"Well, he's not going with you." Deborah clutched Will's arm to underscore her point. "He was in the river, Lucille! He could have drowned."

"I will be with him. I would give my life to protect him."

"And who is going to protect you, Lucille? You're a

sixty-six-year-old woman. And I'm supposed to allow you and my twelve-year-old to sail into a hurricane and snatch a relic from—what?—a thug riverboat captain, whom my son thinks is a demon? No, thank you. Dan was right. Will should have stayed at home. And he is staying here with me."

"Deborah!" Aunt Lucille shrieked as no one had heard her shriek before. "Will can see things the rest of us cannot. He is a *Seer*."

"That's just what the Captain called me. He called me a *Seer*!" Will exploded.

"The muddy shadows he saw as a child, the fleeting blurs of darkness, are becoming clearer to him," Aunt Lucille continued. "He sees what we accept on faith. He saw this demon. It is his gift, Deborah, and as much as I would like to keep him from using it, there is no other way." Emotion welled up in her voice. "I know—more than most—the grave consequences of exposing a gift . . . but we have no choice. That demon is out there whether we see it or not. Will can see it! If we do nothing, it will destroy this town and take many, many lives."

Deborah stiffened. "What are you and Will going to do?"

"We will do what I have done all my life. We will fight the Enemy—the *Sinestri*. The major demons."

Deborah rolled her eyes and walked in a circle. "Do you even hear yourself? Demons and enemies . . . He could have been killed, he and his friends—" She stopped in midsentence. "Will, where are Simon and Andrew?" Deborah asked.

Will's guilty glance traveled to the open golden door near

the altar of the church. "They're trapped in the last chamber. It's flooded, but they know how to get out, Mom. All they have to do is turn the St. Thomas statue around."

"When were you going to share this information with us?" Deborah clopped down the main aisle toward the altar and the trapped boys. Leo trailed after her, carefully folding Elijah's mantle as he went. Marin wasn't far behind. Will meant to follow them, but Aunt Lucille held him back.

"They can stay here and help your friends. You must come with me now," she said, steel in her tone. "We have to stop this Captain of yours. I have a hunch where he went. I'll explain on the way. If we don't get there soon, Tobias Shen and countless others will die."

"He's really dangerous, Aunt Lucille. He smacked me pretty hard." Will rubbed the side of his face, which was still red from the blow. "And he's got that eye!"

"I know exactly what we are dealing with," Lucille assured him. "Believe me, I have means of protecting you."

Will so wanted to remain in the church with his mother and siblings and friends. But he knew that his actions had set events into motion that he had to correct. However foggy his vision, Will had seen the beast up close. He could only imagine the damage it would do now without the relic's protecting the town. It had to be stopped. Then there was the voice he had heard when Elijah's mantle covered his face. . . .

"Deborah, I'll have Will back as soon as I can," Aunt Lucille announced, slipping on her raincoat. "We're headed to Dismal Shoals."

"No, you are not! You are not!" Deborah turned heel and headed back down the aisle.

"Will should decide what he wants to do. It is his path. Time is of the essence." Lucille held the door open at the rear of the church, rain splattering inside.

Will carefully placed his pith helmet on his head. "Mom, I have to go. I saw this thing, and I delivered the relic to him. I've got to try to get it back."

"If we don't retrieve the relic of St. Thomas, this town will flood," Aunt Lucille said rapidly. "Unspeakable things will devour all of us. Do you want to be responsible for that, Deborah?"

Deborah Wilder looked thoroughly confused. Her anger faded into resignation. She ran over to Will and locked him in an embrace. "Go. But be careful. And Lucille, you bring my boy back."

"I will, dear. Or he will bring me back. We'll see you all in a jiffy either way." Lucille turned her attention down the aisle of the church. "Oh, and Leo, keep hold of that mantle. It is irreplaceable—and the property of Peniel."

Leo bashfully nodded from the other end of the church.

Aunt Lucille and Will exited through the solid church doors and stepped into the tempest.

"Mommy, you'd better come see this," Leo exclaimed, staring into the open gold-edged doorway next to the altar. He and Marin wore stricken looks.

Deborah Wilder rushed down the aisle. From inside the

open chamber she could hear the sounds of inhuman, guttural hissing and the high-pitched screams of a boy in distress.

Dan Wilder squirmed uncomfortably in a stiff leather chair facing Mayor Ava Lynch's rat-gray desk. In the other red leather chair sat Heinrich Crinshaw, tapping a fountain pen against his front teeth.

Mayor Lynch stood over the two men, both hands planted on her desktop, explaining her plans for the investigative task force.

"I've taken the liberty of assembling identical folders so we can get right to work." Her heavily made up eyes indicated two manila folders at the edge of the desk.

"Inside you'll find the identities of some figures who were in the vicinity of the crime scenes along the river. For some inexplicable reason, law enforcement failed to properly investigate these people. We will make no such mistakes." She lowered herself into the high-backed red leather chair behind the desk, crossing her legs. "Go on, read your briefing reports. I know them inside out."

Behind the mayor, through the huge double windows of her office, dark skies unleashed a hellish rain on the town. It was so dark that Dan Wilder couldn't help but stare outside.

"Dan, read the report," Mayor Lynch ordered. "We need

to assign cases and jump on this investigation before the trail goes cold."

Dan adjusted his tortoiseshell glasses and leafed through the folder. He didn't recognize the first four of five people pictured, and the one-page descriptions didn't help either. "Ava, I don't, uh, see how we can investigate all these . . . Where did you get these names? I mean, we just authorized the task force. How did you pull this together so . . . fast?"

"You should know me well enough by now, Danny. Before any vote, plans have to be in motion." Mayor Lynch leaned back in her chair. "After you review all the individuals in your folder, I think you'll agree that Sheriff Stout and his deputies were negligent. They just didn't interview enough people, sugar. The net must be thrown wide until we solve these cases."

Dan bolted upright. "Ava, in every case, the victims were attacked by something in the river—an animal—a gator, or a . . . a . . . creature. It wasn't an individual. There wasn't a plot. . . . Do you think an individual—a person—did this?"

"Well, I don't know, Dan." The mayor could not have been more serene. She fiddled with her diamond-studded earring. "That's why we're having an investigation. What is there to fear from an investigation? The truth does set us free, after all."

"But it was clearly an animal or something. It isn't as if someone unleashed these gator things into the river." Dan smiled to underscore the ludicrous nature of the suggestion. No smiles were returned.

"That is an interesting suggestion, Dan. Some crazy person could very well have released these killer crocodiles into the river. Who's to say? I just don't know why the sheriff's office wouldn't pursue any and all leads," the mayor said.

"Maybe because they . . . have nothing to do with these cases. This seems like a huge waste of time to me. As I said in the council room, we are amateurs. The sheriff probably eliminated these people because they're innocent. None of these folks strike me as criminals." A crack of thunder outside drew Dan's attention back to the window behind the mayor.

"So now you're a psychic? You know who's guilty and not guilty? Who needs a criminal justice system when we have Dan Wilder?" The mayor let out a throaty laugh. "Just read the names in the briefing report."

Dan was on his feet near the window. The hundred-year-old trees on the front lawn of city hall were beginning to arch under the pounding of the storm. He had never seen rain like this.

"Dan, are you even listening to me?" Mayor Lynch asked. She shot Crinshaw a bothered look.

"I just don't see how we can investigate people . . . who, uh . . . people who . . ." Dan was speaking, but his thoughts were clearly elsewhere. "What criteria did you use to come up with these names—these persons of interest? These people are innocent."

"How do you know they are innocent?" The mayor swiveled in her chair, looking miffed that Dan had turned his back to the room, pressing his face to the window. "Were you ever at the crime scenes, Dan?"

"Wh-wh-what are you implying?" Dan turned to her for a moment.

"I'm not implying a thing. Just wondering if you've been near any of the crime scenes? Otherwise you best read that folder."

"I will in a minute. The weather is really—really . . . bad." Outside the window, a manhole cover wobbled in the parking lot, arresting his attention. The round metal cover jumped as water spurted from its sides. One edge of the lid slowly rose higher and higher.

"This is interesting," Heinrich Crinshaw said, reading the folder on his lap. "Tobias Shen, the groundskeeper at St. Thomas Church . . . He was spotted at two of the crime scenes but never interviewed by your pal Stout."

Dan tried to focus on the conversation. "Tobias Shen had nothing to do with this. He—he's a decrepit old man my son's been helping plant trees—"

"Your *son* was helping this man—this Shen, Dan?" Mayor Lynch inquired, her eyes narrowing.

"He . . . uh . . . Will, he helps a lot of people." Dan started to sweat.

"How did he meet Mr. Shen?"

"I don't remember. . . ." The lightning made Dan turn toward the window once more.

Mayor Lynch threw open her own copy of the report. "This wouldn't have anything to do with your aunt Lucille, would it? Funny how she was at the crime scene today—motoring around in her little boat."

From beneath the elevated manhole cover, Dan could see a scaly snout emerging. He anxiously smoothed down his hair at the sides.

"Did your aunt Lucille arrange for your son to help this Shen person? Does she know him?"

Dan was paralyzed by what he saw outside the window. *"Fo-Fo-Fomorii. Fomorii,"* Dan stuttered under his breath.

"For who? For Maury? Who's Maury?" Mayor Lynch asked.

Dan Wilder was fixated on the office window. In the parking lot, the front half of a Bottom Dweller flopped out of the manhole, sending the cover clattering on its side. Soon bubbling water carried the scaled creature's entire body to the surface. Behind it were claws and more Bottom Dwellers. Dan watched at least eight escape the manhole and scamper toward downtown.

Then what appeared at first to be mounds of black goo came out of the hole. But as Dan squinted he realized the goo had shape and form. A cascade of slimy long-limbed creatures exited the manhole. A small tan dog lost in the rain began barking at the gooey beings. All at once, one of the black slimy bodies, like a wave, crashed over the dog and it was gone. No barks, no yelps. Just the black goo creatures leaping forward as they had before.

Glancing down to the end of the front lawn, Dan could not see the curb. Main Street was already flooded.

"I've got to go." Dan tossed the folder of suspicious persons back on the mayor's desk. Pictures skittered across the glass top and onto the floor.

"Go where?" Crinshaw asked. "What's the rush?"

"Look at the—the weather. I'll be back later." Dan fled the room.

An intrigued Mayor Lynch watched him leave. She bent over and picked up a stray picture that had flown from Dan's folder: a fuzzy shot of Lucille Wilder in her boat on the river. She held it up as if looking at an X-ray.

"Hen, sugar, call the motor pool and get us a driver and a photographer. People we can trust. I want to go down to the river now."

Crinshaw was out of his seat, worriedly considering the storm outside. "Why do we have to go now? It's flooding. There may be wisdom in waiting until the storm passes."

"Dan got awfully jumpy when I brought up Lucille and his son. An informant tells me that Lucille Wilder has been chugging up and down that river all day with other suspicious individuals. She's out there right now. We want to catch her in the act. How much you want to bet these Wilders are more involved in this trouble at the river than meets the eye?"

"Why do you say that?"

"Instinct, Hen." Mayor Lynch shoved the picture of Lucille Wilder into the folder, smacking it shut. "Instinct."

CHAPTER 13

THE BOOK OF PROPHECY

High waves and sheeting rain rocked the *Stella Maris*, slowing her progress. The stinging spray hit Will and Aunt Lucille from all sides as they bounced upon the Perilous River. Even with the Plexiglas windshield in place, there was no escaping the wet assault.

"So where is this Dismal Shoals place?" Will yelled to be heard. He wore an oversized yellow slicker he had found on board the boat.

"It's a few miles downriver." Aunt Lucille kept her hands firmly on the wheel, and her focus on negotiating the rough waters. "Dismal Shoals is an old pagan site—a ruined temple. It's been abandoned for decades." Aunt Lucille checked Will's reaction. "If your Captain is the demon you think he is, he could well be sheltering there. It is said to contain a

Hell Mouth, a portal to the underworld. My father used to call it a 'watery doorway to hell.'"

"And it's here—near Perilous Falls?" Will swallowed hard. "How do we know Captain Balor will be there?"

"We don't. But it's where Bartimaeus believed the demon was headed when it very likely kidnapped Tobias— and it would be a logical place for him to dispose of the St. Thomas relic. Of course, there is always Wormwood. . . ."

"How does Mr. Bartimaeus know where the Captain went? And why would the Captain take Mr. Shen and the relic to this Shoals place?"

"Listen very closely, dear. We haven't much time." Aunt Lucille pulled him near while piloting the boat. She raised her voice to compete with the storm. "Like you, Bartimaeus has a gift. He is a *Sensitive.* He can prophesy. Many times he intuits events and foresees their outcomes. Bart had a strong sense that the demon was headed to Dismal Shoals. It would be the ideal spot for a demon to destroy a holy object. Once the relic is gone, your Captain probably hopes Perilous Falls will be drowned in this deluge. He has already released the *Fomorii,* which explains all the violence on the river."

"Wait, wait—who are the *Fomorii*?" Will's hands were shaking. He popped a handful of mints into his mouth, which he sometimes did to calm his nerves.

"The *Fomorii* are a legion of water creatures—they're minor demons, actually—vicious killers under the control of a major demon," said Aunt Lucille nonchalantly.

"The major demon that I gave the relic to?"

"Very likely."

"How did he release the *For—For*—whatever they are?"

"The *Fomorii*," Aunt Lucille said, smirking. "These particular creatures—the Bottom Dwellers—are very agile and destructive. I've seen them. But there are other species of *Fomorii*—all commanded by a major demon who, through its own power, can release them from the depths at will."

"You mean he sort of awakens them?" Will asked.

"The demon's power derives from an absence of faith and the acceptance of darkness. When the faith of a people recedes, its power grows. Once the demon is strong enough, it can do incredible damage. Raising the *Fomorii* is but a small part of what the beasts are capable of. My father thought he had contained the seven major demons—he thought the relics and the Brethren—" She sighed and frowned at the thought. "Ah, well, even the prophecy speaks of the demons rising again. . . ."

Will gazed out at the raging waters and into the deep darkness he had unwittingly unleashed. He feared what awaited them at Dismal Shoals. In his mind's eye he kept seeing Balor, huge and menacing, seven heads writhing in all directions, tentacles thick as pillars swinging toward him. Then he recalled the voice—the one that had given him such hope.

"Aunt Lucille," Will croaked, coming back to the present, "when I was under the mantle, the one that belonged to Elijah—I heard a voice. It was so clear and kind. It said,

'Believe and keep your heart pure and I shall be at your right hand always. Will you heed my words? Will you heed my words?'"

"That's what you were saying yes to?"

"Yeah. But I'm not even sure what his words are."

"I know you're not."

"Aunt Lucille, what are we supposed to do?" Will whimpered. "I mean—what is our game plan?"

"I don't really know, dear. But you will." Aunt Lucille's eyes sparkled even in the gloom of the storm. She wriggled an arm out of her raincoat and removed the fabric satchel hanging from her shoulder. She handed it to Will. "This contains the Book of Prophecy that your great-grandfather entrusted to my care. Anyone can read the inscription on the cover. It speaks of a very special person, a chosen one, who will do battle with the demons. It also states that only the chosen one can read the entire prophecy. There are seven locks on the side of the book. If the locks open for you, Will, then you are the chosen one."

Will scrunched up his face and puckered his lips. "The book is going to tell me what to do?"

"The book will prepare you for what you *must* do. Words have particular power, Will. Men and women have died to protect these words—to ensure that they reach your eyes."

"But it's just a book."

"Then like any book, it contains special words for you alone. They will open to you just when you need them most—when you are ready for them. Heed those words."

She shoved him toward the door in the middle of the boat and shouted, "Take the book to the cabin below, and after you read it, put it in your backpack. Then return to me. Go. Now."

Will stared at the rough black satchel in his hand. It was heavy. Through the fabric he could feel the gnarled metal locks along the book's edge. Without another word he opened the maple door to the lower cabin and ran down the ladder. He flipped on the hurricane lamps below and placed the satchel on the rich lacquered table in the center of the cabin.

Will slowly shook the thick volume from the cloth bag onto the table. He was startled by the craftsmanship of the book. The curled metalwork on the cover shimmered. The locks on the right side of the volume were shaped like claws, each one distinct from the others. The first had scales and long talons that reached from the back cover to the front. The scaled lock held the entire volume shut. The next lock down looked like an animal's paw, its extremities nestled inside the book. A clasp fashioned into the claw of a rooster followed. The digits of the successive locks were shoved between pages, each one a little closer to the back cover.

Will's hands hovered over the ornate prophecy, as if being warmed by its power. The slap of the waves on all sides and the thunder spooked him. He was afraid to touch the olive-colored volume, so he began to read the inscription on the cover, folding his hands behind his back. Will's mouth slackened as his eyes scanned the golden letters.

The Prophecy of Abbot Anthony the Wise

The Lord came to me upon the waters and said:

"Take thee a great book and write upon it as I instruct thee."

My spirit trembled, for the visions He placed in my head
*   frightened me.*

Still, I write in obedience:

In those days, when the people have grown hard of heart and
*   belief has dwindled;*

when wickedness has become commonplace; and the Brethren
*   have broken their unity;*

then shall I raise up a young one to lead them.

He shall be the firstborn of the root of Wilder.

He shall have the sight of the angels

and perceive darkness from light.

Behold, when his time is ripe, he shall come riding on a colt,
*   the foal of a donkey, and his blood shall spill.*

This shall be the sign that the battle is near

and all must prepare.

For in those days the beasts shall rise from the pit

to test my people.

Truth shall go further away while falsehood and darkness

draw near.

The inhabitants of the land shall multiply evils

and the Sinestri shall deceive many.

But in those days of tribulation and darkness,

I shall pour out my Spirit upon all flesh; sons and daughters shall
*   dream vivid dreams and sing angelic songs;*

the young shall heal and see visions; and their elders shall
    prophesy and make war on the foul beasts.
Behold, my chosen, the firstborn of the house of Wilder,
will lay hands upon this great book,
and its seven locks shall be opened to him alone.
This too shall be a sign.
These visions shall prepare him for all he must endure,
confront, and conquer. For without him, there can be no victory
    for the Brethren or for my people.

"Beasts shall rise from the pit"? . . . "Days of tribulation and darkness"? How do you make war on "foul beasts"? Will won-dered. Can I really be the chosen one? The one to lead them? . . . That could be kind of cool. Good thing I got on that donkey. . . . But who are the Brethren? And what am I supposed to do about them?

Will yearned to read the rest of the prophecy. The boat bumped up and down suddenly, knocking him against the hull. He grabbed the brass rail that surrounded the cabin to steady himself and straightened his pith helmet. Feel-ing a little queasy, he extended his hands to take hold of the Book of Prophecy and to see if the lock would open to his touch.

Simon screamed his head off at the approach of the Bottom Dweller making circles in the oily pool of the third chamber. The creature swam very near the boys' platform, eyeing them like the last two pieces of shrimp on an all-you-can-eat buffet.

"It's coming! It's coming! Aahhhhahhhhhh," Simon caterwauled.

Across the pool, Mrs. Wilder tried to calm the boys through the golden grille of the Keep. "Get away from that—that animal. I'll try to distract it."

She fretfully searched the Keep for something to throw at the beast. But loud scraping and hissing noises forced her back to the golden bars. The sounds appeared to be coming from the other side of the inscribed black granite slab in the Keep. She pressed her face against the bars, trying to find an angle that would afford her a view of whatever was on the flip side of the slab.

"Oh my—" Deborah caught sight of the second Bottom Dweller. It was only a few feet away from her, wrapped around the Jesus statue on the other side of the grate. The creature saw her as well. It stretched upward, sticking its snout through the bars above the granite slab. Spooked, Marin and Leo backed out of the Keep into the church, opting to watch the proceedings through the open doorway.

"Stay in the church, kids," Deborah barked, hunting desperately for anything to distract the Bottom Dwellers. That's when she spotted the cutout near the golden door.

With an armful of brass keys, she rushed back to the grate. Deborah wildly pitched the keys across the water at the creature stalking Simon and Andrew. She quickly got its attention. From the oily soup, the Bottom Dweller nearer the boys turned its snout to Deborah and hissed.

"You big ugly thing, come over here." She hurled another key, pegging the floating Bottom Dweller on its head.

"Yee-haaa," Deborah yelped with pride. "Guys, you've got to get away from these crocodile things. Hide in those tunnels behind you while I distract him."

"We just came out of that chamber, Mrs. Wilder. It's flooded," Simon explained. "There is only one *little* ledge in that chamber, and if it chases after us—AAAH—"

Andrew put a hand over Simon's mouth, muffling the scream. "What if we go back in there? What did the notebook say about the tunnels?" Andrew started to remove his hand from Simon's face. "No screams."

Simon nodded.

"I obviously don't have a copy of the notebook," Simon heaved. "This will be purely from memory. It said . . ." Simon closed his eyes, elevating his chin. Then, rapid-fire, he pronounced, "'Enter by the narrow gate, for the wide gate brings death and pain.' That's right. That's it exactly."

"Thank you, Googleman."

"What did you call me?"

"Goog— Never mind. Miz Wilder's runnin' out of keys. Get in the hole!"

"I refuse to go back into that dark tunnel," Simon said.

"Then you're going to be swimming in the dark tunnel of that thing's belly." He pointed to the approaching Bottom Dweller in the pool.

Deborah Wilder threw the last of her keys with more passion than precision. But the creature was no longer paying the keys any attention. It was focused on the boys.

"Give me your backpack," Andrew demanded.

Simon was too frightened to resist. Andrew pushed Simon toward the tunnel they had passed through earlier, the one with the rocks and stones bulging from the walls.

"Get in," Andrew insisted.

"It will come after us!"

"The tunnel is too tight for it to pass through."

"And what if it does pass through?" Simon started to make his shriek face.

"Don't scream! If the reptile comes our way, I'll shove the backpacks at him."

Simon lifted an eyebrow. "You're going to choke the gator monster with our backpacks? That's your plan?"

"Do you have a better idea?"

The Bottom Dweller's claws ripped into the edge of their stone platform. It was coming out of the pool for a visit.

"Get in the hole. Get in the hole now!" Andrew shoved his smaller friend into the slit in the wall. He then squeezed himself in, holding the two backpacks with his left hand.

On the other side of the pool, Deborah staggered back from the grate. The Bottom Dweller closest to her had climbed up the reverse side of the grille and was now perched directly in front of her. It jammed its muzzle through the bars, snapping its serrated teeth together and hissing. Though the Dweller's body couldn't pass through the bars, its five-foot razor-tipped tail stabbed the air, trying to spear the woman.

"You might have been right about this, moron," Simon kindly observed as he and Andrew moved halfway through the tunnel. He pressed the light on his wristwatch, illuminating his narrow face in a greenish glow. "If the gator monster goes into the other tunnel—the 'wide gate'—it could experience 'death and pain.' That's what Will's great-grandfather's instructions said, anyway: 'the wide gate brings death and pain.' On the other hand, if it follows us . . ."

Growls and a clawing sound like a chisel cutting away stone filled the tunnel.

"We got the other hand! Or the other claw!" The light on Simon's wristwatch went out. "Aaaaahhahhahhhhhh!"

"Put the geeky light back on, would ya? I can't see this thing," Andrew demanded.

The snarling and clawing sounds moved ever closer. Simon pressed the two buttons on his wristwatch and shone a bright light down the cramped corridor. The head of the Bottom Dweller thrashed just three feet from them. Simon renewed his screams.

"Shut it," Andrew said, nudging Simon. "It's stuck in the tunnel! It can't move."

Simon and Andrew sidestepped deeper into the passage, away from the creature's cruel jaws and bad breath.

The Bottom Dweller, in seeming frustration, started to retreat. It wriggled violently, backing its body out of the tight tunnel.

"What's it doing?" Simon asked.

"Leaving, I think."

Behind the bars of the Keep, Deborah Wilder kept trying to get a clear visual of what was happening inside the boys' tunnel. But each time she moved to a new location, the Bottom Dweller would crawl along the bars and block her view. Its hisses now seemed like chortling to her.

Marin stuck her head in the golden doorway and asked, "Where is the boys, Mommy?"

"They're in that tunnel and I'm worried because the other croc thing followed them," Deborah said, trying to see around the dangling Bottom Dweller. "Oh wait, it's coming out. The croc thing's tail is coming back out!"

Sure enough, the Bottom Dweller pursuing Andrew and Simon exited their tunnel. Its head swiped side to side in apparent anger. Then it quickly slithered inside the wider tunnel to the right. Within moments of entering the tunnel, a terrible grinding sound greeted the Bottom Dweller. It clawed at the walls, attempting to back out, but it was too late. The smooth walls pressed in on the creature, smashing its body in the darkness.

From across the pool, Deborah could see only the flailing backside of the beast. Its bloating tail stiffened. The razor-sharp tip pointed straight up in the air before drooping lifelessly onto the platform.

"I think the croc thing got crushed," Deborah said, still trying to see clearly. The Bottom Dweller in front of her, clutching the grate, swung its head around and let loose a ferocious screech. "Eeeeeeeeaaaaaaaah."

Marin covered her ears at the doorway, while Deb rushed to comfort her. Leo could not have been less concerned. The boy sat on the floor of the church sanctuary, a large Bible propped open on his knees. He leafed through the book with great intensity.

"Leo, what are you doing?" Deborah asked from the doorway.

"Trying to find the Second Book of Kings," he said, his attention never leaving the pages. He bent his head low and eyed his mother over the top of his glasses. "Remember Mr. Valens told me about Elijah's mantle? He said there was a story in the Second Book of Kings."

Deborah helped him find the book in the Old Testament. "You and Marin stay out here for now. I've got to go check on Andrew and Simon."

"Wait, Mom, this is kind of neat," Leo said. His finger pointed to a passage in the book, the mantle bundled under his arm. "The Prophet Elijah hit the water of the river Jordan with his mantle, and the water split. Then, after he goes up to heaven, this other guy, Elisha, gets the mantle. So he tries to do the same thing. He whacks the water with the coat, and it says here: 'the waters were *not* divided. And he said: Where is the Lord, the God of Elijah? And he struck

the waters and they *were* divided, hither and thither.' Wow."
Leo's eyes were dilated in wonder.

"Sweetie, that's fascinating, but I have to make sure
Andrew and Simon are okay." She kissed him on the head
and dashed into the Keep.

Looking down at her brother, Marin broke the silence.
"The big lizard is really mean."

"I don't remember asking you if the lizard was mean,"
Leo muttered, continuing to read the Bible.

Marin quietly slipped off one of her flats, picked the
shoe up, and whacked Leo over the head with it. "The lizard's not the only one who is mean!"

"I'm telling Mom, Marin. I am," Leo threatened. But a
racket on the other side of the golden doorway startled both
kids. It sounded as if the metal bars were being struck by a
hammer. Moving into the doorway, the kids saw Deborah
Wilder standing in the middle of the Keep, her arms wide.
Before her, on the other side of the grate, swinging from
the bars like a wild baboon, the Bottom Dweller screeched
angrily. It repeatedly slashed its claws along the bars as if
trying to rip them open.

"Stay back, kids," Deb said, facing the beast. "I don't
think it can get in here. At least, I hope it can't."

"That lizard *is* mean," Leo admitted, the Bible under one
arm, the mantle under the other.

"Told ya so." Marin closed her eyes and nodded with
some satisfaction.

"I think we're safe," Deborah assured the kids. "Will said the only way to get in here was to turn the statue of St. Thomas around. I doubt if the croc thing will be able to figure that out. I'm more worried about Simon and Andrew right now."

The Bottom Dweller dropped from the grate, out of sight behind the rounded black granite slab.

Deborah called to the boys across the water. Andrew tenuously stuck his head out of the narrow tunnel. "We're okay, Miz W—" Suddenly, strawberry blotches started to appear on Andrew's cheeks. An uncommon look of fear washed over his face. "Mrs. Wilder, the reptile—the monster—it's standing on its back feet. It's turning the statue of St. Thomas around!"

Simon popped his head out of the tunnel at that moment. He could muster only one reaction: "Aaaaahahhah-haahahhhaaaaaa!" He immediately retreated into the dark hole. "They understand us. They have intelligence. That's it, we're gator grub—we're doomed!" Simon's squeaky voice echoed from the darkness.

In the Keep, Mrs. Wilder called Leo and Marin to her side. "Get on the black platform here. Quickly." The children and Deborah stood flat against the inscribed slab. They could hear the Bottom Dweller scratching away on the other side. A pronounced click reverberated through the black disk beneath their feet.

"Mrs. Wilder, he—it—turned the statue to the right,"

Andrew reported. "That's what Will did to make the platform spin. The reptile's coming your way!"

Seconds later, Deborah, Marin, Leo, and his Bible were facing the pool. The Bottom Dweller had switched places with them. Marin clung to her mother, terrified. Leo could hardly believe that he was now inside the chamber with Simon and Andrew. "This is so cool!" he exclaimed.

"It is not cool, Leo. Andrew, listen to me," Deborah whispered. "You and Simon swim over to this side while the croc thing is gone. You'll be safer over here. Start swimming."

The Bottom Dweller slammed itself up against the bars inside the Keep, furious that its prey had escaped. It climbed the grate and hovered over the black platform behind Deborah and the kids. Jutting its elongated green mouth through the bars, it desperately attempted to catch one of them in its jaws. The grate kept the Dweller from getting close enough to do any damage. A shoulder pressed to the bars, the Dweller tried to slash the Wilders with its long, green-scaled leg. Then suddenly it stopped all movement, unblinkingly staring out at the pool.

Andrew had managed to get Simon into the water. As they progressed toward Deb and the kids on the other side, Andrew encouraged his frightened friend. "Remember, it's a short swim, it's a short swim."

A few feet behind, Simon, energetically doing the dog paddle, bleated, "It sees us. It is looking right at us!"

"Keep swimming and don't freak. We're almost there," Andrew said, reaching back and pulling his pal along.

The Bottom Dweller released the grate and disappeared from sight.

"C'mon boys. Quickly," Deborah urged.

The only sounds that could be heard at that tense moment were the splashing of the two boys and the grinding of the marble statue of St. Thomas inside the Keep.

Talon by talon, the brass claws of the first lock lifted from the Book of Prophecy in the cabin of the *Stella Maris*. The very moment Will laid hands on the book, the lock opened for him. He gasped, nearly dropping the volume—his hands trembling beneath it.

Oh no. I am *the chosen one!*

The book gaped open with a creak. A musty smell filled Will's nostrils. He tried to make sense of the strange, elegant calligraphy before him. . . .

Woe to you, Perilous Falls
if the finger of the Apostle is displaced.
For then darkness shall stir
and the beasts of Wormwood
and the underworld shall arise
and a great sign shall appear:
When the river spills over its bounds

the twisted serpent shall break the water's surface
with a great wrath;
for he knows his time is short.
Woe to the earth and sea when this beast appears,
for it is only the first of the SEVEN
that shall test my people.
The finger of the Apostle
must not be desecrated or destroyed.
To protect this relic and all of Peniel,
my chosen one must reject the Darkness.
His sight shall only be as pure as his thoughts and actions.
But if he be deceived, his vision will darken,
and ALL shall be blind.
For only with a pure heart and belief that is strong
can he ever hope to crush the heads of Leviathan.

Leviathan?

Will was even more confused than he had been before seeing the book. He reread the prophecy once more, committing key lines to memory. His hazel eyes were aglow, a thousand thoughts crashing in his head as he closed the volume. He returned it to the fabric satchel and hid it in his backpack. He then charged up the ladder to Aunt Lucille.

Behind the wheel of the boat, Lucille struggled to keep the *Stella Maris* from tipping into the black waters. Her drenched coat and hat were glued to her body. Rain lashed her face. Zealous waves crashed over the sides of the boat, soaking Will's feet as he approached.

"Did the Book of Prophecy open for you? What did it say?" Aunt Lucille asked, wiping rain from her eyes.

"It said, 'I wish you had read me last week!'" Will smiled, pulling the pith helmet down to protect his face from the stinging rain. "Who exactly are the *Sinestri*?"

"The Enemy and his forces. They are powerful demons—the dark ones we have pledged to cast out and destroy."

"We? You mean the *Brethren*?"

"Yes, Will." She turned a hard eye on him. "The Brethren. Your grandfather and your great-grandfather were members, as am I. There'll be plenty of time to share all that history with you, and I will introduce you to the Brethren at Peniel once we return. But I must know what the prophecy says."

"There are Brethren at Peniel? At the museum?"

Aunt Lucille shook her head, frustrated by the rain, or perhaps the question. "Peniel is not *exactly* a museum. It's a refuge for the sacred antiquities and relics entrusted to us. The Brethren who are *here*—"

Will blinked in confusion. "Wait. There are other Brethren?"

"Oh, Will—there are Brethren scattered all over the world. This battle is much larger than you can imagine. But you must tell me what the prophecy said."

"It said that we can't let the finger of the saint be desecrated or destroyed."

"My father said the same thing. . . . Go on." Aunt Lucille fixed her stare on Will.

"Because St. Thomas's finger was disturbed, it said 'a twisted serpent' has risen and he is going to test the people. He's only the first of seven beasts."

"SEVEN?"

"Then it went on and on about keeping my thoughts and actions pure so my sight can be clear."

"You are the *Seer*! I knew it. We haven't had one since . . . Oh, this is good. Now listen. I am a *Repeller*. That means I can repel a major demon when I touch my fingers together— well, you'll see soon enough. I can't expel them for good or lock them away. Only *Vanquishers* like Abbot Athanasias can do that—he'll want to meet you soon. Just listen . . ."

Aunt Lucille now spoke firmly. "When we get into Dismal Shoals, keep your eyes open and tell me precisely where the Beast is—this Captain of yours. You are not to converse with it or interact with it in any way. It is a demon not to be trifled with."

Will sputtered, "The prophecy said that with a pure heart and belief I could crush the heads of *Leviathan*."

"Shussssh. Do *not* say its name." Aunt Lucille sternly pressed a finger over Will's lips. "It can hear you. Merely uttering the name of the Beast can attract it—or send it away, which is a different skill set altogether." She slowed the speed of the boat as they neared the shore. Rocks protruded from the water. "Repeat the last bit of the prophecy—but *not* that name."

"It said only with a pure heart and strong belief could I ever 'hope to crush the heads of . . . ' you know."

"Crushing and hoping to crush are two separate realities. Now listen to me. You will abide by my rules or I will lock you in that cabin." Aunt Lucille pointed over her shoulder. "This old serpent has risen and he is very powerful—as are the others. When we go in, you are to walk behind me. You are to point out exactly what you see—and do nothing else, Will. While I *repel* the serpent, I want you to find the relic. Once you've located it, take it and run. Do you understand me? No matter what happens to me or Tobias or any of us, take the relic of St. Thomas and get it back to the church or to Peniel. Am I making myself clear?"

"Yes, ma'am." Will sobered. His trembling hands grabbed the collar of his slicker, but Aunt Lucille saw them instantly.

"Don't be afraid." She touched his wet cheek. "You will face much worse than this, dear. For now, obey the prophecy and simply believe. Look on the bright side: at least you can see the beasts. The rest of us wander in a fog, never knowing how close they are. Or we delude ourselves into thinking they don't exist at all."

She steered the *Stella Maris* between two rocks that looked like a pair of hunched monsters ready to pounce. Alongside the boat, knees of cypress trees and a string of smooth stones jutted from the water. Dropping anchor, she told Will, "This line of rocks leads into the Shoals. Bartimaeus should be nearby. Stay close and move with me."

She sprang from the boat with stealth and grace, landing on a rock five feet from the vessel. Will fearlessly, if unsteadily, followed her.

A deep voice, soaked in fury, thundered within the central cavern of Dismal Shoals.

"SHEN . . ."

Columns of wet, pimpled rock formations interrupted the vast space. On the slick, craggy floor along the walls of the cavern, pools of flame cast light upward at odd angles. The weird lighting made it appear as if the shadows themselves were dancing. But for the occasional battered brazier there was no other light.

"SHEN . . . Wake up or yer liable to miss all the fun."

It wasn't the voice that woke Tobias Shen but the feeling of being hit on the head by something hard and metallic.

"Up, Shen. Get up."

The old man's eyes fluttered, but only one would open completely. He tried to reach for his face but soon discovered that both his hands were restrained. Turning his head, Shen realized that he was attached to a slick, rocky wall. Neon-green tentacles bound his wrists and ankles. The tentacles sprouted from enormous purple funnels of sea anemones growing on the rock's surface. Shen stood, but the tentacles held him down, making movement impossible. His feet and hands felt numb, as if they had been stung—or were still being stung.

WHAP. The metal object slammed against his head once more. When he looked up, he saw a dirty cage holding the relic of St. Thomas levitating in the air. It suddenly whipped toward his head again, but he ducked the blow.

"There he is," the unseen voice rumbled. "Our chosen witness! Congratulations. Shen, ye'll be the only member of the Brethren to see the end—as it begins."

Lounging on the slimy ground before him were four Bottom Dwellers, their tails wrapped around one another. To his left, busted columns flanked a wrecked, brown-stained altar. More than half of the altar lay on its side. The other portion stood erect, a bit of jagged slab covering a foul pond as big as a wading pool. A thick black substance bubbled in the pond, steam escaping intermittently.

"Yer precious relic will be no more," the cold voice threatened. "Even now, Perilous Falls is taking on water. 'Twas us that brought down those boats and the pier. Soon the people, the Brethren, and the fortress Jacob Wilder spent his whole miserable life building will be totally submerged. Ye and Lucille thought yeh were so clever, didn't yeh? Training little Will in the ways of the Brethren. Making him plant that old walking stick. Yer a fool! None of it will save him or any of ye. It took almost no effort to tempt the Wilder spawn. We're getting quite adept at flipping Wilders."

Tobias Shen strained to locate the speaker in the dark caverns of the chamber. No one was there.

"Little frozen Willy can't help yeh now, Shen. But ye *will* help us offer a nice sacrifice to the *Darkness*. First the relic—and then yerself."

Tobias Shen closed his eyes and began quietly mouthing something. He tugged at the neon tentacles holding him.

"There's no use struggling, old man. We raise those sea anemones special here. They're a new breed of *Fomorii*. Ye probably don't feel much of yer limbs now, do ye? Their tentacles deliver a venom worse than many snakebites. Makes the victim very pliable."

Shen did not respond or open his eyes. He only continued mumbling.

"Look at the good Mr. Shen now—the kind Mr. Shen. What lies!" Two clamshells flew out of the darkness, hitting Shen in the chest and head. "How many of our lovely Bottom Dwellers did ye slaughter today, Shen? A hundred? Two hundred? What happened to 'Blessed are the peacemakers,' Mr. Shen? Here's my peacemaker."

CRACK.

The cage holding the relic flipped sideways and struck Shen hard on the lower leg.

CRACK.

CRACK.

After repeated blows, the old man's shinbone gave way with a dull snap. Fresh blood pooled on his gray pants. His entire body stiffened, though he neither screamed nor uttered a word of protest. Instead, he whispered something urgently under his breath.

"Stop it. Stop that racket, Shen!" the voice howled. "Shut up! STOP IT!"

But Shen continued to whisper.

"Is that Latin? We hate Latin. Silence. NOW."

The cage flew up, cutting Tobias Shen's lower lip. Again and again the cage pummeled the old man from different angles. Still he offered no response, save for his intense whisperings.

"Hurry, guys. The croc thing is moving the statue again," Deborah Wilder warned the boys. She crouched on the edge of the black granite disk, stretching her hands out over the water. Andrew and Simon were not yet halfway across the oily pool. Leo and Marin, touching hands, pressed their backs into the engraved black granite behind them and braced themselves.

"Quickly," Deborah begged the two boys in the pool, urging them to the black overhang she and the children occupied.

But the boys could move no quicker—Andrew stroking broadly through the water, Simon sinking under the weight of another panic attack.

CLICK. The black granite beneath Deborah and the kids shuddered.

At that very moment, Dan Wilder stumbled through the doorway into the Keep. He wore two iridescent-yellow flotation devices around his neck and a policeman's tool belt. His glasses were completely fogged over.

"Deborah? Kids?" he absently asked, realizing that something was moving in the small room. In an attempt to see more clearly, Dan yanked the glasses from his face. There, meeting his glance, stood the Bottom Dweller, its front legs pushing the arms of the white marble statue. "No—no," Dan's voice cracked. "This is not happening."

Dan's eyes bugged out of their sockets. So did those of the Bottom Dweller. But before either of them could so much as flinch, the black granite platform rotated once more.

The Bottom Dweller was gone and three petrified Wilders had taken its place. Deborah was splayed out on the black surface. Leo and Marin stood ramrod straight against the slab, holding each other.

"Daddy, what are you doing here?" Marin asked.

Dan remained frozen, as if waiting for the creature to devour him. His eyes were tightly closed, his arms extended in a defensive gesture.

"I—I came looking for . . . You all should get out of here," Dan demanded, taking charge. "Let's go. Everybody out."

"Eeeeeeeeeeaaaah." The Bottom Dweller on the other side of the grate released a primal yowl.

"Andrew and Simon are in there with that thing." Deborah scrambled to her feet, assisted by the children. "We have to help them." She ran to the grate, grabbing the bars. The Bottom Dweller stood on the end of the black granite platform, yowling in frustration. It repeatedly whipped its head from side to side, tracing a U in the air with its snout.

"Boys, go the other way! Swim back to the tunnel! Now! Quickly," Deborah urged, her face flushed with worry.

Simon didn't need Mrs. Wilder to tell him to swim away from the reptilian terror across the pool. He was closer to the tunnels than Andrew and was already moving through the water like an outboard motor.

"First she tells us to hurry *that* way, then she tells us to hurry *this* way. If I keep this up, I'll qualify for the Summer Olympics," Simon whined.

"Shut it," Andrew ordered in between strokes. "We've got to get inside that tunnel. Stop talking and move."

Simon did as he was told. He pulled himself up on the stone platform and started to scurry inside the tunnel.

"Go ahead. I'm almost there," Andrew panted, swimming hard. "I don't want to get caught in the water with the—"

"It's coming!" Simon screamed, prancing helplessly in a circle. Across the pool the Bottom Dweller clambered up to the top of the grate, then, like a cliff diver, threw itself backward into the air. The twelve-foot green torpedo's eyes never left its target.

Andrew didn't wait to hear a splash. He swam toward the stone platform as he had never swum before. With each stoke he wondered whether he could outpace the creature now plunging beneath the surface of the water he labored to escape.

CHAPTER 14

DISMAL SHOALS

"Y'all best be careful where you set them tootsies," a deep voice rang out from the edge of the river.

Will and Aunt Lucille stopped in their tracks. They were perched on a pair of flat stones leading to what appeared to be a half-sunken temple entrance near the shoreline. Both turned their heads in the general direction of the voice: a gigantic pile of algae-covered rocks rising to the left.

"Loo-ceele. They got Stickers running around out here. Ain't seen one of them in goin' on forty years." Bartimaeus shambled out from under a jutting rock, where he had taken refuge. "So the two of you better scoot in from this rain and let me fill ya in." Propped on his crutches, he beckoned Will and Lucille toward his stony nook.

"What's a Sticker, Mr. Bart?" Will asked, relieved to see a friend instead of Captain Balor.

"Stickers are evil tar critters. They're a type of *Fomorii*—low-down demons. They surround their prey and swallow 'em right up. Got acid all over their gooey bodies. So once they get hold of ya—forget it. You're toast. Good news is ya can hear 'em comin'. They make this 'bubble, bubble, bubble' sound."

Aunt Lucille and Will joined Bartimaeus in the rocky grotto where he had been hiding. Stiffly the old man lowered himself onto a smooth rock that looked like a melted recliner. With his crutch he indicated a rotted log, where his guests were expected to relax.

"What have you seen, Bart? Is the Beast here?" Aunt Lucille asked, shaking the water from her hat.

"Did you let this boy read the book? I sure hope you did, because it's going *down* up in here, Sarah Lucille."

Before his great-aunt could respond, Will starting talking. "It opened for me. The minute I touched the Book of Prophecy, the first lock opened."

Bartimaeus's face softened, and he nodded. "You've done good, Lucille. So now it's on you, young man. What did it say?"

Aunt Lucille interrupted, quickly recounting all that Will had told her of the prophecy: the seven beasts that would test the people, the need to recapture the St. Thomas relic, the importance of Will's vision to the Brethren, and the mention of crushing the heads of—she whispered—*Leviathan*.

"Makes sense. Makes total sense," Bartimaeus said, tapping his crutches against the ground. He turned to Aunt Lucille.

"So about fifteen minutes after you dropped me off, you won't believe what I saw. I felt this coldness, so I knew something bad was coming. Stank to high heaven—which is always a tell with the major demons. I'm hiding up in here and *whoop*—who comes flying by upside down? Tobias Shen! He's struggling—but couldn't move too much. I knew a demon had him. Dragged him right into that old pagan temple over there."

Will's nose itched. *What did the demon do to Mr. Shen?* he thought. *What will he do to Aunt Lucille and me?* Will felt icy all over.

"About twenty minutes later, this cage comes out of the temple and floats right by me. Big long thing—probably used in their pagan rituals back in the day. So a little after that, *zooop*—the cage comes back through here. Only this time it had a reliquary inside it. I was thinking, 'That looked just like the one from St. Thomas Church.' Now I know it is." Bartimaeus stared out of the cave with a grim look. "Once the relic went in, *Fomorii* came pouring out that old temple. Bottom Dwellers and Stickers everywhere. Hundreds of 'em. I thought, 'Oh, bless you, Perilous Falls, because you're in for a world of trouble.'"

"Tell me about Levia—that demon whose name I can't say?" Will asked.

Bartimaeus looked down at the ground, scratching his

head with his big mitts. "Lord, now that one's nothing but trouble."

Aunt Lucille interjected in her clipped manner: "The creature you asked about is the twisted serpent, an ancient demon who has been given the watery realms. Some demonologists contend that his purpose is to stoke envy in the hearts of men and drive them into the pit of loneliness and despair." She put an arm around Will. "My father told us that this demon guards the *Hell Mouth,* an entry to the Inferno—and not the only one. In truth, you know more about this Beast than any of us. You have seen it, dear. Now you must resist its invitations. It will doubtless try to deceive you again."

"Oh, no, Aunt Lucille, I'm onto his tricks this time," Will bluffed.

"That's the kind of talk can get ya killed. You don't play with a demon, son. Look here." Bartimaeus hitched his pant legs up, revealing webs of raised pink scars on his dark skin. They crisscrossed over both of his bent legs. "So you mess with demons and you pay the price. Ya got me?"

Will bobbed his head.

"All you have to do, Will, is tell me what you see, grab the relic, and get out. Nothing else," Aunt Lucille said, checking the two holy-water vials attached to her belt. In a swift gesture, she popped her rain hat back on her head. "We'd better be going. No telling what condition poor Tobias is in."

"Lucille, you shouldn't go into that cave without a *Vanquisher.* That thing's been yowling somethin' fierce."

Aunt Lucille was already up and stepping into the rain. "There's no time to go back to Peniel. We've already waited too long. With Will's eyes I can handle this."

Bartimaeus and Lucille turned to Will, who remained seated on the crumbling log. His usual pluck and determination had vanished. He could only summon a look of uncertainty. "I'm ready," he said, nodding awkwardly beneath his pith helmet, suddenly looking younger than twelve.

Aunt Lucille jumped out of the grotto onto a rock formation and approached the dimly lit entryway at the center of the dilapidated temple ruins. One of Bartimaeus's walking sticks blocked Will from following her.

"Not a word to that devil. You hear me, boy? Get the relic and get out of there." He rested a hand on Will's arm. Squinting, he trained two milky eyes on the boy. "I'll be with ya in spirit. Believe—and there is nothin' you can't do. Now go ahead."

Will mumbled a "Yes, sir," and sprinted off after Aunt Lucille, his red sneakers slipping on the rocks outside.

Cracked, mold-covered columns and half-submerged statues carrying tridents surrounded the collapsed opening. Much of the marble facade had sunken into the marshy ground. From inside Will could hear the deep, sticky voice he knew too well.

"That's him. It's Captain Balor," the boy said, ducking into the glowing mouth of the temple ahead of his great-aunt.

"Will," Aunt Lucille pointedly whispered, stomping a foot

on the ground. "Behind me. The *Fomorii* could be anywhere. Keep your eyes open and your mouth shut—behind me!"

As Will opened his mouth to speak, a sneeze formed. "AH . . . AH—" To muffle the sound, he brought both hands to his face.

"And please keep that under wraps," Aunt Lucille said softly, walking past him.

Nature had reclaimed the hallway once lined with marble. Muddy roots covered the walls, and water dripped from the ceiling. Puddles formed on the broken tiles below. The only barely discernible light came from deep within the dank corridor.

Advancing down the main passage, Will was disturbed by the dark caverns and niches on either side. He kept searching the blackness of the side grottos, worried that something was lurking there. After a few minutes, curiosity got the best of him. He leaned next to Aunt Lucille's ear.

"Can I use my flashlight?"

The woman startled, placing her fingers into a triangle formation. She quickly relaxed.

"No, William. Walk, dear, and only speak if you see something."

"I can't see down these side halls at all."

"Shhhh." Lucille touched her index fingers and thumbs together just in case they encountered any surprises.

BLUB . . . BLUB . . . BLUB . . .

Will got close to Aunt Lucille's ear again. "Do you hear that?"

"Do I hear what?"

"That!"

BLUB . . . BLUB . . . BLUB . . . It seemed to be speeding up.

"It's very likely a fountain dripping down that passageway there," said Aunt Lucille, dismissively waving a hand at one of the side tunnels. She continued down the corridor toward the firelight.

Will stopped and stared down the side shaft. He saw nothing but an impenetrable inkiness. A deep, dark blackness. It puzzled him because the sound was so clear, so close he could almost touch it.

BLUB . . . BLUB . . . BLUB . . . BLUB . . .

This time the noise caused Aunt Lucille to spin around in an instant.

"Will, get down," she ordered in a harsh whisper.

Her fingers in the triangle formation, Aunt Lucille extended her arms. A ray of red light shot from her hands over Will's pith helmet. It struck the dead center of the side hallway. In the illumination, Will realized that he had not been staring into darkness, but at the midsection of a *Sticker* hanging from the passageway in front of him. The neon-red ray hit the middle of the creature's body, creating an ashy blossom whose petals soon spread in all directions. In seconds, the thing was transformed to ash. Aunt Lucille dropped her hands.

"Blow on it," she said.

Will teetered up. When he blew on the *Sticker*'s ashen

form, it fluttered and crumbled to the ground. Will jumped backward to keep the remains from dusting his sneakers.

"Don't linger, and stay close," Aunt Lucille instructed. She held her lightly touching fingers out like a weapon and moved toward the firelight. Will was practically on her back this time.

Every so often a stalactite obstructed their view as they descended to the subterranean center of the temple.

A chorus of accusatory voices spilled from the main chamber. At times the voices spoke individually, at other moments in unison. ". . . Ye will now hear the pained cries we once heard when yeh destroyed our temples. Do ye remember, Shen? Ye were more energetic in those days. Time for ye and the whole putrid Brethren to taste death. As soon as the waves sweep over that fortress on the hill, the faithless cries will go up from yer people. We can't—"

Suddenly a new voice with a high register and an almost soothing tone took over. "Oooohhh, we have visitors, Shen. Company's come a callin'. Where are you? Show yourselves! Your timing is perfect."

"Perfect. Perfect. Perfect," a sextet of strident and gravelly voices echoed.

"I hope my *aim* is perfect," Aunt Lucille murmured.

Will clutched his aunt's shoulder. The determined look returned to his eyes.

For the first time since entering the cave, Will felt a surge of confidence. He could face this demon once more and maybe even secure the relic—so long as he wasn't eaten or burned by a *Fomorii,* he thought.

In the final chamber of the Undercroft, Andrew kicked and paddled through the greasy water toward the stone platform. He was nearly there. Eight more strokes and he would reach the completely hysterical Simon, who twitched and gyrated on the elevated surface.

"The monster is on top of you! It's right there!" Simon's thin arm quivered as he pointed beyond Andrew. The shaky boy jammed half his body into the stone opening just in case the Bottom Dweller devoured Andrew and started looking for dessert.

Dan, Deborah, Leo, and Marin pressed their faces between the bars on the opposite side of the pool.

"How can we help him, Dan?" Deborah pleaded.

"I—I have no idea," Dan stuttered.

In the water, the Bottom Dweller undulated within a few feet of Andrew. Like a mad conductor, Dan tried to direct the creature, waving his arms energetically. "Go! Get away from him! No, no, no . . ."

Leo covered his eyes with the Bible.

An anxious Marin backed away from the gold grille, gasping for air, her shoulders up near her ears. She looked as if she were going to be sick. Lost in fear, Marin opened her mouth and produced an ear-stabbing, glass-breaking, make-a-dog-bury-itself scream. Her mother tried to shake the girl out of her fit, but to no avail. The high-pitched tone went on and on, Marin's face a mask of desperation. And when she finished, Marin inhaled and let fly another sustained scream.

A half smile crept across Dan's face. He was still looking out at the pool. "It's backing away—the Bottom Dweller is moving away from him," Dan said.

As if attached to a leash, the Bottom Dweller was whipped backward across the pool by the roof of its mouth. The creature's jaws hyperextended and its body lifted out of the water, away from Andrew. The Dweller's retreat gave Andrew just enough time to scramble up onto the stone platform so he could join Simon near the thin tunnel opening.

With the immediate danger past, Marin stopped screaming. Deborah embraced her daughter, keeping a vigilant eye on the reptile beyond the bars flipping on her end of the pool. The creature soon recovered its bearings, shook its head up and down, and once more pursued the boys standing on the platform.

Andrew jostled Simon into the opening in the wall so he could enter. But Simon wasn't moving quickly enough. The snout of the green monster was only a few feet from the stone platform.

"Marin, scream again, honey," Deborah said.

"What, Mommy?"

"Scream, scream!" Deborah demanded.

The child balled her fists, inhaled, and let out a screech that made the gold grille vibrate. Once more the Bottom Dweller lunged backward, flailing and yowling as it flew halfway across the pool. It obviously loathed Marin's shrieks.

Dan Wilder was distracted by Leo, who curiously knelt on the ground and opened the Bible near the golden bars. The boy drew Elijah's mantle from beneath his cast.

"What is . . . Wh-wh-what are you doing, son?" Dan asked. "Don't do that. . . . P-p-put that down, Leo. Put it away!"

"I just want to try something, Dad." Leo stuck the weathered fabric through the bars and glanced down at the open book.

The Bottom Dweller caught sight of Leo's arm poking through the grille and swiftly swam in his direction.

Dan Wilder yanked at Leo's shoulder. "The Bottom Dweller! Son, pull your arm in."

Leo could not be deterred. He held his position, reading loudly from the book on the floor, "'Where is the Lord, the God of Elijah?'"

The Bottom Dweller opened its lethal jaws, creating space for Leo's arm.

The boy shut his eyes, raised the mantle, and struck the oily water with it.

A mighty gust of wind pushed the Wilders against the bars of the grille. Had Simon not been holding his friend's arm, Andrew might have been swept away by the blast.

Starting in the middle of the pool, a rush of air split the water in two halves. It shot upward along the side walls of the chamber, rolling toward the ceiling. Like an exotic fish in an aquarium, the Bottom Dweller swam in circles, trapped in the water along the left side of the chamber.

The black granite pool had been completely emptied. Stunned and scared, the Wilders didn't move. The water clung to the sides of the room unnaturally, like free-floating brown Jell-O.

"You did it, Leo. You got rid of the croc monster," Deborah squealed, holding on to Marin.

"I guess I did." Leo was just happy to still have his arm. He withdrew the dripping mantle to his side of the grille—and the moment he did, the levitating water in the chamber fell in a swirling gush. A raging whirlpool of water spun around the lower part of the chamber and coursed through the open iron door between the stairs. The Bottom Dweller's head slammed into the corners and walls with such force that by the time the creature jetted through the doorway, there was no fight left in it. When the last of the oily water had evacuated, the iron door slammed shut, a bolt engaging.

"It's all over. You can come out now, Simon," Andrew said, rapping on the wall behind him. "The reptile's gone."

Simon clung to Andrew's arm, but there was no movement inside the tunnel. "If it's all right with you, I may just wait in here until an adult comes to get us. It's kind of relaxing for me," Simon bellowed from the hole.

Andrew smacked the bony hand attached to his arm.

"What'd you do that for?" said Simon, poking his head out of the tunnel. "If I hadn't held your ungrateful arm, you would have been swallowed up by that whirlpool. Where's the thanks? Where's the gratitude?"

An exhausted Andrew shuffled down the stone staircase leading to the lower level.

"I guess you're embarrassed to admit that I saved you from sudden death, moron," Simon continued from atop the stone platform, tugging at the waistband of his over-sized shorts. "Yeah, I can be pretty indispensable in a crisis situation. I identified the danger, found a safe haven, and then, in the darkest hour, saved a friend. Do the Boy Scouts offer some kind of medal for valor? If they do, you should nominate me for it. I mean, look, we have witnesses and everything."

On the black granite floor below, Andrew began yelping in a frightened voice. "Three of the reptiles are coming through the door down here. One is headed up the stairs. Come help me, Simon. Please, come help me."

The brave hero on the platform didn't even respond. Instead, Simon dove into the tunnel, only his bony legs visible.

"Well?" Andrew called out, dropping his scared routine and laughing uproariously. "I'll give you a medal! The Yellow Heart for Cowardliness in a Crunch."

Dan Wilder had found some rope in the church broom closet, which he busily tied into knots inside the Keep.

"What are you doing?" Deborah asked.

"My thought is to lower this down. We can pull the boys up to our level. Get them out of that room." He continued making knots in the rope.

"Dan, why did you call those green things Bottom Dwellers?"

"Because that's what they are—they're . . . they're Bottom Dwellers."

"How did you know that?"

He hesitated, his eyes fluttering. "I read it in a book—in a book."

"You're lying." Deborah placed her hands on her hips, suspicion filling her blue-purple eyes. "Why are you lying to me?"

"I'm not lying." His face turned crimson, his jaw muscles pulsing.

"You've seen those things before."

Dan's face betrayed him. He nodded sheepishly and resumed tying the rope.

Deborah stopped his hands and exploded in a tense whisper. "Our son thinks he sees demons. He told me he broke in here, stole the relic of St. Thomas, and gave it to a *demon*! Leo just smacked a piece of cloth on top of a pool full of water, and it parted. It flew into the air, Dan. You saw it, and so did I."

Dan's face went blank. He avoided Deborah's glare.

"What is going on Dan? What is happening to us?"

"I . . . I . . . *Where* is Will?"

"He's with your aunt Lucille. Oh, and she says he has a gift. He's a *Seer.*" Borderline hysterical, she searched his eyes for an answer, or even a reaction. "And are you ready for this? They are out on the river right now, getting the relic back from the demon."

Dan was nearly catatonic. "It's her old fables. . . . She's feeding Will all of this. She's been telling these stories for so long, she can't distinguish reality from pious lies. I don't know anything about it, Deb."

"This is your family! You *have* to know something about it."

"I don't. I don't." Dan took the rope, turned from his wife, and stomped angrily toward the black granite slab bearing the inscription "Blessed are they that have not seen, and yet have believed."

Will and Aunt Lucille tiptoed through the three inches of water that swamped the end of the hallway. They were nearly upon the blighted temple, the central circular cavern of Dismal Shoals. As they climbed a few steps the firelight brightened and the cold cacophony of voices grew louder.

"Lucille! This is cause for celebration. A living, breathing Wilder. Just what we needed. Haaaaa-haaaaa-haaaaaaaah." The cruel laughter felt like a chilled stiletto slowly entering Will's chest. It was similar to the feeling he'd had lying on the shores of the Perilous River, watching the relic float out of sight.

The first thing Aunt Lucille spied was Tobias Shen, hanging limply from the wall, his face badly bruised and bleeding, red stains soaking the legs of his gray uniform. She quickly sized up the rest of the room: four Bottom Dwellers in the center of the chamber, one bubbling pit in the rear that resembled her father's sketches of the *Hell Mouth*, and twenty feet off the ground a levitating cage holding the gold reliquary of St. Thomas the Apostle. On the periphery of the room, damaged marble braziers held plates of hot coals, providing a dying light.

Will leaned his head slightly to the right of his great-aunt to peek at the cavern, his hands resting on her shoulders. "He's right there, Aunt Lucille," Will blurted into her ear. "Levia . . . the Captain . . . *It's* right there under the floating cage."

Will couldn't stand looking at the horrible creature. His sinuses didn't much care for it either. AH-CHOO! AH-CHOO!

The demon's seven heads, suspended by their long, barrel-sized necks, suddenly snapped in his direction. Four of the wicked faces began chanting, "Will Wilder . . . Wilder . . . Will Wilder."

That's when Nep Balor's head, at the center, stretched toward the boy. His yellow eye glowed with kindness. "If it ain't our old pal Will. Did you have a good rest? Glad yer up and about. We couldn't have done any of this without yer help, lad." Rumbling laughter ricocheted off the walls of the cave.

"Don't speak to it," Lucille reminded Will, holding her hands out in assault mode.

"Doesn't matter what yer old auntie says about ye. Yer an asset—a treasure—to us, boy," the demon cooed.

"Treasure, treasure, treasure," a wispy chorus intoned.

"Keep silent," Aunt Lucille cautioned.

"'Don't say this, don't say that,'" Balor mimicked mockingly. "Yer auntie is not in charge here. This is not Peniel. Ye may say whatever yeh please, Will. We're all free here."

Will's vision of the demon was sharply focused. For the first time he could see the entire body of the beast, unobstructed. Its seven necks like scaled tree trunks blended into a massive chest. Two arms of reptilian muscle as thick as boulders rested on a tangle of squid tentacles sprouting from the sides of the torso. The ridged belly gave way to a gargantuan tail. On either side of the tail were legs that made Will think of a T. rex poster he once had in his room. He watched in fascinated horror as the flat gray claws of the creature propelled its monstrous form to the pit at the rear of the circular chamber.

"It's only right that ye see history in the making, Will," the demon said. The cage hovered near the pit. "Now begins the rise of the *Sinestri* and the end of the Brethren." The demon raised the caged relic high over its writhing heads. . . .

Aunt Lucille, her eyes locked on the relic in the cage,

hissed over her shoulder, "Where is it exactly? Under the cage?"

"Yes, ma'am. Just to the left."

She asked no more questions. A red-and-white-rimmed ray escaped the triangle of Aunt Lucille's fingers. The surging light struck the demon at the base of its necks. Upon impact, the cage was tossed sideways, near the rocky wall holding Tobias Shen.

"Caaaaaaaaaahhhhhhhh," the demon wheezed. Its seven heads wriggled wildly in anguish as if they were roasting from the inside. Aunt Lucille showed no emotion. She simply stood her ground, projecting the steady laser of light.

Will stepped from behind his aunt, wide-eyed, as the Beast's knees buckled. The thing clawed at the walls, trying to steady itself. As it struggled, the seven heads glared at the *Fomorii* in front of Aunt Lucille and Will. The demon suddenly opened a scaled hand, causing the Bottom Dwellers to stir. All four rose up on their hind legs.

Aunt Lucille continued to pound the demon with her ray. Like insane dogs, the Bottom Dwellers sprang at Will, their jaws wide and bloodthirsty. Aunt Lucille somersaulted in front of the boy and directed her beam at the advancing Dwellers. One by one the reptilian crawlers were turned to reeking purple ash.

That was all the time the demon needed.

Terror filled Will's eyes. "Aunt Lucille, he's coming this way. He's on your right. Two o'clock! He's at two o'clock!"

By the time Aunt Lucille had finished off the last Bottom

Dweller, the demon had overtaken her. It jammed its tentacles between Lucille's forearms, separating her hands and snuffing out the red ray.

"No more of your tricks, Lucille," icy voices cried. Will helplessly watched the clawed hands of the demon throw his great-aunt's body against the rocky surface opposite Tobias Shen. The creature's huge claws grabbed her by the waist, its tentacles stretching her arms wide.

Purple anemone funnels affixed to the wall wormed toward Aunt Lucille's limbs. The funnels spewed neon tendrils that wrapped around her wrists and legs.

"Will, do as you were told. Now!" Aunt Lucille ordered, splayed out on the wall. She winced as the venom of the sea anemones began seeping into her flesh.

With tears forming in his eyes, Will tugged at his great-grandfather's pith helmet for confidence and made a run for it. He scooped up the cage holding the relic and tried to wrestle it open. Over his shoulder, Will glanced up at poor Mr. Shen. Though badly beaten, the old man's lips formed gentle words.

"—*defende nos in proelio, contra neqitiam et insidias diaboli esto praesidium. Imperet illi Deus*—"

Will could not pry the cage open more than a few inches. He stepped on the attached rod and tried to unlatch the enclosure with both hands. Losing patience, he violently yanked the cage this way, then that, sending the rod swinging in all directions behind him.

Across the wrecked subterranean temple, Aunt Lucille

commanded the demon's full attention. Though she could not see its form, she could feel the Beast's icy breath on her face as it spoke.

"The Brethren are near extinction and they send a child and two broken-down fossils to do battle with us. Oh, how yeh've wasted yer life. Yer the relic now, Lucille. Ye could have been such a help to us."

She turned her face away from the stinking frosty breath and closed her eyes.

The voice spoke softly now. "As we devoured Jacob Wilder and yer brother, so we shall devour yer entire line. Even the boy! Yer enduring hope! We shall crush every member of the Brethren down to their last bone. Daddy Wilder may have demolished our temple, but tonight his own blood—his precious Sarah Lucille—will be sacrificed on our ruined altar and thrust into the pit. Once the *Darkness* receives the relic—"

The demon stopped short as if suddenly reminded of something. It spun around, all its faces searching the corners of the cavern. It sought out the reliquary.

Feeling multiple eyes on him, Will froze, his hand caught in the relic cage. The demon opened its arms. Like excited snakes, the tentacles on its sides reached for the frazzled boy. Will shook the cage, unsuccessfully pulling at its metal jaws.

The demon drew closer.

"Go," Aunt Lucille whimpered. "Run."

In his frenzied bumbling, Will inadvertently knocked

over one of the braziers with the cage's metal rod. Hot coals scattered across the ground with a sizzle. Seeing how close the demon was, Will stumbled backward.

"This was not part of the plan," Will said to himself. Suddenly the scent of burning rubber filled his nostrils. The soles of his red sneakers were melting!

"Aaaah! Hot, hot, hot!" Will sputtered, doing a chicken dance on the flaming coals, his hand stuck in the cage.

"It's all right, lad. I know yeh want the relic," said Balor, comforting the boy. "And I want yeh to have it—forever." The demon caught the end of the metal rod, hoisting the cage and Will high into the air. "Let's awaken some of our friends."

The Beast dragged Will along the ceiling of the chamber, which at first appeared to be covered with jagged rocks. But now that Will was closer, he realized they were dangling gray clams, big as footballs. As Will brushed by them, the unhinged shells released black goo, which collected on the floor. From the puddles, long, slick arms emerged, then legs. Within seconds each of the puddles started jiggling. Then, of their own volition, the goo was off the ground and began to stand. The demon had created new *Stickers*. . . .

Will desperately took hold of the relic in the cage, yanking at the bottom of the metal lattice with his other hand. His hanging weight caused the hinge to give, and the cage popped open.

Will and the relic tumbled to the floor. When he hit the ground, his helmet bounced off and the reliquary escaped his grasp. Recovering the hat, he scrambled on all fours toward the reliquary. It was only three feet away from him. As he reached for the golden artifact two prehistoric legs appeared, blocking his path.

"Do ye ever get the feelin' that we've done this before?" Balor asked from overhead.

Will slowly glanced up. Seven corpselike faces smiled down at him.

"Go. Go," Aunt Lucille demanded, with effort, from the wall.

"Shut up, Lucille," a barnacled face gurgled, twisting its neck backward. Balor continued placidly, his face never leaving Will. "She doesn't understand us, lad. She's so afraid of what we might give yeh. What's Lucille ever seen except the inside of that musty museum of hers? Nothing. She lives in the past. We are the future. We command the waters, sail the seven seas. We've adventured with emperors and kings. Why shouldn't ye be next, lad?"

Will was transfixed by the Captain's words.

Balor's neck bent low so that his face was very near Will's. The seven horns atop his head were now quite pointy. The closeness of the dripping, sick eye made Will want to gag. He pulled the pith helmet brim low, covering his eyes.

Balor whispered urgently, "Perilous Falls will be washed away in a few hours. But with us ye can have a future: friends, more power than ye ever dreamed—and oh, think of the adventures that could be yers, Willy. How many times did yer auntie and that cruel groundsman over there"—

the demon flicked a paw in Tobias Shen's direction—"keep things from yeh? We'd never do that, Will. They want to control the relics, control yer gift, hold us all down. But we're here for ye now—and more are coming. The Brethren are finished. Ye poor thing—bet yeh don't even know who the Brethren are?"

"I do," Will said indignantly. "And I know who you are. *Leviathan! You* didn't tell me that you were *Leviathan.* Why should I believe you?" When he looked up, though his vision was fading, the demon's six extra faces seemed angrier than before.

Balor's face remained undisturbed. "Don't know where yeh got that name from. Never heard it before. Expect Auntie's been filling your head with more fibs. Let's make a simple deal: during the terrible water-soaked days to come, we'll protect yeh—and yer family and friends. That's a promise. Help yeh realize yer true power. We only ask one favor."

"What is it?" Will asked, keeping his eyes off the demon's face.

"Help us rid the world of that relic. There are other bones and trinkets. That one's caused so much trouble, Will. Toss it into the pit over there." Balor turned to the bubbling black pool, half covered by the broken altar.

"Why don't you do it yourself?"

"Oh, we've never liked touching dead things. Against our religion . . . and what with the busted cage and all . . . But ye could carry it to the pit for us—and earn protection in the days to come."

Will was visibly frightened by Balor's words. In the grip of fear, he considered making a deal with the demon. With Perilous Falls sinking under the angry waters and his aunt Lucille and Shen trapped, Will's choices were limited. Disposing of the relic to save his family and his friends might be a fair trade. . . .

Then the prophecy's warning came back to him. The relic should not be "desecrated or destroyed," it said. Soon other words echoed in his head:

"*. . . without him, there can be no victory for the Brethren or for my people. . . . For only with a pure heart and belief that is strong can he ever hope to crush the heads of Leviathan.*"

Some of the demon's faces wore pleading expressions; others were dejected. His vision of the demon was steadily dimming. Nep Balor had tears in his good eye—as far as Will could tell.

"Ye have to end this suffering, boy. Help yer family. Help yerself. There'll be no orders given here. Ye'll be free to do as ye please once we get rid of that old bone." The demon's razor-sharp tail pointed to the relic for emphasis.

BLUB . . . BLUB . . . BLUB . . .

Will knew those sounds. Behind him, the *Stickers* were closing in. *BLUB . . . BLUB . . . BLUB . . .* Like an alarm clock in his bedroom, the bubbling noises startled him. They pulled Will from his thoughts and out of his conversation with Balor. Shifting into a sprinter's stance, Will made a decision.

CHAPTER 15

REPELLING LEVIATHAN

Gazing through the front window of his home, Max Meriwether fell asleep in his wheelchair. He had been watching the torrential rain pound Dorcas Drive outside. The sweet classical music that calmed him filled the cramped living room courtesy of his mother, Evelyn.

The round, soft center of the Meriwether household ducked in and out of the living room every few minutes to check on her little boy. The pudgy and perpetually flushed woman continued chatting with Max from the kitchen despite his snores. Her voice was a bit too loud, possessing the sunny tone of a kindergarten teacher instructing students to put their finger paints away.

"Raining hard out, huh?" Evelyn asked, absently adding water to her bread mixture on the kitchen counter. "Daddy emailed and said he saw a crocodile swimming up Gall Lane, outside the shop. Can you believe it? You don't see any crocs out there, do you, Maxie?"

Max slept soundly, his head resting on a rubber cushion attached to his wheelchair.

"Haven't heard from Cami. I hope she's okay in this downpour. Hope she had the sense to stay at the museum." Evelyn flipped on the television to check the weather.

A young female reporter in a blue windbreaker with tousled blond hair hugged a lamppost on Main Street. She battled the relentless downpour to stay in front of the camera. Her false eyelashes and bloodred lipstick were the only things standing between the audience and her clueless expression.

"It's the most unbelievable weather event I have ever seen—I know I've only been here a few weeks, but there are hurricane-force winds on the streets. Signs are blowing off buildings, trees are down—holy cow! Now, I'm not a weather expert"—she giggled to underscore the obvious—"but the meteorologists tell me they didn't even see this system coming on their radars."

During a meaningless chat with the anchors, the reporter was distracted by something happening off camera. Her eyes suddenly widened and she began to shiver. The wind-ravaged woman shrilly cut the anchors off.

"I can't talk anymore because . . . Okay! I'm going to go in. The guys in our van are, like—being attacked! Holy cow! There are two, like, *huge* alligators scratching at the door of our news van. I'm not kidding—they're breaking the windows—holy cow! Rachel Riker Rutledge reporting from Main Street for Sidon News, Channel Eight. . . ." She finished with an insincere smile, dropped the microphone, and fled the scene.

"Maxie, I wonder if those are the crocodiles Daddy saw," Evelyn mused, staring at the TV. "We certainly can't count on Rachel what's-her-name to tell us." She struck the dough before her with a rolling pin. "Poor girl's a mess. . . . Reporting's just not her bag. She should try track and field."

The kitchen door burst open, rain splattering on the golden-yellow linoleum. Cami slammed the door behind her, soaked to the bone and breathing hard.

"Mother, where is Max?"

"Oh, just look at you, Cami. You look like a waterlogged squirrel, honey." She raced into the laundry room, wiping her plump hands on her red calico apron. Within seconds, she was wrapping Cami in a fresh towel. "You're shivering, hon. This weather is crazy. Why didn't you stay at the museum?"

"It's kind of a long story, Mother." She shot into the den, drying her hair. "Max. Max." After a few shakes the boy stirred, his eyes filled with sleep.

Cami knelt next to his chair. "What happened at the end of your dream the other day, Max? After the bad one got the golden treasure. Did the town flood? Was Will hurt?"

Max used his left wrist to rub at his eyes. "I keep having a new dream. A totally new dream, Cami."

"Tell me about the old dream first. What did the 'bad one' look like?"

"The bad one is ugly. An ugly monster with many faces. It goes away in the old dream. The bad one goes away. But today . . ." He beat his head against the cushion supporting it. "Today . . ."

"Was Will the bad one? Is he with the bad one?"

Max shook his head, indicating a definite no.

"He wants to get the golden treasure back from the bad one—the *Sinestri*. Only Will can get it. Nobody else." Max clenched his teeth and got very still. His eyes locked on his sister's. "Today I had a new dream—a nightmare," he panted.

Evelyn Meriwether stood in the doorway of the living room, watching her children. "Why are you badgering your brother? Maxie is tired. Aren't you, darling?" she said, an edge in her voice.

"Just a minute, Mother," Cami insisted. "What did you see in the nightmare?"

"A dark raven. A black, black raven comes. It's nice, so nice at first."

"Does the raven come here? To Perilous Falls?"

"Yes." Max seemed almost afraid. "Then it makes blood. Blood . . . everywhere."

"Here in Perilous Falls?"

"Can't you see you're upsetting your brother?" Evelyn said, gently interrupting. She took hold of the wheelchair handles. "Maxie, come see the bread I'm making for you in the kitchen."

As he was wheeled away he reached an arm out toward his sister. "Blood in Perilous Falls . . . blood everywhere."

Stunned and confused, Cami stared through the front window at the debris and water swirling outside. What she couldn't see beyond the maelstrom were the two Bottom Dwellers clamoring up the big oak on the front lawn—or the one balancing at the end of the tree limb just above the Meriwethers' roof.

The demon towered over Will, awaiting a response to its offer. The boy crouched before the Beast, his legs bent, balancing on the fingers of one hand.

BLUB . . . BLUB . . . BLUB . . . The Stickers crowded in behind him.

"So do we have a deal, lad?" Nep Balor asked. The heads of the demon formed an eerie semicircle around Balor's face, like sickly planets orbiting a dark sun. "Deal? . . . Deal? . . . Help us . . . Power . . . Adventure . . . Deal? . . . Deal?" they begged in a series of low moans.

Will nodded. In one swift move, he lunged between the demon's legs for the relic. The seven heads followed Will's movement, necks straining downward and under the scaled legs. Their wicked eyes watched Will take hold of the reliquary's gold base. He rolled to his side and found his feet.

"Good lad," Balor sang, his head cocked beneath the gray legs. "We have a deal, then! Throw the filthy thing into the pit over there."

The relic began to glow an electric blue in Will's hands. His whole body warmed and he could clearly see the demon once again.

Aunt Lucille struggled on the wall, pulling on the tendrils that held her fast. "You have it now. Go. Go, dear," she gasped.

"No, Aunt Lucille. The prophecy said I had to drive it away with belief and a pure heart." He pressed the relic against the rubber band–like strings covering her wrists and ankles. The neon tentacles instantly recoiled, releasing her. "I *believe*, Aunt Lucille."

BLUB . . . BLUB . . . BLUB . . . Five Stickers stood behind the demon, advancing toward the pair.

The Beast's seven necks extended to their very limit. In one undulating movement the heads whirled, as did the entire grotesque body, to face Will.

"Back, Leviathan!" Will cried in a strong voice he hadn't expected to produce. He brandished the relic in front of him like a sword. A slim blue light emerged out of the top of the reliquary, striking the demon in the stomach. It staggered backward.

"What about our deal? Our friendship?" Balor cried. "Speak! Won't ye even speak to us? Where is yer pity? Killer! Plunderer! Just like all the Wilders before yeh."

"Not one word," Aunt Lucille cautioned Will.

"I hear you," he responded. Hard as it was, Will remained silent, directing the relic's blue light at the writhing creature. "I'm not sure what I'm doing."

"You're *repelling* him. Keep it up." Lucille stood behind him on feet that had gone numb, shaking her sore hands. She could feel little below her elbows. With great effort she repeatedly made fists. Then, placing her fingers in the triangle formation, she aimed her red-and-white beam at the Stickers. One by one they were reduced to steaming statues of ash.

"You'll have to show me how to do that sometime," Will muttered out of the side of his mouth.

Aunt Lucille did not respond, but followed Will's lead, turning her beam toward the demon. *"Reppéle, Domini, virtútem diáboli, fallacésque ejus insídias ámove,"* Lucille said with vehemence, *"procul ímpius tentátor aufúgiat."*

"Will, she'll take control of yeh the first chance she gets. She'll manipulate yeh to do her biddin'. Is that what yeh want?" The demon teetered backward, stumbling toward the black pit and the broken altar.

Back, Leviathan! Will so wanted to yell. And though he didn't, the moment he thought it, the Beast flew against the rear wall and slipped into the bubbling black *Hell Mouth*. Will could feel a power surging through his hands.

Her blast never yielding, Aunt Lucille continued to mutter strange words the boy had never heard her speak before.

"Leviathan will not be controlled by an insolent child and an old hag," the demon swore, all the voices speaking in unison. It dug claws into what remained of the broken altar, trying to stop its descent into the black pool.

"Perilous Falls is flooded. Others will come, Wilders!

Others less kind than we, Will!" The black tarry waters began to swallow the Beast. Its unyielding claws snapped off the last bits of the altar, dragging it into the pit.

Will edged closer to the demon, keeping the blue ray of the relic trained on Balor's head. Leviathan's multiple faces sank beneath the surface of the pool.

"Where is yer sympathy? Yer mercy, Will?" Balor asked in his most sorrowful voice. Then, raging, he screamed, "We'll be watching yeh!" Balor's diseased eye opened. Aiming the relic's beam on the sickly pupil, Will looked away. Though she could see nothing, Aunt Lucille also averted her gaze.

Consumed by the black liquid of the pit, only the horns on Leviathan's last head were still visible. Will pressed the relic against the highest horn until it vanished. Within seconds the center of the black liquid turned hard and the entire pit transformed into gray concrete.

"Not bad for an insolent child and an old hag with a musty museum," Aunt Lucille said, dropping her hands and throwing her head back in exhaustion. She laughed in her knowing way.

"Did I kill it? It's gone, right?" Will asked, clutching the glowing relic.

"It's gone for now—and you've closed up the *Hell Mouth*. But we've only repelled the demon. It'll take a *Vanquisher*—an exorcist—to lock the beast away. We'd better help Tobias." She turned her attention to the unconscious groundskeeper slumped on the floor. When the demon was drowned in the pit, the tendrils holding Shen had retreated, causing the wounded man to fall into a clump.

"Is Mr. Shen going to be okay?"

"Touch him with the relic, dear."

Will did as he was told. The reliquary's blue aura intensified. Tobias Shen let out a pained gasp and bolted into an upright position.

"Stay still, Tobias. We're going to help you out of here," Aunt Lucille said.

"Did you get the relic? Where is the demon?"

"It's gone. And Will has the relic."

The boy moved it in front of Mr. Shen, who noticeably relaxed after seeing the illuminated reliquary.

"It agrees with you, Mr. Wilder—you could be your great-grandfather's twin in this light," Shen said weakly, his swollen, bloody lips forming a smile. "Now we must secure the relic in St. Thomas Church once more. Very quickly."

"Not so fast, Tobias." Aunt Lucille turned her attention to Shen's blood-soaked trousers. She took Will by the wrists, directing the relic toward Tobias Shen's battered legs. He quivered at the touch.

"It's very warm. Ohhh. Look, look." In amazement Shen ogled his bent limbs. The bloodstains dissolved from the gray pants, and his legs straightened. The pain that had afflicted him for hours melted away.

"Keep it there for a moment, dear," Lucille instructed, closing her eyes, a hand on Will's back.

Will could have stayed there all day, watching the old man revive and feeling the surging warmth pass through his hands into the reliquary. Tobias Shen's lips returned to their normal size, and the gashes on his head and face closed. A peace filled the chamber, which only moments earlier had reverberated with chaos.

"That ought to do it," Aunt Lucille said, tapping Will's shoulder. He lowered the relic solemnly, extending it toward Aunt Lucille.

She refused its touch. "I'll be all right." She straightened her long neck and tugged at her collar. "There is not a moment to waste."

"Let's go," Shen said, bouncing up and striding to the exit. "We have been spared for important work. Come, come, come. We must get the relic to safety—inside the Keep. Now."

"We're right behind you, Tobias," an exhausted Aunt Lucille said, rising. She winced as she walked. Each step felt as if she were being impaled by broken glass. Her hands didn't feel much better, but she soldiered on.

The trio hastily abandoned the soggy chambers of Dismal Shoals. Outside they discovered Bartimaeus sitting inside the rocky niche, exactly where they had left him.

"Go ahead, take ya time," he called out sarcastically from the grotto, black beads in his hand. "Good to see y'all relaxin'. Probably gives you comfort knowing I'm out here doing the heavy lifting while y'all were playing around inside."

They laughed and helped Bartimaeus into the *Stella*

Maris. Once everyone was on board, Aunt Lucille situated herself in the captain's chair and turned the boat upriver toward St. Thomas Church.

Along the riverside, cloaked by trees, a camouflaged military vehicle observed their leaving. Behind tinted glass, a long-lens camera repeatedly snapped images of Aunt Lucille, Bartimaeus, Tobias Shen, and Will exiting the wrecked temple and boarding the boat.

"Now, what are they so happy about?" Mayor Ava Lynch asked Heinrich Crinshaw, who was seated tensely beside her in the back of the vehicle. She turned to the police officer manning the camera in the front seat. "Keep taking shots of this. We need all the photographic evidence we can get, sugar."

"What's the Wilder boy carrying?" Crinshaw asked.

Mayor Lynch brought a compact pair of binoculars to her eyes. "It's some kind of gold sculpture. One of those superstitious voodoo things Lucille keeps in that museum of hers, I'm sure." She tossed the binoculars aside with annoyance. "Now, will you all explain to me what Lucille Wilder, a couple of old guys, and Dan's kid are doing in a cave during a thunderstorm? Because I would love to know. And why are they in the exact cave where all these murderous crocodiles are coming from? That is the location you all traced those crocs back to, right, officer?"

The man in the driver's seat nodded crisply. "Yes, ma'am."

"That is curious. Killer crocodiles attack our towns-people, but Lucille and her merry men go in and out of their breeding ground without so much as a scratch. Are they raising those things? It's all very curious."

"Maybe they were out in the boat and got swept down-river, Ava," Crinshaw offered, stroking his mustache. "Perhaps they were seeking shelter from the storm, which seems to be lessening now."

"Noooo," Ava Lynch droned. She was lost in thought, her eyes flatly staring out at the *Stella Maris* gliding on the rough waters. "Lucille Wilder is responsible for all of this somehow. She has a lot of explaining to do. Not to me, mind you—to the people of Perilous Falls. They deserve answers."

CHAPTER 16

THE SUMMONER

Sitting in the passenger seat next to Aunt Lucille, Will tightly gripped the reliquary as they proceeded up the Perilous River. The change in the river amazed him. As the *Stella Maris* moved along, the choppy waves on all sides calmed. Will could see the shoreline receding from the nearly topped levees. Overhead, black clouds separated, permitting the sunshine to burn away their edges.

In the aftermath of the battle with Leviathan, Will was anxious and filled with questions.

He turned to his aunt Lucille, who struggled to keep a firm hold on the steering wheel with her injured hands. "So what happened to Levia—you know, the Captain?"

"Don't personalize it that way. It's a demon. A cruel deceiver. What was that name it gave you?"

"Captain Nep Balor."

Aunt Lucille released a trilling laugh. "Nep Balor? *Neptune* Balor. Could have been *Poseidon* Balor. The Aztecs called this one *Atl,* the Illyrians, *Rodon.* The demon has gone by many names—mostly those of pagan sea gods. The only name that matters is the true one. The one it responded to. The one you used to control the serpent."

"But where did he—uh—it go?"

"Back to the underworld. It has been weakened. But you heard what it said. You read the prophecy: others will come."

"Look, look at the Bottom Dwellers," Mr. Shen yelled from the back of the boat, pointing to the shore.

The creatures charged over the banks toward the river in a frenzy. They seemed to be gasping for air as they stampeded over one another. Fighting their way into the water, the Bottom Dwellers belly flopped into the river and disappeared from sight.

"Where are they headed?" Will asked, looking over the side of the boat, bracing for their sudden reappearance.

"Back where they came from," Bartimaeus said from the bench seat at the rear. "Without a demon to keep them goin', they've got to find a power source. They'll swarm near Wormwood, I expect. Don't worry, they'll be back."

"I'm not worried. Aunt Lucille can always roast them with her death ray."

Lucille grinned, steering the boat. "It's not a death ray."

"Then what is it?" Will asked.

"*Rebutting illuminance.* That's what the old books call it, anyway. It's merely spiritual light that repels evil. I told you we all have gifts. The *illuminance* is mine."

"Can you teach me to do it?"

"No, dear. It's a gift. One I didn't even know I had until I was confronted by a demon. I was about thirteen. Walking home one night from a friend's house, the beast set upon me. It slashed at my arms and threw me to the ground. Of course I couldn't see it. I screamed and put my hands out in self-defense—what else was I to do?—and the *illuminance* appeared. The beams went in all directions. I torched a number of trees behind the house, ruined a fence. My mother was not happy. It took me many months of training to control it. Daddy helped quite a lot. . . ."

Lucille slipped out of her raincoat and deftly steered the boat around the boulder tips jutting from the water. Every so often she slowly stretched her hands. From the way she bit her lip each time she made the gesture, Will could see she was in pain. After a long pause, Aunt Lucille continued, "Gifts must be honed, Will. Mastered and understood. Or they are of no use to anyone. After seeing what you did with the relic, it is your time to be trained."

"Trained at what? Trained where?"

"At Peniel. At the archabbey there. It's where the Brethren live."

Raising a brow, Will asked, "They *live* in the museum?"

"Below it, around it, above it—yes. It is the community house of the Brethren. They've been there since the founding to protect the relics and the artifacts within. It's the main citadel in this part of the country—and our most important defense against the *Sinestri* and the *Darkness*."

"You mean there are other abbeys—citadels?"

"Yes. We're all in contact, though not as close as we once were. There's been a lot of infighting and disagreement. But you may be able to help with that."

Will remembered the line in the prophecy about the Brethren and their broken unity. "The prophecy said the chosen one will lead them. Will I have to lead them?"

"In time . . . It's very important that you receive training as soon as possible. We can teach you skills and awaken talents you'll need to protect yourself and perhaps all of us— skills you'll need to fulfill the prophecy."

The pressure Will felt caused a dull nausea to roll through his stomach. "Is this like a school?"

Bartimaeus rose from the cushioned seat in the rear and hobbled forward on his crutches. "It's individual training— highly specialized. So don't expect a prom or a report card. If ya live and we all survive, ya passed. If we don't—ya failed. You got me? This ain't a regimented kind of thing. Push on over, let me share your seat. I'm old—my legs are worn out."

Bartimaeus leaned the two crutches against the brass rails along the side of the boat. With his hips, he nudged the boy across the cushioned seat. Half of Will's backside fell off the chair. "Kinda tight, huh?" he complained.

"But that's a lesson right there, ya see? In community

living, you learn important things . . . like *sharing*—even your chair—understanding people's failings, seeing a little deeper than what the world sees. We'll teach ya discernment, defense against evil, how to control your visions—"

"How to keep your hands off items that don't belong to you"—Aunt Lucille turned her eyes like daggers toward the reliquary—"items that must be respected." She spun the wheel hard to the left with a smile. "Aha. We're here."

St. Thomas Church rose up beside the boat. The *Stella Maris* pulled as close to the rocky shore as Aunt Lucille dared to pilot her. Tobias Shen cast the anchor over the starboard side, grabbed a line, and jumped into the receding water near the shore. He tethered the boat to a nearby tree.

Aunt Lucille waddled toward the church, moving much slower than usual thanks to her aching feet. Her algae-smudged silk pantsuit fluttered at the wrists as she spoke. "When we get inside, Will, if your father is here, let's not share too many details of our little adventure. He has a propensity for disbelief and might not take kindly to our instructing you in the ways of the Brethren."

Will nodded.

"Might not take kindly?" Bartimaeus chucked. "He might take your aunt Lucille's head off. That's what she meant to say—I know that's right."

Tobias Shen cracked a knowing smile but said nothing.

Aunt Lucille spun around at the door, removing his smirk with a withering glance. "I'd better take the relic from here."

Will held the reliquary all the tighter. Deep down he felt

he should be the one to return it to the Keep. He couldn't bear to part with it when he was feeling so unsteady—so uneasy about the future.

"Can't I bring it back in?" Will asked. "I took it out and I know where it goes. . . ."

Aunt Lucille flicked the top of his pith helmet with her index finger. "You're a Wilder through and through—head like a brick. Deliver it directly to the Keep and go no farther, dear. I don't even want to think about the condition of that Undercroft. It's going to take us weeks to drain those chambers and reset the security down there. Which reminds me—" Even though it ached to do so, she opened a flat palm directly before his eyes. "Where is my daddy's notebook?"

Will held the relic under his arm for a moment while he rummaged through his backpack. Bypassing the Book of Prophecy, he felt the slim volume. Wordlessly, he placed the green lacquered book in his aunt's open palm, then grabbed the reliquary again.

Will, Aunt Lucille, Tobias Shen, and Bartimaeus were shocked by the reception that greeted them upon entering the church. Dan quickly hid the two drawn flares he was prepared to ignite depending on who or what walked in; Marin let out a head-rattling scream of glee; Deborah thanked the Almighty, burying her face in her hands; and Leo jumped out of the rear pew, throwing both his cast-covered and cast-free arms around his brother's waist.

"All right, Leo. Thanks. That's plenty," Will said, trying to shake his brother off while protecting the reliquary. "Give me some space. I've got to put this back in the Keep."

"I'm so glad you're alive. Dad told us he was going to have Aunt Lucille arrested if anything happened to you," Leo said, nuzzling his face into Will's side. He clung to his brother like a human fanny pack all the way down the center aisle.

"You can let go now."

"I missed you." Leo tightened his embrace. "I hit Elijah's mantle on the water in the flooded room and saved Simon and Andrew."

"That's great." Will passed his two friends, who were sleeping in a pair of pews near the front of the church. "You've got to let me go. I can't get into the Keep with you hanging on me."

Leo refused, holding fast.

"Don't worry. We'll make it in," Leo said, lifting his legs off the floor.

Will elbowed his brother until the boy finally relented, releasing his grip.

Leo straightened his glasses and continued excitedly. "You should have been here, Will. If I hadn't saved Mom and Marin and your friends, you'd be in big-time trouble. That croc monster was going to eat the whole family. All you did was steal a relic. I smacked down a monster."

Provoked by his brother's boasting, Will's pride and his bottled-up fears rose to the surface. His face held a feverish glow. "Call me when you see demons, okay, Leo? You tell me the next time you see a man turn into a seven-headed monster—and all seven heads want to rip you apart. Call me when your knees are shaking and you're so scared all you want to do is lie down and cry, but you still have to fight the demon," he shouted. "Do you see demons, Leo? DO YOU? DO YOU? DO ANY OF YOU?"

His face screwed up, turning beet red. He intently stared down at the reliquary in his hand, the natural color returning to his face. "I'm still supposed to be a kid, and I can't be a kid for too much longer . . . because I am the only one who sees these things. I know what they can do." Tears dropped from his eyes. Embarrassed, he swiftly retreated into the Keep with the reliquary.

"I blame you for all of this," Dan seethed, thrusting a finger at Aunt Lucille. "You're . . . confusing him. Filling his head with y-y-your . . . ancient demon stories. I suppose you told him about the prophecy?" From her tightening lips he could tell that she had.

"The Hand of Providence and Will's vocation are not ours to control," Aunt Lucille said, slipping her hands into her silk pockets.

"You're the one trying to—to—control everything—engineering it all. Jacob Wilder has become an idol to you. When are you going to let him go? Your father's dead, and so is mine."

"It was Will's decision to mount that donkey—which *you* rented, incidentally. Will found his own way into the Keep. He removed the relic of St. Thomas *himself*. I had *nothing* to do with any of it. I wasn't even there—and neither was my father!" Aunt Lucille squarely faced Dan, her strawberry-blond curls quivering. "Did you see the weather today? The sudden flooding? Did you see the *Fomorii* crawling all over town? How do you explain their reappearance?"

"Deb, we're leaving." He tried to gather the children on the other side of the church.

Lucille pursued him as best she could on a pair of stinging feet.

"You saw the *Fomorii*, Dan. I can see the fear in your eyes. You know the truth. Delude yourself if you wish, but don't try to delude me."

Inside the Keep, Will returned the reliquary to the top of its elevated stand. He felt so alone, as if no one in the whole world could truly comprehend what he had gone through— what he had experienced. The proximity to raw evil had sapped his energy and left him weary. He wanted to lock himself in the Keep and never leave—to avoid all of it: the prophecy, the training, the demons. Unconsciously, he ran his thumbs over the inscribed circular base of the reliquary as if trying to release some secret it held.

"Do not be unbelieving, but believe . . ." it read.

Easier read than done, Will thought. How much easier it would be to believe if he knew the end. If he knew what monsters, what demons tomorrow held. But not even the prophecy gave him that knowledge. He stood before the reliquary, considering each carved word, while fear rose within him. "Do not be unbelieving, but believe . . ."

When he finally emerged from the Keep several minutes later, Aunt Lucille and Dan were still going at it.

"So moving a relic caused boats to sink? Caused a pier to collapse? Caused th-th-the river to flood? Really? You've gone off the deep end."

"That *relic* should never have—"

"The only *relic* here is *you*," Dan exploded. "You're the relic. You and your band of misfits clinging to the past. It's a compulsion. Now you want to drag my boy into your madness. Aunt Lucille, y-y-you need help. Let's go, kids."

Lucille had no more words. She'd been struck to the heart by the man she had raised—by the child she could still see in her mind's eye racing down the stairs of her Victorian home, sitting in her lap, running delightedly through the halls of Peniel. . . .

Bartimaeus rapped one of his crutches against the side of a pew and rose to his full height. "Danny. Don't you disrespect this woman. Ya hear me? I remember what she did for you—what we all did."

To avoid the heat of the conversation, Tobias Shen retreated to one of the side aisles and began sweeping.

Will stood quietly behind a column in the shadow of the sanctuary, pith helmet in hand, listening.

"This could be our last chance," Bartimaeus continued.

"That boy has the gift. So we either teach him to use it, or God have mercy on us all."

"Let's go." Dan shoved Leo out the back door of the church and exited. Deborah begged that they wait for Will and the two boys still napping in the front pews. She and Marin hurried down the center aisle toward the back of the church.

On her way out, Deb grabbed Aunt Lucille's hand, causing her to flinch at the touch. "I'm so sorry. You know he doesn't mean it. By the way, you were right." Deborah sidled close to Lucille. "There were two Bottom Dwellers in those chambers. I saw them. They were here in the church. What I don't understand is Marin's screams. Each time she screamed, those creatures were yanked backward in the water. She prevented Will's friends from being killed. I'll tell you about Leo and the mantle later. . . ."

"How do you mean, she kept them from being killed?"

"When she screamed, and only when she screamed, the Bottom Dweller—that's what it's called, right?—backed off. Flew backward."

An impish smile crept across Aunt Lucille's face. She took Marin's little chin in her hand. "You're a very special girl. And I am proud of you. Hard as they may try, don't let anyone ever quiet that voice."

"I love you, Aunt Lu-silly," Marin laughed, taking the woman's hand.

The smile vanished from Aunt Lucille's face instantly.

Her body visibly contracted. She gazed at Marin in awe as if the child had just insulted her.

"What's wrong, Lucille?" Deb asked.

"Nothing, dear. I'm fine." Though her look was pensive.

"Bye, Aunt Lu-silly." Marin blew her great-aunt a kiss and bounced out of the church, carefree as ever.

"Let me go check Dan's temperature. I'll be back for the boys in a minute," Deborah said, running into the sunlight after Marin.

Bartimaeus tottered in front of Aunt Lucille, flashing nearly every glittering white tooth in his head. "So the child is a *Summoner*. Lord, Lord . . . What are the chances of a man having a *Seer* and a *Summoner* in the same household?"

Aunt Lucille opened and closed her hands with ease. "She's also a *Healer*. My hands, my feet—there's no pain at all. I could feel the heat of her touch. It's remarkable that Marin—"

"What's a *Summoner*?" Will asked loudly, stomping down the central aisle wearing a grimace.

"You may as well tell him." Aunt Lucille continued flexing her hands in fascination.

"A *Summoner* is one who can call down the angels in times of need. The good ones," Bartimaeus said. "So sis has got a gift too. Don't that beat all?"

Aunt Lucille directed Will to a nearby pew. She sat beside the agitated boy, training her deep blue eyes on him. "I know that look. None of us who encounters evil is left unscathed, dear. But you mustn't cling to the terror or it will darken your days and cloud your future. Don't fear what's coming, Will. Light banishes darkness—always—and you will be given what you need when the time is right."

Will fiddled with the pith helmet in his lap, twisting the pelican medallion on the front. Nausea pinched his stomach. "I don't know if I can do this. I'm not even sure what I'm supposed to do. It's scary. I don't want to *see* anymore. . . ."

"Be at peace. Don't be afraid of the future; stay here in the present. Every gift, every calling, Will, is a burden. Within you is the substance to carry that burden well. I only ask this . . ." Aunt Lucille lowered her voice. "You must exercise *discretion* with those in the outside world; especially with your friends and school chums. We can discuss anything, particularly at Peniel. But don't tell others about your gift or your sister's. It could endanger you both, and people . . . well . . . they won't understand."

"Yes, ma'am," Will said.

Aunt Lucille lifted her father's pith helmet, straightened the medallion, and placed it on Will's head. He unexpectedly flung himself at his great-aunt, holding her in a long embrace.

"Thank you, Aunt Lucille. Thank you—for being here."

As if that was his cue to move, Bartimaeus teetered over to Andrew and Simon snoozing in the front pews. "It's wakey time, buttercups," he bellowed. Trying to rouse the boys, he poked a crutch at them, with little effect.

A great thud suddenly resounded through the church.

Bartimaeus and all those not sleeping turned toward the

sound. It was Tobias Shen latching the golden door of the Keep, sealing the St. Thomas relic away once more.

"Safe and sound," Shen said, patting the door. "All is as it should be."

"Not quite." Aunt Lucille gripped Will's bony shoulders. "Late Saturday afternoon, I want you to come to Peniel. It's time for you to meet the Brethren."

Butterflies in his stomach, Will started to respond, but Tobias Shen interrupted. "He can meet the Brethren after he finishes his gardening duties. The big trees and little one still need your attention, Mr. Wilder."

A smirking Will accepted both invitations.

CHAPTER 17

THE SARCOPHA-BUS

The following Saturday morning, Will met his friends for breakfast at the Burnt Offerings Café on High Street. While chaining his scooter to the bike rack out front, he couldn't help but overhear a conversation between two old men.

Lounging on the park bench in front of the restaurant, they flipped through a copy of the *Perilous Times* newspaper. A bloated codger with the wrinkled neck of a manatee, a toothpick just barely hanging from the side of his mouth, read to his pasty companion: "'The injuries and fatalities have yet to be explained. While some eyewitnesses suggest they might have been alligator attacks, others believe them to be paranormal in nature.' Oh, brother. Here we go. They always gotta interview the fanatics. 'Alton Taylor, a member of the Full Holiness Church'—that explains a lot—'who

survived a mauling in the Perilous River last Tuesday'—
blah, blah, blah—'fervently believes that whatever attacked
him was no animal, but a "creature with demonic character-
istics."' This paper has become a comic book. . . ."

"Stop reading that junk," the gray man sitting at the
other end of the park bench said, dragging on a cigarette.
He wore a stained seersucker jacket and wheezed a bit when
he spoke. "Sick and tired of those Holy Rollers myself. Always looking for some airy-fairy explanation when a simple
one will do. A gator bites some folks, and we're supposed
to believe the devil is running around Perilous Falls? It's
nuts. Though if he'd fix this economy, I'd welcome the devil
here myself. He could stay at my ex-wife's house—he'd fit
right in."

The big man in overalls giggled merrily, running a finger over the column. "Get this. They're having a prayer rally
down at the river to 'remember the dead and beg protection
against evil.' Oh, these fanatics! It's like a time warp. Why
don't they dig Jacob Wilder up from the dead and carry him
around town? He used to go on with that demon stuff, remember?"

Will quaked like a volcano on the verge of an eruption.
He so wanted to confront the men—to loudly tell them
what he had seen and knew to be true. But instead he pretended to lock up his scooter, while eavesdropping on their
conversation.

The hefty man continued. "Here's the only good news
in this whole story: 'The mayor's office is in the midst of

an extensive investigation. Sources tell the *Perilous Times* that the mayor herself has assembled a list of suspects who she believes may be connected to the river attacks, the deaths, and the destruction of Gareb Pier. Suspects could be charged within a matter of weeks.' I hope they include that Full Holiness Church character in their dragnet. The more of these extremists they lock up, the better."

"Every war ever started—all the problems of the world—was caused by some religious nut," said the other man, a cigarette between his yellowed fingers. "Let 'em have their guilt trip. Don't need nobody telling Harry Johnson what God's saying. 'Less I hear him with these two ears, I'm not listening." He flicked the cigarette to the ground and crushed it under his boot.

"Will-man! You coming in?" Andrew had stuck his head outside the restaurant's glass door. "How long does it take to lock up one scooter?"

The question caused the two men on the bench to focus on the squatting Will, who suddenly looked very guilty.

"You going on a safari, son?" the fat man asked, staring at Will's pith helmet.

"No."

"Mikey, Mikey," the ashen Harry Johnson said, swatting the arm of his bench mate. "You wanted Jacob Wilder back from the dead. Somebody heard you. There he is! Hat and all."

Will angrily stormed into Burnt Offerings, leaving the old men guffawing on the street. The restaurant had the feel of a sprawling French provincial cabin with bowed wooden floors, low-beamed ceilings, and wall-sized fireplaces in every room. Will and Andrew headed to the back of the restaurant, where they always met for Saturday breakfast.

"Did you know those guys?" Andrew asked. "Was one of them the Captain?"

"No. Forget about the Captain. There was no Captain."

"You told us there was a Captain."

"Not now, Andrew," Will said, approaching the table.

Cami looked steamed before Will even said a word.

"I'd ask how you are, but you must be fine because you're late," Cami said, legs crossed, flipping her ponytail with an index finger.

"So, I guess this means you don't want to hear the good news," Will said, raising an eyebrow at Cami. "That's fine."

"Come on, Will-man, what's up?" Andrew asked, taking a seat.

"Leo's arm is healed, and my mom and dad said our trip is back on! We're going to Florida!" Will beamed.

The boys high-fived across the table. Will glanced over at Cami, who he knew was trying to hold back a smile. He picked up a menu and coolly began studying it. "So, what are we having?"

"Oh, I already ordered for everybody," Simon said. The stark white thumb outlines burned onto Simon's cheeks during the Undercroft adventure were still visible. "Rhonda's bringing pancakes, muffins, and eggs for you all. Gluten-free, peanut-free pancakes and muffins for me. Fries on the side for Andrew."

Rhonda Blabbingdale, a cousin to Simon's father, Judge Blabbingdale, owned the restaurant. Six months earlier she had invited Simon and his friends to her café for a complimentary Saturday breakfast. She meant to have them in for just one Saturday, but the kids never stopped coming, and Rhonda was too polite to send a bill to the table.

Simon leaned over the table, his intense eyes jumping behind the rectangular frames of his glasses. "We need to get our stories straight. My father has been asking all kinds of questions. Especially about the thumbprints." Simon flexed his thumbs and manically pointed to his cheeks.

Andrew said, "My dad cornered me too and asked—"

"Just a minute, big boy," Simon said, interrupting. "If we don't get our stories straight, it will not be good." He fell into a panicked whisper. "There are criminal cases moving forward—that's what my father told one of his clerks on the phone the other day—criminal cases! Your aunt Lucille, the yard guy at the church, and some other people are going to be named. We can't be involved. I can't be involved. So we've come up with a story. Muttonhead—you're on."

Without a word, Andrew shoved Simon off his chair.

"Totally unnecessary," Simon complained from the corner, straightening his legs and his shirt. He quietly repositioned his chair between Cami and Will.

Andrew explained. "Look, Will, we decided to tell our

parents that we were helping you plant trees in the church-yard. After we planted for a while, we all strolled down to the river to soak up some rays."

"That explains the burn on my face."

"He got that, Simon," Andrew said, striking the table. "So we need you to go along with this, Will-man. Technically, it ain't a lie. We did go to the church to help you, and we were by the river. We're just leaving out the breaking and entering, destruction of property, the croc monsters, water flying in the air—which I still don't understand—and your parents."

There was a pause at the table as the food arrived. Andrew shoved four fries in his mouth at once. Simon sneered at him.

"What? I'm hungry," Andrew mumbled in response. "So can you agree to the story? You don't think your parents will go all state's evidence on us, do you?"

"My parents won't say anything," Will said.

"What about the Captain?" Simon gnawed on a petite brown muffin.

"There was no Captain," said Andrew. "So he won't be talking."

"I knew it," Simon exclaimed triumphantly. "Imaginary friend! Imaginary friend! Will has an imaginary friend."

"Hate to interrupt you, but can I get a word in here?" Cami asked. "Thanks. I have to tell you about Max's dreams because they've been eerily accurate."

Cami told the table the details of Max's first dream, his

vision of the sparkly gold treasure taken from a gray castle by the bad one—the *Sinestri.*

Will swallowed hard as he listened, thinking only of the prophecy: *". . . in those days of tribulation and darkness, I shall pour out my Spirit upon all flesh; sons and daughters shall dream vivid dreams and sing angelic songs . . ."*

"If nothing had happened, I would have just ignored it. But I think Max sees things before they happen. How could he have known about the relic? And I don't know who the bad one or the *Sinestri* are, but at least he got part of it right. Anyway, a few days ago during that horrible storm, Max was really upset," Cami continued, her slender hands painting pictures as she spoke. "He told me about a nightmare he'd had. He's been having it every night since."

Andrew finished off the fries as if watching a movie. Simon was so engrossed he reached for a second muffin without even looking down.

"Max keeps saying that a raven is circling Perilous Falls. 'A dark, black raven is coming,' he says. It brings blood. He says the blood is everywhere. Does any of that make sense to you?"

"Nope," Will said, feeling a slight chill.

Cami's green eyes cut through Will, watching him intently. "Do you know anything about an ugly monster? Max said the bad one, the *Sinestri,* was 'an ugly monster with many faces.' Have you seen anything like that?"

Will went as white as the milk before him. He involuntarily shoved his lips to the side, trying to think of something to say. He couldn't talk about the *Sinestri* or Leviathan without discussing his gift—which he had promised to keep to himself. His mind was racing.

"Well?" Cami asked.

Just as Will opened his mouth to speak, Simon began wildly waving his half-eaten muffin at them. He was trembling and turning red.

"Wrong muffin. Wrong muffin," he choked. "I ate the wrong—EpiPen! Get the EpiPen!" Only air and rasp escaped his mouth. His eyes flipped backward.

Will ripped open Simon's backpack, joined by Andrew.

"I'll have Rhonda call an ambulance," Will said, handing the found EpiPen to Andrew. "I've got to run anyway—"

Cami fanned Simon but stayed on point. "Before you go, Will—answer my question. What about this monster with many heads?"

"What about it? We're in the middle of an emergency, Cami," Will said, throwing on his pith helmet. "See you guys later. Feel better, Simon—we need you in tip-top shape for the Florida trip next week!"

Andrew was already jamming the EpiPen into his friend's thigh before Will had disappeared down the hall.

"Thanks, moro—Andrew," Simon sighed gratefully.

Will had to keep his promise to Tobias Shen. With all the troubles he had caused at St. Thomas, Will figured it was the least he could do. Rolling up to the yard on his red scooter, he ran into Father Ulan Cash exiting a taxi.

"Billy," the chubby priest bellowed. He wore an extra-large teal Hawaiian shirt and a fishing hat that matched nothing. "I go out of town for a few days and all hell breaks loose. Bad storm, huh?"

"Yep." Will nodded, a frozen smile plastered on his face.

"How's the planting coming?"

"We're getting there, Father." He forced a laugh that Father Cash returned for no reason whatsoever.

"Less laughter, more planting," Tobias Shen blurted, appearing at the edge of the yard with a shovel in hand. "Good to have you back, Father. Mr. Wilder, the trees' toes yearn for warm earth. Dig, dig, dig."

"That's our Tobias. Always on the job," Father Cash announced. He yawned and shuffled up to the rectory for what he called "a vacation-recovery nap."

Before Will could start digging a hole, Mr. Shen led Will toward one of the few things he had actually planted in the yard.

"Did you see how your tree is faring?" Tobias stood over the visible half of the walking stick poking from the ground, as if it were something precious.

Getting closer, Will could not believe his eyes. Along the shaft of the stick, seven small green buds had sprouted on the wood. The bud near the top had even released a spray of tender white blossoms.

"It is small, as all things are at first. But he who is faithful

in small things is *great*, Mr. Wilder." A wide smile broke over
Shen's face, age lines spreading in all directions. "Go on,
touch, touch. It is your tree."

Will laid an unsure hand on the ridged top of the stick.
A second later the swollen buds on the rod expelled more
white blossoms. Ripe almonds soon hung amid the clusters
of petals. A wondrous, awe-filled look covered Will's face.
"Did you see? . . . Did you see it bloom when I . . . ? I can't
believe it."

"Believe it." Tobias Shen plucked two of the almonds
from the plant, snapping the shells open for Will. "Here,
take and eat the fruit of obedience."

The sweetness of the almonds erupted in Will's mouth.
He had never tasted anything so satisfying. They were like
treats—candy corn, Will thought.

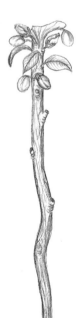

"Keep watch over your tree. Nurture it,
and it will nurture you. Protect it, and it will
protect you," Mr. Shen said. He turned his
back to Will, facing the yard. "Now we have to
plant bigger trees, but none more important
than your tree."

The pair spent much of the afternoon
planting more saplings in a circular pattern
around the St. Thomas churchyard. Throughout the day Will found himself gravitating to
the flowering stick, marveling over what had
happened. He even pinched off a few more
almonds in between shoveling and tree lifts.

By the time twilight's brilliant pink haze fell over the river, Will had said goodbye to Mr. Shen and watered his little "tree." Even though it was out of his way, he rode his scooter to Peniel, having promised Aunt Lucille he would stop there before going home.

Approaching Peniel's walled collection of structures, something within him stirred. The first sight of the main Gothic hall, with its steepled towers and attached buildings, made his heart race. Will thought it looked like a little village unto itself. As he got closer, the dome and the seven-story rectangular tower at the rear of the compound faded from view, blocked by the massive Bethel Hall. Hanging on the wrought-iron gates out front were a pair of banners advertising a new exhibit. They held images of a bearded old man wielding a staff. Will didn't bother to read them.

He dodged a stream of exiting visitors and slipped beyond the outer library to the main hall. It was empty and shrouded in darkness.

"Aunt Lucille. Mr. Bart," he called, but there was no response.

He proceeded past the antique case holding Elijah's mantle. "She must have finally wrestled it from Leo," Will said to himself.

At the rear of Bethel Hall he entered the arched central passageway and called his aunt's name again. A guard sweeping out the last two stragglers directed Will to the Egyptian Gallery.

Oversized square stones and the pair of black dog statues

guarding the corners made Will feel as if he had just entered a pyramid's burial chamber. At the center of the room, a young man in a purple linen vest and yellow tie placed a rectangular piece of glass over a display case. Aunt Lucille and Bartimaeus gave him direction.

"Over to the left, Valens. There it is, dear. Perfection."

"Let's lock her down," said Bartimaeus, handing Valens the keys to the four small locks on the exhibit.

Aunt Lucille introduced Will to Valens. "Very nice to meet you," Valens said, offering a strong handshake. Will enjoyed the English accent and took an instant liking to Valens. "I know we'll be seeing more of each other. Do tell your sister and brother and mother that I send my regards. Oh, love the hat." He winked and was on his way.

Aunt Lucille brought her great-nephew close to the display case at the middle of the room.

"What do you think of the new exhibit?" Aunt Lucille placed two hands atop the glass, gazing inside. "The Staff of Moses. Now, the exterior you see there is an ornamental covering—a loaner from the British Museum."

A gold gem-studded staff lay on a black velvet cushion beneath the glass.

Will stared at the bent object. "The staff is inside that gold and jewel thing?"

"Correct. You can see the top of it there. The dark blue shiny knob poking out of the gold sleeve is the actual rod of Moses. We've always kept it in a simple bronze container. But for this exhibit I thought it needed a spectacular setting. The staff is over thirty-five hundred years old. Very powerful. And what a history . . ."

As she spoke, Will was distracted by Valens, who walked purposefully into the adjoining room, striding toward a sarcophagus—a stone casket—in the corner.

"Usually the staff is locked in the vault, but once this exhibit opens to kick off the Jacob Wilder Day celebration, it'll be out here for a full year. Will, before it gets too late, Abbot Athanasius asked to meet with you . . . in the arch-abbey."

Will wasn't listening. He couldn't take his eyes off Valens's activities in the other room. The man casually stepped into the open stone sarcophagus and lay down.

"Hello. Hello!" Bartimaeus said, waving a hand at Will. "Your aunt's talking and ya ain't even looking at her."

Will was waiting for Valens to rise out of the casket in the other room. He couldn't tear his eyes away.

"Uh, that Valens guy just got into the—the tomb thingy." He was very concerned and padded to the doorway for a closer look.

"Here we go," Bartimaeus said, advancing his crutches toward the main entryway. "I'll be locking up Bethel Hall."

"Come with me," Aunt Lucille said, leading Will into the room that had riveted his attention. The gallery featured stone works: empty fountains, the tops of antique wells, and four sarcophagi.

Aunt Lucille neared the stone casket in the corner, the one etched with scenes of demons fleeing robed men with extended hands. "There are multiple ways to enter the archabbey. But this one's more efficient than the others. Go ahead, look inside."

Will leaned over the sarcophagus—the same one Valens had crawled into just moments before. There was no trace of the man.

"Where did he go?"

"To the abbey."

"But how?"

"*Sarcophagal peregrination.* He traveled by sarcophagus. When we were your age, my brother Joseph—your grandfather—used to call it the sarcopha-bus." She giggled. "Every sarcophagus in this museum has a destination point elsewhere. This one terminates at a stone coffin in the abbey's crypt. So if you need to get to the archabbey in a hurry, use only this one." She then pointed to the richly sculpted sarcophagus resting on two marbled lions across the room. It was decorated with Grecian figures who seemed to be enjoying an outdoor party. "That one leads to another community out West, at the Getty Villa. You don't want to go there now. One of these others goes to the Cleveland Museum—or is it the Walters? I can't remember which."

"You mean I can use the sarcopha-bus? I can travel in it?"

"That's the idea. Step in." He did so. "Lie down. Cross your arms over your chest. Now you'd better either hold your helmet or put the chin strap on. *Sarcophagal peregrination* can be a bit aggressive, dear."

"How aggressive?"

"Tornado-like."

His chin strap in place, palms sweating, Will asked, "What's next?"

"You have to recite a formula. It's very simple. Close your eyes. Say it quietly, and brace yourself. Whatever you do, don't move your arms or legs while you're in motion. You could lose them."

"Okay, okay. What's the formula?"

Aunt Lucille stooped over and whispered, "*Morte in vitam*—it's Latin. I'll be right behind you. So step out quickly once you arrive."

Will took a deep breath, shut his eyes, and repeated the formula.

"*Morte in vitam. . . .*"

The floor of the sarcophagus beneath Will suddenly disintegrated. He fell backward, a mighty wind surrounding him. It was as though he were plummeting from the top of the Empire State Building . . . and yet, strangely, the violent gale supported his weight.

In the darkness, plunging faster and faster through space, Will was needled by an unwelcome sensation. It started as a slight itch, a tingling. Unable to move his hands, he tried to suppress it mentally, tried to distract himself by thinking of something else. He wriggled his lips from side to side. All the while Will hoped its arrival wasn't a warning as it had been in the past. But there was no holding it back.

This could be a problem, he thought.

AH-CHOO! AH-CHOO! AH-CHOO!

❖ ACKNOWLEDGMENTS ❖

Writing fiction is like entering an extended dream while trying to capture what is seen and heard. Without the indulgence of four very special people, I might never have had the time to enter Perilous Falls, and her residents would have certainly remained unknown.

Will Wilder was born aside a bathtub. When they were younger, my children would often ask me, during bath time, to tell them stories while they played in the bubbles. One night, Will Wilder and his slapstick, scary adventures came tumbling out of my imagination, and they refused to go back. At the urging of the kids, Will would reappear in installments each evening, usually accompanied by suds. So I first must thank my children, Alexander, Lorenzo, and Mariella, for demanding an original story and for their willingness to hear the Wilder saga in its various iterations over many years. They have made my story (and my life) so very rich. But it was their mother, Rebecca, who allowed me hours and hours of time to commit Will and his wild exploits to the page. Without her sacrifice and loving support, I know I would not have been able to complete this first book in the series, nor plan any of the forthcoming adventures. Dear Rebecca, I love you so.

Many people collaborated with me to bring the Will Wilder series into existence. Their sage counsel inspired me to reshape this work and remake it in ways I never originally intended.

To my publishing family at Random House, what a joy it is to be back home. My editor, Emily Easton, at Crown, with taste and care helped me refine this story in incalculable ways. She is now an honorary citizen of Perilous Falls, and I am so grateful to have gone on this journey with her. To Phoebe Yeh, my publisher at Crown, and Barbara Marcus, president of Random House Children's Books: you both took Will Wilder under your wings from the start. The love you showed this story and its author will never be forgotten. I am humbled and so thankful to have you as collaborators and to have been the beneficiary of your wisdom and advice. You are simply the best in the business.

I am absolutely thrilled to have Jeff Nentrup's splendid, action-packed art gracing the cover of this book. For the stellar line drawings that punctuate the text, I am indebted to the very talented Antonio Javier Caparo.

Dominique Cimina and her crack PR team; John Adamo in marketing; Ken Crossland, our designer; and Isabel Warren-Lynch, our art director, all took a personal interest in the series from the very beginning. Your professionalism and devotion to this series showed at every turn. My thanks to each of you.

Outside of Random House, there were others who offered perceptive notes and kind assistance as I shaped the story. They are Diane Reeves, Rachel Abrams, Hannah Sternberg, Marji Ross, and my friend Cheryl Barnes, whose artistic eye helped guide me in many ways.

Then there are the other dear friends and mentors without whom this first book in the Will Wilder series would not exist. My friend Francis "Chip" Flaherty at Walden Media has been devoted to this project for literally years. He encouraged me to rethink my first take on these characters and never failed to provide passionate support and fantastic suggestions. It was he who proposed taking this work to Random House. How right you were, Chip. Thank you for always being there. Ron Hansen, one of our great novelists, offered pointed advice early on that fired my imagination and greatly helped me to expand this story. Joseph Pearce, an accomplished man of letters, also provided critical notes on the manuscript that proved extremely helpful. You all have my deepest gratitude.

For their inspiration, friendship, and support, I must thank William Peter Blatty, Dean Koontz, Jim Caviezel, Anne Rice, Laura Ingraham, Randall Wallace, Christopher Edwards, Umberto Fedeli, Monica and Kevin Fitzgibbons, Joe Looney, Stephen Sheehy, James Faulkner, Cristina Kelly, Peter Gagnon, Lee South (with the mercilessly wonderful editorial eye), Deborah Giarratana, Mary Matalin, Loretta Barrett (my agent of happy memory), Father Gerald Murray for the Latin course, Bill Donahue, Michael Warsaw,

Dorinda Bordlee, Corey Frank, Michael Sortino, Doug Keck, Mother Angelica, her nuns, and my parents, Raymond and Lynda Arroyo.

To the librarians, bloggers, and lovers of kids' lit who carry the stories forward—who *storyent* our lives, touching souls and shaping the future—we are all in your debt. Finally, I want to thank you for taking the time to read Will's first adventure and for supporting me for so many years. I can't wait for you to see where Will goes next. . . .

❖ ABOUT THE AUTHOR ❖

RAYMOND ARROYO is a *New York Times* bestselling author, producer, and lead anchor and managing editor of EWTN News. As the host of *The World Over Live* he is seen in more than 250 million homes internationally each week. When not visiting Perilous Falls, he can be found at home in Virginia with his wife and three children (none of whom wear pith helmets or steal relics for kicks). You can follow him on Facebook and on Twitter at @RaymondArroyo.